ALSO BY MARY ADLER

Shadowed by Death:
An Oliver Wright WWII Mystery

In the
Shadow
of
Lies

An Oliver Wright WWII Mystery

by

MARY ADLER

Dancing Dog Books

IN THE SHADOW OF LIES

Cover and Interior Design by Kerry Ellis

Published 2018. Printed in the United States of America. For
information, address: Dancing Dog Books, P.O. Box 1308, For-
estville, CA 95436

ISBN: 978-1-7320097-3-8

Library of Congress Control Number: 2014930012

"Everyone sees what you appear to be, few experience what you really are."

Machiavelli

For William, Benjamin, and Nicholas Ardine,
my father and his brothers, who went to war.
Two came home.

AUTHOR'S NOTE

It is difficult for me to think certain words found in this book, let alone express them. You will find them where they would have occurred in real life: in the dialogue and thoughts of characters whose actions are motivated by the ugliness of racism and prejudice.

The book is set in a real place and time. The characters are my invention, save Thurgood Marshall, an extraordinary and courageous attorney, and General DeWitt, a man who acted ruthlessly against the people the United States had labeled "enemies."

THE CHARACTERS

The Families

The Flemings

Maude

Ellie, Joe, and Sammy—her children

The Wrights

Oliver—a homicide detective

Elizabeth—his wife

Charley, their son

Harley, their German Shepherd

Peter—Oliver's brother, an Assistant District Attorney

Jennie—Peter's wife

Zoe and Theo, their children

The Judge, Oliver's father

The Fioris

Bennie—a farmer

Michael and Mia, his children

Jack—Bennie's brother, a fisherman

The Slaters

Wade—a homicide detective

Cora (Lundgren)—his wife

Sandy—Wade's uncle

The Buonarottis

Harry—District Attorney

Paola—his wife

Steve and Anna Maria, their children
Lucy Forgione—Harry's aunt and owner of the Café
Avellino
Isabella—Paola's sister, Harry's sister-in-law
Dom—Isabella's husband, Harry's brother-in-law
Cesare and Tomaso, Dom's sons

The Hermits
Edna—the Wright's housekeeper and Lucy Forgione's
friend
Nate, her son and Steve Buonarotti's friend

The Community

Luca Respighi, an Italian Prisoner of War
Roan (Harmonica Man) and his dog, Emma
Andrew Semmel, Veterinarian
Doc Pritchard
Louis Carlton, owner of Carlton's Blues Club
Hershey, Oliver's Sergeant on Guam
Harmon, Oliver's partner in Point Richmond
Jonah, a welder and Oliver's friend
Regis Simmons
Paul Butler, a policeman
Ralph Robinson, owner of Ralph's Restaurant
Auntie Josephine
Becky
Monica

Contents

Point Richmond,
California

1941

1

Corvid Dreams

Ribbons of ebony crows streamed across the cobalt sky and disappeared into the centers of redwood trees, guiding me, it seemed, to the ridge where my friend Paul lived. A fitting escort. My wife had loved crows. She had told me more about their intelligence and complicated family structure than anyone needed to know, and I had become as fascinated by them as she was. For her last birthday—her last ever—I had written a poem about the flock settling for the night, rustling and murmuring as they closed their eyes and dreamed their corvid dreams. She had wanted me to write more poems about them. For a book she would illustrate. That wasn't going to happen now.

The crows vectored in from all directions to the trees around Paul's porch, perhaps a tribute to Elizabeth, perhaps not. He and I sat in rocking chairs and set about drinking the neck and shoulders off a bottle of bourbon, our private wake for her. Harley, my German shepherd, gnawed on a knuckle bone Paul had given him and kept us company.

"I thought the judge was going to stomp his foot and disappear like Rumpelstiltskin when he saw Harley. *Oliver, one does not bring a dog to a funeral.*"

I smiled at his exaggeration of my father's quasi-English accent. I had broken one of the unwritten societal rules that separated *us* from *them*—and had only made it worse when I dismissed the cemetery workers and reached for a shovel. My father had asked what I was doing in a stage whisper, trying not to be observed by his friends who were hanging on every word while appearing not to.

I simply answered, "She's my wife."

I had to swallow hard when Charley picked up a shovel and said, "And my mother."

He and I filled in the grave slowly, not wanting to let her go. Harley lay as close to it as he could. His sorrow, the depth of loss in those dark eyes, broke my heart. I couldn't explain to him why she was gone. I couldn't explain it to myself or to Charley. Finally, we smoothed the dark earth, covered the mound with red sunflowers from Elizabeth's garden—ones that had bloomed after they recovered her body. Harley had risen slowly and trailed us down the path, away from the windswept hill overlooking the bay.

Paul clicked the bottle against my glass—an invitation to leave the cemetery behind for a while. We talked about the last war, our war, and the Marine Corps' plan to create a K-9 unit if we were drawn into the fighting in Europe. If Charles Lindbergh and his America First movement had their way, the United States would ignore England's pleas for help. We agreed that we would rather fight in Europe again than watch the United States become more and more fascist.

We drank to absent friends, lamenting the lust for power that had sent them and other young men to their deaths. The sky deepened to purple, and a screech owl rattled and glided through the dusk, hunting for dinner along the edge of the dry meadow.

2

A Cooling Light

Maude Fleming leaned against her porch railing and breathed the hot bay smell lingering from the ridge trees.

She was tired of things ripening all at once and forcing her to spend the hot fall days canning. It would be even harder after Ellie started seventh grade next week. She would miss her daughter's singing spirit, her chatter that made the work go faster. She had to find time to make up those plaid yard goods into a back-to-school dress for her. The child had surely earned it, cutting the beans and watching her brothers, when all she wanted was to finish *The Wizard of Oz* before she had to return it to the library. She would probably read under the covers with a flashlight all night, struggling to stay awake.

The children should be coming back soon. She had sent them with a picnic into the woods by the creek, where the boys could play in the trickle that was left of it and Ellie could read the book she had slipped into the dinner sack. Before bedtime, they would eat pudding and listen to the jar lids pop, Ellie and

Joe jumping in their chairs as if the pings startled them, reducing Sammy to giggles.

She leaned on the post, half asleep and half dreaming about a summer kitchen where she could work outside and feel the afternoon winds blowing inland from the Golden Gate, although the breeze setting the glass chimes dancing felt more warm than cool.

A sudden clatter of crows unsettled her. They erupted into the sky, circled and gathered, then screamed away from the ridge. Something wasn't right. She smelled smoke. Who would have a fire on a night like tonight?

She grabbed a flashlight from the kitchen and ran toward the woods.

The flaming cross exploded into hundreds of burning shards and ignited the long, thin stalks at the edge of the clearing. The fire crackled like a swarm of locusts as it gobbled through the grass, moving almost ten miles an hour and heating the air to more than a thousand degrees.

Ellie looked up at the ridge, at the crowd of panicked crows that filled the sky. Something had spooked them, maybe a mountain lion. The big cats stalked so silently, and Sammy was small enough to be easy pickings.

"Let's go, boys. Mom told us to get back before it got dark."

She heard a rumbling sound and looked around, uneasy. Behind her, the sky seemed foggy, blurred gray and white, like a low cloud. Then orange and yellow flickered through the gray, and a wave of flame rounded the hill and flowed like a river toward them.

She picked up Sammy and screamed at Joe to run. They were far from the safety of the trees. Too far. Fear whitened his face when he turned to help her.

"No, run! Run as fast as you can, and don't look back. Run!"

He hesitated, and she screamed at him. "Go. Get help!"

She faltered when the world of Oz slid to the ground, then clutched Sammy tighter and ran. He clung to her and whimpered, a baby again. When she coughed, his grip loosened, and she almost dropped him. The heat scorched the backs of her legs as she stumbled through the smoke silently screaming for her mother. Her eyes smarted and burned, and she ran blindly for home.

Harley whined, a tentative, questioning sound, then ran off the porch, nose in the air. I peered into the gathering dark trying to figure out what was worrying him and the crows who had left the safety of the roost.

"Listen." Paul held up a hand for silence. A low roar came from the hill, and a hot burst of wind carried the smell of burning grass. We said the terrorizing words at the same time: Wild fire.

He called the station, and I banged on the doors of his neighbors. One of them grabbed hoes for us, and we scrambled to clear a firebreak.

An anguished scream of *no* cut through the night. Harley took off and I dropped my hoe and tore after him.

A boy stumbled toward us, coughing and crying. A eucalyptus tree burst into flames and illuminated a woman running toward the fire. My heart sank when Harley raced after her. He closed the distance between them quickly and grabbed her dress in his mouth. She struck his neck and head again and again, but he held her until I picked her up and carried her away from the heat. She clawed at me and screamed and slapped at my face. Finally, neighbors surrounded her and dragged her back to the boy. She collapsed on the ground, gathered him in her arms and rocked back and forth.

I don't think I'll ever forget the keening sound she made, calling her daughter's name while we hunted for a way through the flames.

At last, the moon spilled a cooling light on the charred hill. Wisps of smoke snaked and danced like cold morning fog on a warm river, silence its dark companion.

As soon as we could, before we should have, we ran into the meadow and swept the hill with our flashlights, calling the girl's name. When I saw a mound not far from the edge of the woods, I stopped dead, but the heat penetrating my boots forced me to pick up my feet, to go toward what I knew was the girl.

She might have made it on her own, but it looked as if she had carried her brother until the smoke and the heat overcame her. I didn't think this child, as brave as she was, could have stayed and sheltered him if she had been alive when the flames reached them. At least, I hoped not.

I had to tell the others, but I couldn't speak. They would have to wait, just for a minute.

3

Stick to Your Own Kind

The wily old fox had timed it perfectly: the rainy September day, the cemetery, the weeping mother huddled with her son under a black umbrella, a clichéd study in grays and blacks that evoked a memory of another coffin's descent into the earth, a memory that stirred my guilt and made me so deeply tired that I slid into the thankless habit of trying to please my father.

When we returned from the Fleming children's funeral, he summoned me to the study.

"Not the dog, Oliver."

"Harley, find Zoe." I sent the him off with a wave of my hand, and he bounded away, nose to the floor, on the trail of my niece.

My father motioned me to a chair.

"It is fortuitous, Oliver, that circumstances have brought you back to Richmond."

Coming home to bury my wife was fortuitous? I had forgotten that my father had no more empathy than a hanging judge should have. I drew back in my chair, but I didn't think he noticed.

"We've had a breakthrough on the fire that killed the Fleming children. It was a warning to a Negro professor at Berkeley who was buying a house in a white neighborhood. The Klan threw a brick through his window with a note advising him to stay where he belonged, or *his* children would be next."

"Was his family hurt?"

"No, but he decided to move to a black neighborhood in Oakland."

"Do you have any other evidence the Klan set the fire?"

"As a matter of fact, we do. Normally, people don't hide their Klan affiliation. Hell, they marched up MacDonald Avenue on the Fourth of July." His lip curled in disgust. "They're proud of themselves, keeping America for Americans, and a lot of people sympathized with them. But now they've killed the children of a longtime Richmond family—white children—and we had a secret witness willing to talk about it."

"Had?"

"He's gone. He left town when the Klan threatened him."

"Couldn't have been much of a secret if the Klan found out about him. Who else knew?"

"My office, the police chief, and the prosecutor's office. That's all." His lips tightened. "It had to be the police or Buonarotti's office. My staff would never breach a confidence." He leaned across the desk. "That's where you come in."

"Me?"

"This was a serious breach, Oliver. Serious enough for the police commissioner to ask me to convince you to move back to Richmond and join the police force. We know we can trust you to help clean out the corruption. I insisted they instate you at your present rank and salary."

He hadn't changed one bit. *Here's what I want you to do with your life, and while you're at it, you can be grateful.* I was tempted, mainly because I still wasn't ready to go home. My captain in

Seattle had told me to take as much leave as I wanted, and I *had* told Maude Fleming I'd try to find out who had killed her children. The problem was the Klan. It could take months to find out anything about them, and I didn't want to stay away that long.

"I wish I could help, Judge, but I need to get back home."

He held up a hand.

"Seattle can wait. You'll only sit around feeling sorry for yourself."

"Feeling *sorry* for myself?" I threw up my hands and walked toward the door.

"I need your help. Please."

How had those words slipped out of his mouth?

"Look, I'd help if it made any sense at all, but I'm an outsider. Worse. My father is a judge and my brother is a prosecutor. Who in his right mind would let me in on a Klan conspiracy?" I sat on the arm of the chair. "I'm not the right person for this."

He reached for the whiskey decanter behind his desk and half-filled a crystal tumbler. "It's no secret you would prefer to have nothing to do with me and your brother. It wouldn't be that hard for people to believe you had turned completely against us."

It beggared belief. In his mind, my not wanting to be a part of my family's social circle equated to my being seen as corruptible.

He touched his lips with his handkerchief. "There's something else."

Of course, there was. The part that really mattered to him.

"We think anyone who talked to the witness could be at risk."

"For example?"

"Your brother."

"Ah. I see."

I was twelve again, watching blood spatter the principal's white shirt as he shook me, asking why I couldn't be more like my brother. I knew Peter wouldn't have risked getting dirty, let alone hurt, sticking up for the new kid outnumbered by bullies. Right then, with my head whipping back and forth, I had vowed to leave Richmond one day and make a life where being a Wright meant nothing.

"Oliver, please. Do it for me. Do it for your mother."

His trump card. My mother had always wished Peter and I had been closer. If he were at risk, my father might be too. Peter wouldn't know how to protect either of them. And then there was Maude. Maybe I *could* find some peace for her and make sure my brother and father were safe. Besides, it would be good to be closer to Charley for a while, at least until he settled in at Stanford.

"I'll give you some time— till the end of December, but then I'm leaving."

I regretted my promise as soon as he smiled.

The note had been a mistake. We now knew the cross burning hadn't been a random attempt to terrorize Negroes or other non-Aryans but had a specific target—a particular professor buying a house in a particular area.

I talked to the neighbors around the house he had almost bought but came up empty. They said they didn't know who had wanted the cross burned, but their smiles said they knew and were happy it had happened. Some said they didn't want to live next door to a Negro—not always the term they used. They all said they had nothing against colored people, but they were better off sticking with their own kind: Look at the trouble that uppity teacher had already caused.

I made a map, noted who owned the houses, and tracked the man who collected from the people who rented. His involvement ended with the lawyer he gave the rental payments to. If

I tackled the lawyer on my own, he'd clam up, claiming client confidentiality.

I gave the information to my father. He could decide whether he wanted Peter to pursue it.

4

To Shroud the Dead

The seventh of December. Three more weeks and I'd be home. I ran on the hard-packed sand below the high tide mark trying to tire my body and quiet my mind. Music seemed to float above the sound of the waves. When I rounded the point, I found the source. Radio broadcasts spilled from the gaping doors of cars parked along the highway. Men and women, some in church clothes, struggled through the dry sand toward the water.

A teenager shouted, "Have you heard the news? The Japanese bombed Pearl Harbor this morning. A sneak attack."

"How bad is it?" I wanted to ask how it could have happened, but he would have no more idea how than I did.

A man with swollen eyes shook his head and his voice broke. "Bad. It happened early while most of the men were still sleeping."

I looked toward Hawaii and imagined the horror of the attack, men waking to shelling, to flames, to the screams of their shipmates. How many men had been murdered this morning?

How many families were waiting to find out if their loved ones had survived?

I could feel the anger and hatred in the people around me. They had come to see for themselves whether Japs were landing on the beaches. Some carried weapons, ready to defend the coast, ready to avenge the dead at Pearl Harbor. Men on cliffs scanned the kelp beds, lifted binoculars to the sky, and listened for the sound of planes coming out of the sun.

But most of the people seemed to be mourning the men of the Pacific Fleet, California's own. They lit candles by tide pools and cast flowers on the gunmetal swells. They pressed against the water's edge, against the thousands of miles of uncaring ocean separating them from Honolulu. They wanted to help—to tend the wounded, to shroud the dead. This was as close as they could get. What was left of my heart went out to them.

The scent of the night flowed through the open door and filled my uncle's cabin. The day had run long into the small hours of the morning, the precinct switchboard jammed with calls about Japanese planes over San Francisco and rumors of invasions. I had almost felt as if I belonged with my fellow cops as we patrolled the streets and reassured people who had come outside to seek the comfort of neighbors. I quieted their fears, told them they were safe, although I knew little more than they did.

Now I sat in the armchair that faced the bay, rested one hand on my sleeping dog, and let my breath find the rhythm of his chest. I closed my eyes and drifted with Billie Holiday. She flirted with death, invited it, caressed the lyrics that had been banned for romanticizing suicide. Strangely, "Gloomy Sunday" helped me survive.

The man who wrote it knew my pain. Knew the fear, the hope, the waiting. The loss. People said, "I know how you feel," but they couldn't see into my heart or into the hearts of the thousands of people who would wake in the morning remembering a future they would never have, haunted by the laughter of children who would never be.

I wished for sleep, for a moment of stillness in a world of constant motion. In country after country, troops massed along borders and refugees snaked along cratered roads. Earlier, as Harley and I ran on the beach, the war had seemed far away, a distant backdrop to my investigation into the police department. But now it would be our war, too, and once again Americans would die in Europe—and the Pacific.

What little chance I had to keep my promise to my father would vanish like the ships at Pearl, as witnesses and suspects left for the war. Not that he would understand. A man kept his word, war be damned.

I sighed, and Harley looked up, his eyebrows pinched together. I rubbed his worry away, easing my own as the smooth fur slid under my fingers. He stretched and headed for the door. I shrugged on my coat and followed him into the night.

5

My Giggling Assailant

Richmond—the whole country—was a mess. Men were still unaccounted for at Pearl Harbor. Some people had heard from their loved ones, but others waited with dwindling hope. People were terrified that the Japs were heading our way. For the past three days, we had been preparing for the follow-up attacks we publicly denied were coming.

Harley and I were on our way out of the station when I saw Wade Slater, a fellow detective, trying to get away from a man in overalls. A girl about my niece's age held the man's hand. I wasn't about to see if Wade needed help. He had made it his business to make my life as unpleasant as possible. Men who had wanted to learn about fingerprinting suddenly lost interest when he showed up. I was sure he was the informant, that he fed information to his Uncle Sandy—which was the same as telling the Klan—but I would never be able to prove it.

I lit a cigarette and listened to his conversation. The man's son was missing. No one had seen the boy since he had left a friend's house the night of Pearl Harbor.

"Wait. He'll turn up." Wade took the man aside. "He's probably at a bar or getting laid."

The man pressed his lips together and bent toward the girl. He smoothed back her hair and said something I couldn't hear. I looked at my watch. Time to give the judge a progress report. Again.

I had taken two steps onto my father's porch when Harley woofed, and someone flew out of the dark and leaped onto my back. Harley spun around, biting at the shoes of my giggling assailant.

"Zoe, I could have hurt you!"

"I got you that time, Uncle Oliver."

"Oh yeah?" I picked her up and threw her over my shoulder.

"Potatoes for sale. Ten cents a peck." I carried her into the dining room, where the housekeeper was setting the table.

"Hey, Mrs. Hermit, need some potatoes? They're kind of lumpy."

"No thanks, mister. If they're rotten, you can dump them out back in the compost heap."

Zoe screamed while I lugged her to the back door. She was almost twelve. I realized it wouldn't be long before she outgrew the game she loved to play with me. Her brother, Theo, ignored us and went to the table. He had never liked the potato game.

After dinner, I followed my father into the study.

"A colleague saw the witness on Saturday and convinced him the only way to be safe was to tell someone what he knows. We were supposed to meet here Sunday night, but the attack on Pearl

Harbor must have prevented him from coming." He handed me a slip of paper. "Someone needs to go see him."

"And who would that be?"

"This is serious, Oliver. Your levity is entirely inappropriate."

"Is he safe?"

He shrugged. "He was told to stay hidden. No one else should know where he is."

I drove toward Oakland where the witness was stashed, slowed by the masses of people who had streamed into town. A few months ago, Richmond had been a sleepy little place, but the attack had galvanized Americans. Men enlisted in the military, and workers traveled across the country to help build ships and tanks.

The Pacific coast readied itself for an invasion, worried about the Japanese submarines that prowled the western edge of the country, sinking a ship here, firing on a city there. They didn't do serious damage, but they kept everyone on edge.

Immediately after the attack on Pearl Harbor, the Navy had stretched seven miles of metal net across the mouth of the Golden Gate, a barrier to an underwater invasion. The government had been preparing since the thirties for the war they feared would come. Now almost the entire coast, including Richmond, was a restricted military zone.

I eased to a stop in front of a bungalow. Checked the address. A peeling picket fence surrounded the yard, and tufts of weedy grass dotted the hard-packed dirt like patches of stubble on a worn-out face. When I brushed the wild mint that edged the fence, I was reminded of summer afternoons reading with my mother in our garden.

I knocked on the door, then squinted through the grimy window and made out an easy chair and a table. Cigarette butts filled an ashtray next to a crumpled Lucky Strike pack. It looked like the man had a serious habit. Maybe he'd gone to find more smokes.

Harley had disappeared behind the house but was gone only a few seconds before he tore around the corner and barked at me. I followed him to an open back door and called out, drew my gun, and signaled him to search. He streaked out of sight and barked once. I found him sitting by a pool of blood.

6

Tougher Than I Look

I stared at the Café Avellino menu, the one I had almost memorized. The night before, I had called the Oakland police to report what I had found in the empty house. Two patrolmen showed up and took my report, which would probably gather dust until the corners curled. If a body showed up, they'd let me know.

Harley nudged my knee. I looked at the front door where my niece's face was squished against the glass. She took a deep breath, as if she were steadying herself before letting an arrow fly, then pushed open the door, followed by the girl who had been at the precinct looking for her brother.

From head to toe, Zoe's friend was a mess. Her black hair looked like it had been combed with an eggbeater, one edge of her cardigan hung lower than the other, and her scabbed knees showed under her uniform jumper. Probably last year's uniform, or maybe the year before. One sock had slipped down in the space between her heel and the back of her shoe. No caring mother would have let her out of the house like that. Then the girl looked at me, and I had the feeling there was no mother.

"Uncle Oliver, we need you to help us find Mia's brother Michael."

"He went missing the night of Pearl Harbor. Almost four days ago." Mia's voice threatened to break.

When I pulled out chairs for the girls, Harley moved to sit between them. Mia smiled and dropped to the floor to scratch his chest.

"You are so beautiful."

Zoe hugged me and whispered, "My dad can't know we're here."

I nodded.

"Let's get you girls some breakfast."

Mia refused, but I told them if they wanted me to listen, they would have to eat with me.

I gestured at the chairs and signaled to the waitress, but before she could respond, Mrs. Forgione, the café's owner, appeared with hot chocolate and pastry. She listened while Mia told her story. I asked the usual questions: girlfriends, drinking, had Michael gone missing before, did he owe anyone money, did he have enemies? Mia answered me, closing her eyes every now and then, as if reminding herself to be polite.

"We think the government has him, Mr. Wright."

"Why? Isn't he a citizen?" The government had been rounding up Italians who weren't citizens. Japanese, too.

"We're all citizens. Even my dad. But I don't think it matters."

"Uncle Oliver, our music teacher hasn't been to school since we went back after Pearl Harbor. He hated Mussolini. Used to make fun of him and Hitler. Maybe they took him, too."

Mia nodded. "And maybe they took Michael by mistake."

"I want to help you, but I don't know what I can do that you haven't already done, Mia."

"I'm sorry about your brother." Mrs. Forgione patted Mia's hand. "Maybe my nephew Harry can help you, Oliver."

I hadn't agreed, and now I had an assistant. I gave her a look.

"I know Michael from church." She smiled at Mia, then gave me a look of her own. "The girls are right. Michael would never leave without telling his family."

"Okay. I'll do what I can. When do you think I can meet Harry?"

"I'll call him now." She disappeared into the kitchen.

"Harry who?" Zoe sat straight up.

"Harry Buonarotti." I drained my coffee cup. "He's the district attorney, Zoe. Your dad works for him."

The girls stared at each other.

Of course. They were worried about Peter finding out his daughter was "associating" with Italians. I imagined he even harbored suspicions about his Italian boss.

"Mrs. Forgione and I will keep you out of it. Okay?"

They nodded, but didn't seem too sure.

"Honest. It won't get back to your dad, Zoe."

Mrs. Forgione hustled back.

"Harry can meet you tomorrow morning. If that's all right with you, I can tell Mia's father when he comes to deliver the produce."

I told her I'd be there and pushed back my chair.

"Come on. Harley and I will drive you truants to school. I'll tell the teacher you're late because of official business, and if she asks you what business, tell her it's top secret." Maybe I'd ask the school principal about the music teacher, too.

"You better not stay too long at school, or Sister Bernadette will get the truth out of you." When Mia teased me, her face lit up. "They should send her to interrogate German spies."

"I'm tougher than I look." I took her hand. "Stop worrying. Harry and I will find your brother."

7

He Had a Gun

God help me, I'd done it again. Made a promise I might not be able to keep. When I parked on the street where Michael's friend lived, curtains twitched in windows, and women popped out of their front doors like cuckoos striking the hour and called their reluctant children home. People noticed things on this street. Whether they were willing to talk to me was another story.

After I talked to the boy Michael had been visiting, I walked the block catching glimpses of long, narrow back gardens, old fruit trees, and gnarled grapevines. A tire swing swayed on a thick rope.

My door-to-door canvas was useless. No one had seen anything the night Michael disappeared. The Italians shook their heads, said no, and pushed the door closed, if they opened it at all. They were afraid. Italy had declared war on the United States, and they didn't know yet what that would mean. Ireland remained neutral, exhausted from the first war and unwilling to send men to die helping England in another war with Germany, but the Irish families didn't help, either. No one knew anything. The night of December 7, everyone had been sitting in the dark by the radio, desperate for information.

"Hey, mister."

I looked behind me.

"Up here."

I scanned second-story windows and saw movement in an oak tree. Two boys peered down at me from a tree house partially hidden in the leaves. Had to be brothers—maybe twins, with identical, stick-straight brown hair and freckles.

"Are you looking for Mr. Posto, the man in the house up the hill?"

"Why? Do you know something about him?"

"What's your dog's name?"

"He's Harley. I'm Oliver."

"I'm Tim. He's Jimmy."

"Jim," the other boy corrected him.

The boys seemed to confer without words.

"If we tell you what we saw, will you promise not to tell our mother?"

"I promise, but why don't you want me to tell her?"

"We were supposed to be in bed, but we couldn't sleep and we couldn't turn on any lights, so we snuck out the window to look for planes."

"Didn't your mother notice you were gone?"

"There are eight of us."

"Got it." I looked at my shoes to hide my smile. "What did you see?"

"Two men took him away."

"Do you know who they were?"

"We think they were G-men."

I tried to get a line of sight to the street in front of the solitary house.

"How could you see what happened?"

"We were up here with our brother's binoculars when the car drove up. We snuck behind the bushes to see if they were spies."

"What did you see?"

"The men went to the door and took Mr. Posto right off the porch. He didn't even have a coat. They were putting him in their car when a guy ran up and shouted, asked them what they were doing with Mr. Posto. Then Jimmy made a noise—"

"Did not."

"Then how did they know where we were?"

"You made the noise."

"Did not."

"Did too!"

"Boys, what happened next?"

"We ran through the backyards to our friend's house and hid there until we thought the car was gone."

"Why did you run?"

"One of the men looked right at us and pulled back his coat. He had a gun."

8

She Grew Up Too Fast

The next morning, I stood in the kitchen, the heart of the Café Avellino, and inhaled the smells. Garlic and onions, something roasting. And coffee. Cups of coffee and a plate of cookies sat on a long pine table.

Mrs. Forgione's nephew Harry rose and extended his hand. He was dark—dark hair, dark eyes, and now dark circles behind his wire-rimmed glasses. Bennie Fiori, Mia's father, looked worried-thin, his frame burdened by the weight of the black jacket he wore over a collarless white shirt. His hair was slicked straight back, still separated into furrows by the teeth of his comb. He stopped folding and refolding a napkin long enough to grasp my hand.

"Thank you both for helping. We've been beside ourselves worrying about Michael."

"Your daughter is very persuasive."

Bennie shook his head, as if wishing things could have been different. "She grew up too fast."

"I found out something." I filled them in on my conversation with the boys. "The men might have taken Michael when he tried to intervene."

"Mr. Posto is my father's friend. My son would try to help him. But maybe the men were helping. Maybe he was ill."

"I'm afraid that's not what it sounded like."

"Then why hasn't Michael called, told us where he is?"

"The names of the men being picked up aren't being released, and they're not permitted to communicate with anyone."

"Not even a lawyer?" We were at war—maybe due process had become an early casualty.

Harry shook his head. "What we've learned from the few people released is that the detainees are presumed guilty. It's up to them to prove they're innocent—without knowing what they're charged with." Harry's voice was strained.

"Why would they arrest Mr. Posto?" Bennie sounded bewildered.

"Him, specifically, I don't know. A few years ago, the government compiled a list of people considered dangerous: Italians, Germans, Japanese, refugees. The round-up began the day we were attacked."

"How could anyone think my son was dangerous?"

"It doesn't take much to make the list. Rumor, innuendo, knowing fascist sympathizers. They're going after anyone remotely connected to Italian institutions: the consulate, the Italian newspaper or radio stations. Veterans of the Italian army or navy. All those people are suspect. Even if they're citizens. Even if they're antifascists. Even if they fought with us in the last war against the Germans."

"My son isn't any of those things. He has no politics."

"We aren't certain he was picked up, but the timing fits. He might have been in the wrong place at the wrong time." I thought about chance, how a fraction of a second could change your life.

"At least now we know where to look for him," Harry reassured Bennie.

"Where?" Bennie's palms flattened on the table.

"The old Salvation Army building in San Francisco. From there, they go to Immigration or to Fort McDowell on Angel Island."

"I'm going to find him!" Bennie sprang from his chair.

"It won't help if you stir things up." Harry stood and put a hand on his shoulder. "Please leave it to me. If Michael was picked up, finding him is going to be about calling in favors and relying on people who don't want to act like the fascists we're fighting. I'll leave messages with my aunt to keep you informed." He handed him a card. "You can call me at home."

Bennie rubbed his thumb across the raised lettering and nodded—a reluctant agreement.

Mrs. Forgione wrapped a baking pan in a dish towel and followed him to his truck.

Harry turned to me; I knew what he was going to say. "You didn't tell him everything, did you?"

"No. He doesn't need more to worry about."

"What is it?"

"The detainees are being interrogated none too gently. Those thugs think because a man is on the list he must be guilty of something, even if he's on it because someone lied about him."

Mrs. Forgione came back without the pan. She pressed the palms of her hands together and moved them up and down at the wrist. "I can't believe this is happening. Mr. Posto's poor wife died while he was in an Italian prison for speaking out against Mussolini. He barely escaped to America. Now this. It is a nightmare for him."

"Harry?" I hated to burden him further. "I talked to the principal at the girls' school. Their music teacher is missing, too."

Harry swore under his breath in Italian, then smiled an apology to his aunt. Hard to mistake swearing for anything else. In any language.

"He taught music at the Italian culture schools until the fascists took them over. He left when they ordered him to teach "*La Giovanezza*," the fascist anthem. Took the job over here."

I suspected Harry had found the teacher the new job and had been quietly helping other Italians caught up in the politics of war. I wondered what would happen to their community next.

9

Safer Not to Know

Almost two weeks had passed since our meeting at the cafe; Bennie and I were at the morgue. Not a good place to be on Christmas Eve.

Doc Pritchard was uncomfortable, as if he still hadn't gotten used to this part of his job. Maybe that was a good thing.

"Mr. Fiori, this boy fits the general description of your son, but his face is badly damaged. It may be difficult to identify him."

The skin around Bennie's eyes tightened, but he signaled that he was ready, and Pritchard pulled back the sheet.

The farmer brushed the hair from the boy's face, then turned away.

I touched his shoulder. "I'm sorry."

He looked puzzled, then realized what I thought.

"No, no. It's not Michael."

"Are you sure?"

"There is no scar at his hairline from the time he ran into a tree branch. He had a scar here." He pointed, then the momentary relief on his face disappeared. "One of my customers told me her son is missing. It could be him."

"We have no other reports of missing boys."

"He was in hiding. When she didn't hear from him for a while, she got worried, but she didn't want to cause a fuss in case he was okay."

"Hiding from whom? And why?" There were a lot of reasons to hide these days—the restrictions, the draft, the police.

"She didn't tell me, but I think it had something to do with the children who were killed in the fire."

I suspected I might have found my father's missing witness. "Let's go see her."

We arrived at the woman's house sooner than I would have liked. When she opened the door, she closed her eyes and made the sign of the cross as if she already knew why we were there. She hung up her apron and turned off the stove. Bennie helped her to my car and asked her why her son had been hiding.

She told us someone had found out he was talking about the fire that killed the Fleming children. They told him to get out of town if he knew what was good for him, so he ran away, but felt so guilty, he came back. He was afraid to go to the police, but he found someone else to tell. No. She didn't know what he knew or who had beaten him. He had said it was safer for her not to know.

It was late afternoon when I tapped on the door to my father's chambers.

When I told him about the witness, the color drained from his face. I poured him a drink and tried to reassure him.

"Peter should be safe. Whoever set the fire will figure if he had any proof, he would have acted by now. No witness, no threat. Besides, those groups will disband or go underground. The men will be drafted and turn their hatred toward the Japanese. They'll disappear."

"The men I suspect will not sacrifice themselves for the greater good. They'll remain here and turn the war to their own profit."

"We might never know who set the fire, Judge."

"Perhaps not. But nothing prevents you from discovering who in the police force helped them. Police are exempt from the draft, so they're not going anywhere."

"I'm sure it's Wade Slater and his pals, but we'll never be able to prove it. In the meantime, you can stop worrying about Peter."

January

1942

10

A Little Bit Gossip

Wade Slater watched his wife peek around the door of the police station.

"Hi, Mrs. Slater. Do you want Wade? Well, I guess you do— why else would you be here?" Harmon's ears turned red, and the files he held exploded from his hands.

Cora stooped to help him, but Wade caught her by the arm and shook his head. Damn, she irritated him sometimes.

"You forgot your wallet, Wade. It's such a beautiful day for a walk, more like April than January, so I thought I'd bring it by."

"Come on. I'll walk you to the corner." He half pushed her out the door.

"How about lunch? We need to talk. Can you meet me later?"

"Sure. The Hotel Mac at one." He whispered in her ear. "Maybe we should get a room. Forget lunch."

Cora looked up at him from the corner of her eyes, flirting. Lifted an eyebrow, and Wade laughed. Maybe she had changed

IN THE SHADOW OF LIES

her mind about moving to Colorado. If she had, everything might work out after all.

"Hi, Mrs. Slater." A man had stepped out of the fire station. "Wade, can I see you for a minute?"

"Go ahead. I need to stop at the variety store anyway. I'll see you at the Hotel Mac."

The firehouse doorway sheltered him while he listened to the fireman's tale of woe and watched her walk away. He wasn't kidding about the hotel room. Imagine what the Point would think then. It would be all over town before they got home. They still hadn't recovered from the shock of the lovely Cora marrying a Slater.

He never understood what had made him knock a rookie out of the way of a bullet. Maybe he wouldn't have if he'd known he'd be the one to be shot, but the truth was, getting shot was the best thing that had ever happened to him. When he had seen Cora through the haze of his concussion, he'd thought he was seeing a ghost. Or an angel. An angel with pale-blue eyes and skin you could almost see through. Then she had touched him. Cora Lundgren, back in Richmond after all those years. He had drifted in and out of consciousness, worried about what he might have said in his delirium. She'd stayed with him long past her shift, reading to him, putting cold compresses on his forehead. He had responded to her gentleness with a tenderness that surprised him. Still did.

Someone called out to her. Oliver Wright. She turned sideways to greet him and touched the locket she always wore. She glanced back at Wade, then dropped her hand and hurried away. Wright looked after her until she disappeared into the store.

Is that why she wants to stay in Richmond? Because Wright came back? Did she bring me my wallet hoping to see him? He thought he had settled the score with Mr. Golden Boy, full of his family connections and big-shot education, but nothing seemed to faze him. He's ruining everything. Again. For a moment, he remembered that Cora still could have married Wright all those years ago, and she hadn't. Maybe she regretted that now.

He couldn't stomach having lunch with her while she pined for another man. Let her sit there.

Cora sat in the Hotel Mac surrounded by people talking and enjoying their lunches. She didn't look at the plates of food that passed her; smelling them was enough to make her mouth water. She sipped at her coffee, wishing she could order without Wade.

She felt the glances of other diners, and her face began to burn. She took a pen and notebook from her handbag and played at making a list. Gradually, the restaurant grew quiet. Her heart sank when she realized he wasn't coming. Because of Oliver. No matter how much she tried, she could not convince him that Oliver meant nothing to her now. She hadn't even known him when she'd dated Oliver. So much had happened since then. So much had changed.

She left money on the table for her coffee and gathered her packages. She hesitated in the doorway and hugged herself against the chill. The morning's golden sun was now a cold gray glow behind the fog. She braced herself and stepped into the street, dreading the long walk home.

I stared out the window of the Café Avellino, barely aware of Harley's head on my lap, telling me he was hungry even if I wasn't. Running into Cora had been less awkward than I had thought it would be, until she touched her locket. I remembered what it had meant, and how happy we had been. And then she had disappeared. I still didn't know why she left or why she had refused to see me when I went to her house in Santa Cruz. So much time had passed that it didn't matter, but I did wonder why she was still wearing my grandmother's locket.

I had been so absorbed in my thoughts, I hadn't heard Mrs. Forgione coming, but I should have known the promise of food was near when Harley's tail thumped the floor.

"What are you thinking about that makes you forget to order?" She sat down beside me. "Why your police colleagues are not welcoming to you?"

"What? Why do you think they're not welcoming? I mean not the reason for not being welcoming, but whether they are?"

Her hand covered her mouth.

"Mrs. Forgione, quit laughing."

"I'm sorry, Oliver. Which question should I answer?"

"Both, I guess." She was so without malice, that I didn't mind opening up to her.

"Do you know about Chief Anderson. The one Cavanaugh replaced?"

I said no, and she told me to order my lunch. When she was satisfied I wouldn't faint from hunger during her tale, she told me about the old chief.

"This is a little bit gossip and a little bit what I saw myself." She rolled a napkin into a long cylinder. "He was a policeman here, but then he moved to Los Angeles for a better job. His wife wasn't happy—people said he married above him—so she pressured him to come back. We think her family bought him the job as chief."

Our lunch arrived. When the counter girl left, I motioned for her to continue.

"She had money and enjoyed lording it over him. Rumor is ..."

"And the rest isn't rumor?"

"Rumor is"—she ignored me—"that he was having affairs and wanted to leave her, but he was used to the high life. Now, I think he was a good man at first, but he was unhappy. Then Prohibition came in, and all of a sudden, a cop could make a lot of money simply by turning a blind eye."

"This keeps getting better." It was all new to me. I suppose because I had been away. "Now he's philandering and on the take, but this is only rumor?"

"There had to be something to it because there was an investigation and then they fired him. A lot of the men said it was unfair. Some of us thought maybe others had been in on it, but the investigation stopped with Anderson. Then they hired Chief Cavanaugh, and before you knew it, he had brought you in over other men who had been there longer." She was back to rolling the napkin. She didn't seem to be finished.

"What else?" When she tried to look innocent, I pointed at the napkin she was torturing.

She sighed. "Your brother and father haven't made a lot of friends. There's no reason anyone should think you're any different than they are."

Seeing Cora with my grandmother's locket had bothered me on and off all day, and I was still wondering about it while I watched the men leave the station. I had volunteered to man the house so they could go to a retirement party for a beat cop who had spent the last thirty years on the pavement. I used to think I'd spend my thirty years in Seattle at my first precinct, a job I missed more and more each day even though I had lost Elizabeth because of it.

My partner and I had been working a crime scene, one I wasn't even supposed to be at. I had cleared my cases to spend time with my family at Lake Washington, and then the captain had called. There had been a murder, a rare opportunity to show the homicide department the new methods for processing a scene I had learned. He said I'd be done by the afternoon and could join my family later at the lake.

We worked in our shirtsleeves, ties loosened, talking over the drone of a fan that barely moved the heat around. A middle-aged woman in a stained housecoat lay on the floor, part of her face stuck to a whiskey bottle that had left raspberry smudges on the slanted linoleum. The husband sniveled in the kitchen, crying over the spilled Four Roses, over killing his wife, getting caught, who knew why? Maybe he loved her and was sorry. Maybe he was just a maudlin drunk.

Someone cleared his throat. The precinct captain stood in the doorway, holding his cap. He looked at me. I'd delivered bad news often enough myself to see what was coming. Coming my way. My partner shut up the drunk with a look.

"What is it?" I moved toward the door.

"Charley's been hurt. Let me drive you to the hospital."

"How bad is it? What happened? Where's Elizabeth?"

He shook his head. "I'm sorry."

The words knocked the breath out of me. Everything, everyone in the room disappeared. Except the man in front of me.

"How?"

"They were canoeing in the lake. A powerboat lost control and hit them. It didn't stop. Elizabeth went under. Charley kept diving, looking for her. When the harbor patrol got there, he was exhausted, but he dove again. By the time a diver got him out, he was unconscious."

"He would never leave his mother." I felt pain swelling in my chest, filling it, threatening to break me open. I should have been with them. I didn't have to ask the next question.

"They're still searching for her."

They searched while I sat beside my son's bed and willed him to wake up. I told Elizabeth I would never forgive myself for not being there to save her and asked her to send Charley back, if that's where he was, still not able to leave her.

The phone rang, pulling me back to the present, to Pt. Richmond. I was surrounded by empty desks. Looked like this call was mine.

11

The Deadline

Night after night, he sat at his kitchen table with a cup of black coffee and watched the trains snake in and out of the Santa Fe railroad yard. Sometimes he fell asleep in the chair, lulled by the movement of the brakemen who uncoupled the cars, or the switchmen who leaned on the tall rods that moved the track junctions. He knew the language of the signals that commanded the locomotives to speed up or slow down. He knew the red arc and splash of sparks when a watchman threw down a cigarette as a train rolled into the yard. He knew where the trains had been and where they were going. Which settled on sidings and which slid through the lines of engineless boxcars straight out to Ferry Point.

Sometimes the phone rang, calling him out to unlock a house for a customer who had lost his keys, or to fit a new lock on a burgled store. When he returned home, he would walk down the hall to his kitchen, put the dollar bills in the tobacco can he kept in the icebox, and light the flame under the percolator to reheat the coffee.

Tonight, he stood in the shadow of a water tower and looked at his watch. Almost midnight, February 17, 1942. The deadline. He wished his friend had done what he had asked. He supposed he couldn't blame him. He wondered if he would have done it for him. It didn't matter now.

The rain drenched his black suit and the white shirt that chafed at his neck. He ran a finger inside the collar, then touched the breast pocket that sheltered the photo of his mother. He heard the chuffing when the train entered the yard, then the *whup-whup-whup* as it passed the line of still boxcars that hid the approaching engine from his view. He stepped out from behind the water tower, ignored the shouts of a switchman crossing the yard, and lifted his polished shoe over the glistening steel track, careful not to stumble on the uneven rail bed. His hand had barely touched his right shoulder, on the word *Ghost*, when he lifted his head and stared into the window of the cab, into the stricken face of the engineer.

The rain fell, invisible in the darkness until it splattered on the windshield and reminded me of nights in Seattle when my partner and I had ridden together, drinking coffee and talking about nothing much.

The tires hissed along the wet street, and the hooded beams glowed on the pavement in front of me, leaving alleys and door-ways draped in darkness. I cranked down the window, hoping the cold air would keep me awake while I drove to what sounded like my second suicide of the night.

I hadn't gotten over what I had found at the other end of Richmond. A man had jumped, fallen, or been pushed from the roof of an apartment building. It looked like a suicide, but I wouldn't be certain until they had translated the note I had found in the poor guy's pocket. Looked like Italian, that old-fashioned script.

In some ways, I envied the jumper the peace he had found, the ending of pain. For me, the time without pain was in the past, on the other side of an abyss that grew wider each day. My whole working life had been defined by death, but Elizabeth's was the only one to bleach the color from the sky, mute the song of the birds. Muted me, too. Writing had been my escape from the violence and sorrow of my job, but I had lost my words, lost them with Elizabeth.

Now two more people were dead. Both suicides? Had they given any thought to the people left behind, the ones who would have to move through days of grief with no choice but to go on?

A gust of wind sent sparks flying from my cigarette. When I looked down to slap out the embers before they ruined another pair of trousers, the car swerved onto the curb and almost clipped a phone booth. A head appeared in the rearview mirror. Reproachful.

"Sorry. Next time you drive, and I'll curl up in back."

Harley yawned and stuck his nose out my window. I felt the breeze from his tail and leaned my head against his neck. I needed to sleep, but people wouldn't stop dying tonight.

The car stuttered over the steel tracks that crossed and re-crossed the asphalt and stopped outside a small building where a rectangle of light promised warmth and shelter. Harley jumped over the seat and followed me into the rain, threw that black nose into the air, and began casting for something.

A man squatted by a bundle along the railroad tracks. From the back, he looked like a frog about to leap into the pool of the night. He rose and turned toward me. Doc Pritchard. He wiped his round face with delicate fingers.

"Detective Wright. Not a fit night for man or beast, but your dog doesn't seem to mind."

I glanced behind me to see Harley nosing around a water tower.

"What do we have?"

"Suicide."

"You sound pretty sure."

"A switchman saw him walk onto the tracks right in front of the train. Called out to him, but he didn't stop."

"Any chance of an ID?"

"The train threw him off to the side, only ran over his legs."

I winced at the *only*.

"Yes. Well." Pritchard shook his head. "The impact killed him. His face is bruised but recognizable. The switchman thinks the poor soul lived in the house next to the yard. He and the engineer are in the office."

"I'll talk to them, see if we can get into the house. Wonder if anyone else lives there, knows why he did it."

"Oh, I found this in his shirt pocket."

I looked at a creased photo of a small woman standing in front of a church, holding a baby in her arms. She looked foreign. Maybe Italian.

I had fallen asleep while I waited for the Café Avellino to open. I stretched and rubbed my face and let Harley out for a rather prolonged leg lift on the corner of the building. We'd been together three years now, three years since I'd found him bloody and unconscious next to a body and felt for a heartbeat through his soft puppy fur.

"The dog's alive." I glared at the patrol officer.

"Oh, yeah?"

"Didn't you even check? What the hell's the matter with you? How about the woman? Did you bother to see if *she* had a pulse?"

My partner knelt down by the woman. Shook his head.

"Let's get him to a vet. He's young. Maybe he'll make it."

I remembered the weight of him in my arms while a patrol car rushed us to the closest vet, and the sense of loss when they carried him into surgery. I told Elizabeth about the dog, knowing if the family of the victim didn't want him, she would say we should take him. For Charley.

I alerted nearby hospitals after the vet called to say he had removed a chunk of flesh and some cloth from the dog's teeth. We arrested the woman's brother two days later. He might have gotten away with murder if he hadn't gone to the emergency room to have a dog bite treated.

Charley visited the dog every day until he recovered and called him Harley for reasons only a fifteen-year-old boy might understand. He thought it was hilarious for them to be Charley and Harley. Elizabeth had loved to watch them play together.

God, I missed her.

"Come on, boy. Let's get some breakfast."

When I walked into the café, Harry and the regulars were at the round table by the fire where they had sat during the wake for Enrico, Mrs. Forgione's husband. I had been a little envious that her husband had friends who honored him so zestfully at his death. His chair had sat empty, the shot glass in front of it full. "Remember, remember," the men had interrupted each other, laughing, talking, hands moving and circling, as if swirling memories up to their friend. Presumably up.

I ordered frittatas, then made my way to the men's room to wash away some of the gloom of the night. I would eat, then tell the men they had lost another friend—Marino, the man who had thrown himself in front of the train.

The Cafe Avellino's green-and-black-striped awning sheltered Jonah North from the rain. He debated whether to go in. The café looked very Italian. And he wasn't. Italian. But he did like the cosmopolitan feel of the place, and if they had cappuccino in there, he'd gladly bear being treated like an outsider. As his boss always asked when he worried about doing something, "What are they going to do? Kill you?"

It was like walking into a kaleidoscope. White-veined black marble on the floor, red marble on the smaller tables, white marble on the counter, and inlaid rugs of different marbles, on top of which sat chairs upholstered in large-flowered patterns.

When the bell on the door rang, a group of men looked him over, then back at each other. One man nodded to him. Not an invitation, merely a greeting.

A lone man sat at a table, eating an omelet. He didn't look Italian either. English, probably, with straight blond hair and almost invisible eyebrows. He reminded Jonah of a photograph that had been taken out of the developer too soon. The object of his scrutiny looked up, as if he felt Jonah's gaze. His eyes were deep blue, the color of gentians, and reminded Jonah of the deathly flowers of Lawrence's poem. He felt those eyes size him up and memorize him. A cop. The man dropped a piece of bread on the floor, and a long brown snout reached out for it. A dog? In a restaurant? None of his business

12

Enemies in Our Midst

I scarfed down my breakfast and realized I was showing scarcely more manners than my dog. At least I used a napkin. The stranger who came in looked eastern with his pleated trousers and jacket with elbow patches. Gray-blue eyes; about five feet ten; medium forehead; ears close to the head; long, thin nose; full lips; cleft chin. Filed.

Harley lay under the table and held his tin plate with one paw and licked it now and then to let me know he wouldn't be averse to a bit more.

I picked up my coffee, walked over to the round table, and sat down when Harry gestured at a chair. I came out and told them. Their friend Marino was dead.

A man with a handlebar mustache burst out in Italian.

I thought it could be important, or the man could just be asking for another cup of coffee.

Harry calmed him, asked him a question. When the man answered, the other men made the sign of the cross, muttered, and reassured him.

"What did he say?"

"Marino offered him fifty dollars to shoot him last night. He thought he was being dramatic. He had no idea he was serious."

Harry touched the man's shoulder. "Marino couldn't stand the thought of leaving his home, his business. Starting over."

"When was the last time you saw him?"

Sadness clouded his dark eyes. "Last night at the Galileo Club. That's why you're here, isn't it?"

"Harry, you should have been a detective." My dry tone teased a smile from him. "Yes. I found matchbooks from the club in his house. I thought he might be part of your bocce group."

"We were at the club, but not for bocce. We held another meeting to explain why only Italians who are citizens can live or work in the restricted zone. We're helping people find new places to live, new jobs for the fishermen and the cannery workers."

A man with a nose that had been broken at least once interrupted. "It isn't easy. Most of them don't speak English, and no one wants an 'enemy alien' working for them or living in their neighborhood. People with Italian names are losing their jobs, even people born here." He reached out a hand and told me his name was Bruno. "I became an enemy alien overnight, even though I hate Mussolini, and now I have to move to my sister's house in Oakland where I will have to be in the house before eight every night, like a child."

"Why did your friend do it? The war won't last forever."

"Eh, no one tells us what will happen after they make us move, or if they're going to send us away, or when we'll come back. *If* we'll come back. They could deport everyone. I can understand why he did it." He hurried to add, "Not that I would do it. I have a family. He didn't."

"Look what's happened to the fishermen. We can't go near the water. Who's a fisherman if he can't fish? What are they going to do for fish, these people? Think the fish are going to jump up on the docks for them?"

"Joe DiMaggio's father can't even go to his son's restaurant because it's on the wharf." Bruno looked at me, as if expecting me to share his outrage.

"Oliver, it's hard for the older people to move to a strange place." Harry spoke in an even tone, despite the sadness in his eyes. "In Italy, until recently, each region was like a separate country with its own food, its own language, even different saints. People from one area didn't mix with those of another. Many had been enemies and fought wars over land. When they came here, they stayed in those groups, and now they're terrified of being separated from their families and neighbors."

"Not to mention most of them can't read or write Italian, let alone English. How could they pass the citizenship test? Besides, we—they—were too busy earning a living or raising families to study." Bruno forced a short laugh. "And we thought it didn't matter if we were citizens or not."

"We know better now." Harry looked around at the men. "My neighbor had to move away. She lost one son at Pearl Harbor, has two more in the army, and now, when she most needs the help of her friends, her church, she is in exile, alone with her grief and her fear."

He gestured at the newspaper he was holding and asked if I minded if he finished translating it.

I shook my head and read over his shoulder.

War makes possible enemies out of people whom we have considered friendly acquaintances for many years. Yet the dangers attendant on having people who would furnish information to the enemy in our midst is too great to al-

low a relaxation of alertness. Aliens loyal to Mussolini or
Hitler are just as dangerous to us right now as the Japanese.

Mrs. Forgione had refused to put up the government poster that called Italian an enemy language, but I'd noticed that the men had stopped speaking the language of their birth in public. They were tongue-tied, their rolling *r*'s and beautiful vowels stuck in their throats, but I didn't think they could find words, English or Italian, for the way the newspaper made them feel.

Bennie Fiori, Mia's father, pushed through the door of the café with a man who had to be his brother. He told us Jack, a sardine fisherman from Monterey, would be staying in Pt. Richmond a while. Jack looked exhausted. Worse, as if his soul were exhausted.

"How are things in Monterey? What is happening along the coast? With the fishing fleet?" The men peppered him with questions before he had a chance to sit down.

He looked at Bennie, as if asking what he should say.

"Tell them about the boats. It might help." He shrugged. "It can't hurt."

Jack settled in his chair and drank the espresso the waitress had brought him. He nodded a few times, then leaned toward us.

"Before we even knew if our sons and brothers had survived the attack on Pearl Harbor, the Navy knocked on our doors and said they needed our boats to help defend the coast. Most of us volunteered to man the boats and work with them, but they didn't need us. Only our boats. What could we do?"

When Jack grew quiet, Bennie urged him to tell us about delivering the boats.

"Last night, we brought our boats to Treasure Island. We ran without lights through the black night, past the dark light-houses—it was like sailing inside a bottle of ink—and then the ocean began to glow. Shapes flickered against the shimmering water. The curve of a bow, the reflection off a hull." He shuddered. "We looked like a ghostly funeral procession, sailing through the night from Monterey to San Francisco."

The ever-practical men interrupted Jack's lyrical description of the voyage. "With the war, we need canned fish more than ever. Why did they take your boats?"

"The government didn't trust you. It took the boats because Italy had declared war on the U.S." I spoke without thinking, but the men agreed.

"It broke my heart to see the schools of sardines glowing in the water. The runs this year have been better than any of us ever could remember. It should have been a year for paying off debts, putting something away for leaner times. Instead the fishing is over, and our boats are gone."

"What about your crews?"

"They don't know what will happen next. We didn't ask them to come because Japanese subs had been seen off the coast. It should be enough to give up the boat you loved, your livelihood, the future of your sons; you shouldn't have to risk the life of your crew delivering her. But some men showed up anyway."

"What will you do now?" I knew fishermen. They were lost on land.

"Without fishing and the canneries, there's nothing left for Italians in Monterey." Jack's smile reminded me of mothers watching their sons leave for war.

He seemed to realize how defeated he sounded. He looked toward the window, and when he looked back, it was as if he had put his regrets behind him.

"I'm too old to join the Navy, so I said good-bye to the *Stella Maris* and came to see if I could learn to catch vegetables."

Bennie put his hand on Jack's shoulder. I thought the brothers carried the war's burdens with grace. But this was only the beginning.

"Listen up!" A voice killed the moment.

I groaned. Wade Slater.

The men looked at him. He'd never been a friend to them, and now he had the government's blessing to harass them.

He pointed at a *sfogliatella*. Mrs. Forgione set the pastry and a cup of coffee on the counter for him, not waiting for him to ask. Or pay. He scanned the café, paused when he saw me among the men. I had to call his expression a sneer. It looked natural on him.

"Listen up." He was enjoying the men's uneasiness and smiled while he read from a piece of paper: "'All enemy aliens living on the West Coast, that includes Pt. Richmond, for those of you not so clear on your geography, must surrender radio transmitters, short-wave radios, cameras, and firearms. Flashlights. All signaling devices and anything written in invisible ink.' Invisible ink—might have a few choice moments with that last one. 'Come in voluntarily, or we'll search your houses." He smiled. "And you won't like that. Fines and imprisonment if we catch you hiding something." He bit into the pastry. It muffled his next words. "And you won't like that either."

No one spoke. Lots of shrugs and looking at their coffee cups.

Mrs. Forgione broke the silence. "Detective Slater, excuse me, please. I think I have a delivery in the kitchen." A man watched through the glass in the kitchen service door.

Slater banged his cup on the counter. On his way out, he turned. "Don't forget to tell your Wop friends."

Harry tried to reassure the men, but they said it was like living in a fascist state—so many people had disappeared in the night, lost their jobs, had to move.

"I'm sorry." I shook hands with the men at the table, not sure what I was apologizing for. Slater? The restrictions? The men's dead friend?

I signaled for Harley and we walked down the hill toward the station house.

Chief Cavanaugh's voice rolled out of the precinct. I slid into a seat near the door.

"Let me repeat. No more blackouts. It has been determined they interfere with the production of ships and planes. Apparently, we cause more damage to ourselves driving into things than enemy bombers would cause." The chief glanced up, and the men laughed on cue.

He looked back at his notes. "I need teams of men to make sure all the enemy aliens are leaving the restricted zone. The Army is handling the majority of the job, but you know your people: who might hide out, who might have items we need to confiscate. Sergeant Butler will handle that. Slater will take any homicide calls that come in."

He scanned the room, as if he hadn't noticed me and Harley sitting by the door.

"Wright, I'm told you went to two suspicious deaths last night."

"Yes, sir. They appear to be suicides. Italians who killed themselves because they were being forced to relocate."

"No big loss, then."

I didn't know who said it. Could have been any one of them.

The chief smiled. "From now on, I want you on shipyard crime. Thefts, beatings, drunk-and-disorderlies." He raised a hand when I protested. "You've done a great job imparting your *impressive* knowledge about working homicide scenes to the men. Let's see what they can do. Oh, Harmon can help you. I mean Officer Har*mon*, not Har*ley*."

Harmon's face turned red, because of the dog comment or because he'd been put with me. Didn't matter which to me. There were times I'd need backup, and Harmon was so new he couldn't have been involved with the fire. Maybe he'd be a more willing partner than some of the others, less distrustful of the outsider whom the police commissioner had forced on a resentful chief.

"There was a beating at Moore Dry Dock last night. Get over there; get some statements. Any other beatings are yours, too."

I ignored the smug looks of some of the other cops. Barroom brawls and beatings would get me out on the street where I might be able to find a few informants.

13

Forget Me Not

Wade ended up where his aimless drives almost always took him: Keller's beach.

Moonlit waves lapped at the rocks where they had found the broken body. For a while, people had shied away from the rocks, had spread their blankets on the other end of the beach, but gradually they had forgotten, moved closer and closer until boys scrambled over the rocks again and looked for stranded crabs in pools that had once been red with Phyllis Brennan's blood.

Twenty years later, and he still wanted to howl into the night. The silent cry rose from his stomach and filled the hollow in his throat. He clamped his teeth until the bones by his ears ached. He cursed Phyllis, cursed her for loving him, for making him want to be loved, then cursed her for leaving him alone in the world.

She had been perfect. Well, almost perfect. She was always taking home stray cats and dogs and helping the vet with injured birds. She cried when a sparrow with a damaged throat lifted its head and tried to sing. She said it broke her heart.

Wade wanted to shout at her, *Forget about the bird and the dogs. Look at me. I'm injured. Take care of me.*

Instead, he comforted her. She never knew he wanted to wring that bird's neck. Let the wounded vulture and the stranded turtle and whatever the hell she found next fend for themselves. He wanted her to love him, and she did. Until Oliver Wright stole her, then dropped her for Cora.

Cora, who married him and showed him a different world, one where someone looked happy to see him at the end of the day. He had quit going to the bars where the Slater men hung out and hurried home to her. She could tease him into holding a skein of yarn on his hands while she wound it into a ball so she could knit a sweater. For him. He drew the line at going to the yarn store with her, but she brought home samples that she thought would bring out the hazel flecks in his eyes. They sat together and looked at photos of collegiate-looking guys in sweaters, until he finally couldn't take it anymore and stabbed a finger at one. He loved being with her, loved the way she looked at him as if he could never be anything but good. Sometimes he wished it were true; other times he pretended it was.

He looked at the moonlight slash across the bay and wondered if the happiness of the past ten years had been real, or if Cora had been like him, both of them pretending to be something they weren't.

He wanted to trust her. He had tried for weeks to forget seeing her with Wright, to forget seeing the puzzled look on his face when she touched the locket.

He felt himself drawn to the edge of the cliff. One more step, and it would be over, all of it, but maybe the locket meant nothing. He flicked away the cigarette. Its glowing tip traced Phyllis's path to the rocks below. He could almost hear her scream as he turned back to his car.

Death by misadventure. Meant it was an accident, no one was at fault. But he knew that wasn't true. Wright was responsible. Phyllis would be alive if it hadn't been for Wright.

The next morning, Wade snuck the locket out of Cora's jewelry box. He opened it—nothing inside. He slipped out of the house without waking her and drove into town. Time to see what he could find out, maybe put the whole thing to rest.

He walked down Washington Avenue into the old Dietrich's jewelry store.

"Hey, Shelley," he called to the clerk. "Could you take a look at this for me? I need to trace it. Part of a case I'm working on."

"This isn't something we ever carried." She picked up a loupe. "I think this mark is from Tiffany. Probably a special order."

"Where would you get something like that?"

"Maybe San Francisco. Or you could try Powell's in Oakland. Looks like something they might have done."

He waved his thanks as the door closed behind him.

There hadn't been much point in hurrying to the car; the traffic on San Pablo Avenue barely crawled. He cursed the people who gawked and gathered and spilled off the sidewalk into the street. He double-parked in front of Powell's, ignoring the traffic snarl behind him. He pushed through the door and flashed his badge.

"Good morning, Officer."

"Detective."

"Sorry, Detective. How may I help you?"

"I was told you might have ordered this locket." He threw it on the counter.

The portly jeweler blinked, then spread a black-velvet cloth on the glass, placed the locket on it, and took out his loupe.

"I recognize this." He looked at Wade, obviously puzzled. "What are the police doing with it?"

"Who bought it?"

The jeweler looked like he wanted to ask another question, but thought better of it.

"It was a special order from Tiffany." He pulled a large cloth-bound ledger from under the counter, turned the pages one by one, paused, went forward, then back, ran his finger down the lines of tiny handwriting. "Let's see. . . It was in 1914, for the very first celebration of Mother's Day, I believe."

Wade lit a cigarette. Blew smoke in the jeweler's face. He coughed, but didn't hurry his methodical examination. Mother's Day. So maybe it was a family heirloom after all and had nothing to do with Wright. He felt a little ashamed at what he'd done. He'd have to tell Cora he'd taken it to be cleaned, to surprise her.

"Ah, yes. Here it is. I thought I recognized the border."

"The border?"

"It's a wreath formed by two interlocking initials: B.R."

"B.R.?"

"Yes. Judge Wright ordered it. Actually, he ordered two. This is the one with his mother-in-law's initials on it. The other had the initials of his wife."

Wade wanted to smash his fist through the glass counter, or in the face of that smug jeweler, so pleased with himself and his prissy record keeping. He grabbed the locket and turned to leave.

"Would you like to see the special feature?"

"What special feature?"

"If I may . . ." The jeweler held out his palm. "There's a secret catch."

He slid a nail under the lip where there seemed to be no space and pressed. The shallow backing opened to reveal a faded blue flower. Wade grabbed the locket, and the brittle petals drifted onto the counter.

"Oh dear, maybe we can put it back together. A forget-me-not, I think." The jeweler pulled a set of tweezers from his vest pocket. "We must be careful. They look to be quite old."

Wade's hand closed over the locket as if he were going to crush it. A forget-me-not. And she hadn't.

14

Wans

Mrs. Forgione stretched to kiss Harry's cheek. She was worried about how he was taking the news he had gotten the day before, about the death of his friend who had thrown himself in front of a train.

"How are you doing, Harry?"

He waggled his hand, that noncommittal gesture.

"Come. I'll get you some coffee. Have you eaten yet?"

"Yes, Aunt Lucy."

"How about some nice poached eggs?" She headed for the stove.

"No, no, thank you. I'm meeting someone who is having trouble with the new regulations. I'll eat with him."

"*Bene.* You can help me, too."

Harry tilted his head, asking a question. His aunt had been born here.

"Nothing like that. I wonder if you can take something home to Paola. Save me carrying it up the hill."

She pointed at a box almost as big as she was. "Guess what it is."

Powdered sugar dusted the sleeves of her black dress.

"Hmm, let me see. Ravioli?"

"No." She nudged his arm.

"Veal cutlets?"

"Harry, a box this big of veal cutlets, I'd have to cook a whole calf. Maybe two. It would take a year's worth of meat stamps." That reminded her about what was going on at George's Meat Market. Maybe she should tell Harry what everyone in Richmond seemed to know, but he had enough to worry about.

"I give up."

"*Wans!*" She had gotten up at four, mixed the stiff dough, rolled it out into thin sheets, sliced it, twisted it, fried it, then sprinkled the crunchy cookies with powdered sugar.

"You probably worked all morning on these."

"It was nothing." She poured coffee and set out a platter of *wans*. "What's bothering you, Harry? Your friend's death?"

"Paola." He waved a hand. "No, no. Nothing serious. I think she's worried about the way Dom is treating her sister, but she won't complain to me about that buffoon because she doesn't want me to say something to him and make things worse for Isabella."

She shook her head.

"What, Aunt Lucy?"

"I don't like to speak ill of anyone, but I don't like Dom either. I wish he hadn't wormed his way into our family."

"I didn't say I didn't like him."

She smiled. "So, *buffoon* is a term of endearment?"

"Okay. You got me." He took a *wan*, dropping powdered sugar on the kitchen worktable. "Why don't you like him?"

"It's a little bit not fair."

"Go on."

"Our families came from the same town in Italy. Dom's grandfather, Luigi, wanted to marry your grandmother, but her father thought the men in that family were not good men. He figured out a way to let Rosa find out for herself. He waited until the swallows had nested in Luigi's barn, and when the birds hatched, he took Rosa there. A storm of swallows swooped at the closed barn doors, shrieking and battering them in a flurry of wings.

"When your great grandfather asked why the swallows were so agitated, Luigi boasted about his cleverness. Every year the swallows came and made nests in the rafters of the buildings. Year after year he destroyed them, but the swallows kept coming back. Finally, he came upon the perfect solution. He left the barn doors open and let the swallows sit on the nests. The first morning after the eggs began to hatch, he waited until the foraging birds left the barn to gather insects for their mates and the young. Then he shut the doors."

Harry shook his head.

"When Rosa cried because of the high-pitched screams of the birds inside calling to the frantic birds outside, Luigi told her to stop carrying on. It only lasted a couple of days before the birds inside starved to death.

"Rosa couldn't believe his cruelty: to separate the birds who were driven by nature to care for their young and each other. Her father said the anguished cries of the birds should have made the heavens weep. And this man wanted to marry his daughter."

"What happened next?"

"They couldn't interfere on another man's farm. Opening the doors would only have postponed the inevitable, but your grandmother refused Luigi." She nodded her head emphatically. "So, you are a Buonarotti instead of a Criscilla."

"You mean Caputo."

"Criscilla is Dom's father's name. He uses his mother's name now."

"Why?"

Before she could answer, the bell at the back door rang. Dom stood there in his boots and overalls. He always looked as if he needed a shave and a good scrubbing, even when he wasn't carrying a box of meat.

She couldn't understand Isabella's attraction to him. She was a younger version of Harry's wife, both with eyes like picholine olives, black and oval, deeply set above high cheekbones. But now she seemed faded, unsure, always looking to Dom for approval. Perhaps Lucy didn't like him because she knew too well the life Isabella suffered, however she tried to hide it. Dom seemed to be a lot like his grandfather, the torturer of defenseless creatures.

"I have your order."

"Put the box in the refrigerator, please. Help yourself to some coffee."

"Mind if I have a few *wans*?" He stuck his dirty hand into the cookies.

"Of course not. I'll put the rest in a box for you."

15

Bella Vista

Valentine's Day had come and gone, and Michael Fiori still wasn't home. The Army had shipped him to Montana by way of Texas and Tennessee, shuttling the detainees all over the blasted country as if it had nothing better to do. Harry had arranged for us to go see Michael. Even if we couldn't get him out right away, we would be able to reassure Mia and her father that he was okay. They had sent us with food for him—of course—and books and warm clothing.

We drank coffee he made on the wood stove that heated about ten percent of the freezing barracks. He told us that on the day Pearl Harbor was bombed, he was on the way home from his friend's house when he heard Mr. Posto crying for help. The next thing he knew, he was in the back of a car, trying to figure out where he was. Soon the smell of the mudflats seeped into the car, and he knew they were on the Bayshore Highway. The car climbed into the night sky and crawled across the Bay Bridge, feeling its way in the dark. He felt as if he could have been anywhere in the world, that time was suspended, maybe even gravity, and then he felt the car descending.

Mr. Posto had huddled beside him in the backseat, trembling. Michael held his hand, patted his knee, tried to calm him. Soon they were herded along a slippery dock and onto a coast guard cutter. When the boat rocked Michael fell onto a seat, almost pulling Mr. Posto over.

The sailors told him to shut up when he asked where they were going, but another man in handcuffs whispered that they were going to Angel Island, God help them.

Mr. Posto had hung his head and said it was like before. In Italy. When they take you, they can do what they want with you.

Michael had hoped he was wrong, that it was age and fear talking, but for weeks it seemed as if he had been right. Then Harry had sent word that he was working to get a rehearing for them. Not to give up.

"Permesso?" It was the captain of the Italian cruise ship that had found itself on the wrong side of the Atlantic when war broke out. His crew had renamed Fort Missoula *Bella Vista*, the beautiful view, and settled into their barracks, happy not to be fighting a war they didn't believe in. The ship's orchestra was allowed to keep its instruments, and even the captain's little dog got to stay. If it had been a POW camp, life would not have been so pleasant.

"For you." The Captain handed Michael a thick sweater.

He reached for it, then drew back his hand. "Please give it to Mr. Posto. He needs it more than I do."

"I gave him the extra blankets my American friends sent me. He is as warm as possible. If you become ill, it will not benefit him. Take it. Please."

Michael told us Mr. Posto had been coughing all night. The cruise ship's doctor thought it sounded like bronchitis, but he had nothing to treat him with. Harry arranged for the old man to go the army hospital, hoping it wasn't too late. It seemed that taking care of Mr. Posto was all that kept Michael going.

16

Parachuting Into War Zones

Our trip to Montana had left me with a scratchy throat, and I'd finally fallen into a fevered sleep after hours of dealing with drunken St. Patrick's Day revelers. Then the phone rang. *They couldn't need me at the station house. Not yet.* I swallowed, then croaked a *hello*. It was Charley inviting me to meet his math professor.

Harley and I drove down the peninsula. We had started the trip several times but had always turned around before we reached Palo Alto. Being able to see Charley more often had been one of the reasons I had stayed in Richmond, but I let him decide when we would meet.

Besides, I wasn't sure how to be with him without Elizabeth bridging the gap between us. I had been so afraid of being like my own father, that I hadn't known how to be anything at all. Elizabeth's advice had been simple: *Pretend you are Charley, Oliver. Treat him the way you would like to be treated.* But sometimes I froze—my mind or my heart wouldn't work—and

I was incapable of imagining how he would want to be treated. I was never harsh with Charley, but I couldn't quite be the way I wanted to be. Still, somehow, he knew I loved him.

The math professor tried to crush my hand. He looked like a clerk, with his little mustache and bow tie. I knew the type: an intellectual who would be extra-aggressive on the basketball court to prove he was one of the guys, because he wasn't, and never would be. He reminded me of my brother Peter. The professor glowed with affection for Charley who had been put in his course in cryptology. Turned out Charley had a talent for recognizing number and letter patterns, and the military wanted him to become a decoder.

I pictured my son parachuting into war zones and being killed before he hit the ground, but before I said anything that would have embarrassed myself or, worse, Charley, the professor said he'd be in the navy, stateside, and contributing more with his brain than he could with a rifle. He added that he shuddered to think of that mind at risk on a battlefield. I thought maybe I should be insulted on behalf of the men I had fought with in the last war, but I made allowances for the guy. He was an egghead.

After lunch, we walked around campus, threw sticks for Harley, and caught up until I had to leave. When we got to the car, Charley held out his hand.

"Thanks, Dad. I wasn't sure you'd be okay with this. It'll mean I have to go east."

"I know, but the professor made it sound like you might win the war without firing a shot. How could you say no?"

He smiled, and I saw Elizabeth in his face. I remembered her advice and decided that if I were Charley, I would want my father to be honest with me, not try to protect me.

"Um, I've been thinking about reenlisting, but if something happened to me . . . after your mother and everything."

He smiled, as if he knew I wouldn't understand what he was about to say. "Mom's always with me, Dad, and you would be, too, if anything happened to you. I'm not alone. Do it." He looked down at Harley. "What about the big guy?"

"He's coming with me."

I held my son. "I'm proud of you." My eyes filled, and I might have started blubbering if Harley hadn't almost knocked us down when he broke into our hug.

Now Harley bounced along beside me as we neared the station house. He seemed as happy about having seen Charley as I was. We stopped when we heard a woman berating someone.

"I'm telling you, I want to talk to a detective. A *de-tec-tive*!"

I glanced through the window. A girl sat on the chair against the wall, folded in on herself as if she wanted to disappear. Her dusty brown skin was scraped, her crown of braids tarnished, one kinked backward like a dog's leg.

"You can talk to me. I'll take the report and see that someone gets in touch with you."

"No, you won't. You'll do what you did the last time I brought someone in here. I got the same runaround, and no one ever talked to me. You think just because these girls are colored, you can ignore what's happening to them? Or do you think these girls are asking for it? Well, this time he made a mistake. This time he picked a girl that isn't on the street. A good girl."

"There are no detectives here right now."

"We'll wait."

"Maybe she should see a doctor instead."

"You let us worry about the doctor. Your job isn't to send us to a doctor. Your job is to stop this monster. I'm staying here until we talk to someone."

I had listened long enough and went into the station to rescue my partner.

The girl drew up her knees when Harley went through the door.

"Here, Harley." I patted my leg, and he sat by me. "He won't hurt you."

Whoa. A tall, broad woman spun around and almost stood on my toes. "You a detective?"

"Yes, ma'am. What can I do for you?"

She nodded at the girl on the chair.

I understood. Too well. "Come into the meeting room. We can talk there."

I was ashamed for my gender, ashamed we couldn't stop this man. Maybe that was why it was so hard to look these women in the face.

The woman helped the girl up and supported her until she slid one hip onto a chair.

"What's *your* name?"

"Becky." The woman stood over me.

"Please sit down."

She glared at me, then sat next to Becky.

"Have you been to a doctor?"

"We're going when we're done here."

"You need to let her answer, ma'am. What's your name?"

"Josephine Jessup. I'm Becky's aunt. Everyone calls me Auntie Josephine."

"I need Becky to tell me what happened to her." I smiled at the girl. "Take your time."

"Same thing happened to the other girls." Auntie Josephine looked at me as if she thought I was useless.

"What other girls?"

"Don't you all talk to one another?" She bounded out of her chair, hands on hips. Her bushy eyebrows met over a long nose that broadened at the base. She must have been in her forties, old enough to be the girl's mother.

"Sit down! Please." I looked at her until she sat, then uncapped my fountain pen and pulled over a pad. "Let's begin at the beginning. Assume I know nothing about this." I jumped in when those busy lips opened to speak again. "I want to help you. Let's get through this so Becky can see a doctor."

Becky and Auntie Josephine told the story in tandem. Becky answered with single words, and her aunt filled in the details. It had still been dark when the girl had left home for work. She had been running late, and even though she knew it was dangerous, she had taken a shortcut through the alley behind Tapper's Inn. It was a pickup spot, but it was early morning and the women had left. A man had grabbed Becky from behind and choked her until she passed out. She couldn't tell if he was tall or short, dark or light. But he was strong.

Auntie Josephine tapped the table. "This may sound crazy to you, but these attacks remind us of ones that happened a long time ago. Must have gone on for ten years."

"When did they happen?"

"They started a year or two after the first war ended. We were scared to go out."

I wondered if she had been a victim.

She wagged a finger in my face, as if she could read my mind.

"Didn't happen to me, but happened to plenty. Back then it happened maybe every six months. But now it's happening closer together. First Sylvie, walking home in the dark after her own birthday party. What a terrible thing for her. On top of being attacked, she lost one of her new birthday earrings. She thought maybe the man took it, but what's he gonna do with one earring?"

"Did she go back and look for it?"

"A couple of her friends did. They found a lot of trash, but no earring. Then he got Laila, and now Becky. The third girl in three weeks. And you people do nothing. Think the prostitutes were asking for it 'cause they, you know, get paid for doing it." Her voice softened. "But Becky was just a girl in the wrong place at the wrong time."

"Let's get her to the hospital." I stilled her protests. "I'll come talk to you, talk to the other women, but first she needs some care."

Becky flinched when Harmon reached out to help her into the police car. Auntie Josephine rolled her eyes, as if men in general, and Harmon in particular, were completely stupid.

I thought about what Josephine had told me. I doubted it was the same man. The attacks had ended sometime in the early thirties and started again about ten years later. That was a long break, but maybe the man had been caught for something else and been in jail or had moved away and come back. More than likely, Auntie Josephine and her friends had it wrong.

17

The Washington Beehive

Paola ruffled Harley's fur and led me into the garden. "You're lucky to catch Harry. He just got back from Washington." Her hand flew to her mouth. "Whoops. Maybe I wasn't supposed to tell anyone that."

I laughed. "I don't think any harm will come from your telling me."

"Sit down. I'll bring some wine." She waved a hand at my protests and walked back to her house.

"Welcome home, Harry."

He gestured to a chair, inviting me to sit with him under the arbor. Winds off the bay jostled the trailing vines of wisteria that sheltered us, creating sinuous shadows on the tablecloth and Harry's white shirt.

"It's so good to be home. I kept hearing, 'Washington is a beehive of activity.' I didn't contradict them, but clearly the bureaucrats have never seen bees at work, or they couldn't confuse their own conflict-filled activity with the harmonious ballet of a hive." He gestured toward bees flying in and out of white boxes.

"May I ask what they wanted of you?"

"They asked me to become a bureaucrat." He seemed amused by the idea. "To become one of the confused bees at cross-purposes in the Washington beehive."

"I can't see that. But you'll want to do something."

"I'm reenlisting."

"Harry!" Paola set a tray with bread and cheese on the table. "I don't like to be unkind, but aren't you a little old for that?"

"Forty-five isn't old. Besides, I'd be part of the Judge Advocate General's Corps, probably stay in the Bay Area. The more Italians that are fighting, working against the war, the sooner it will all end—the backlash against Italians *and* the war."

"I think that's one of the reasons Steve enlisted." She turned to me. "Our son. He had never thought of himself as different from his friends, but after Italy declared war on us, some of them shunned him and called him names." She waved a hand in front of her as if to rub away the ugliness and walked back to the house.

Harry poured the wine. "So, what brings you here today, Oliver?"

"It seems neither of us knows when he's had enough of war. I came to tell you that *I* reenlisted. I'm not sure when I'll be leaving."

"It's not my business, but I've wondered why you decided to stay in Pt. Richmond."

"My father is convinced someone on the police force is connected to the Klan. I promised to see what I could find out."

"As I suspected, but why is he still concerned about this possible connection."

"He's worried about Peter."

"With good reason. Your brother can be a bit reckless in his exuberant pursuit of the truth."

I thought it was more Peter's exuberant pursuit of his own career that motivated him. Wondered if Harry thought that, too.

He slid the knife through the cheese and offered it to me. "Try it. It's mild."

I took it and a large chunk of bread, in case the cheese wasn't as mild as he thought.

"Have you told your father you're leaving?"

"Yes. He's 'disappointed,' but my son gave me his blessing, and that's all that really matters."

We looked at each other. Two fathers with sons in wartime. A crow swooped from the cypress tree on the point and landed on the rocky shore, setting a flurry of gulls into the air.

"My son, Steve, and his friend Nate Hermit will be leaving for the war in a few days. You know, you and I were lucky, Oliver. We managed to survive one war almost unchanged. Not like some of the men we know. I don't want to think about it happening again." He swept a few crumbs from the table and dropped them on the grass. "I'm meeting my brothers soon to play bocce. Come with me. It's part of a little going-away party for Steve and Nate."

I almost refused, but realized I'd like to know Harry and his family better. Besides, my easy chair would be waiting for me, and I'd still have plenty of time to sit and stare into the night.

The sound of women laughing floated out to the arbor.

"Paola and her friends are probably swapping stories about the restrictions on Italians. They've disrupted our community: men have lost jobs, families are unable to visit a father in the hospital or attend a cousin's wedding."

"Those of us outside the Italian community hear little about what is happening day-to-day."

"One of the women who should be here today had to move from Richmond, where all she could see from her house was her neighbor's washing. Now she lives in a non-restricted zone in San Francisco where she watches battleships heading toward the Pacific, and my uncle isn't allowed to cross the street to work in his store, so he sits at the curb and yells orders to his son all day. Even the police think it's funny."

"But General DeWitt doesn't."

"No. If the politicians hadn't stopped him because of the hundreds of thousands of Italians in the armed forces and the defense industry, he would have interned me and my family. Like the Japanese."

"Well, Japanese gardeners *are* trimming lawns and bushes into directional signals for air attacks." I hoped my tone conveyed how absurd I thought that fear was.

"Yes, not to mention poisoning our vegetable supply. Thank goodness for the good general and his concern for our welfare." Harry's scathing tone revealed his anger.

He poured more wine.

"Enough of the war, Oliver. What are you working on?"

"There have been three sexual assaults in the past three weeks. He's targeting colored prostitutes, but yesterday he got a young girl. She might have been a mistake, or maybe the prostitutes are being too careful."

"Paola's heard that there have been other sexual attacks near the hospital. White women. But no one has gone to the police. The women don't want anyone to know."

"So they don't report it. You can hardly blame them." We both knew the women would only be victimized again by the legal system. "The chief has Slater investigating. He's determined to hang it on a Negro sailor from Mare Island or Port Chicago."

"You have far more experience with serious crime than he does. Why aren't you investigating."

I shrugged. Soon it would be over.

18

Lampante

Dom Caputo watched from the hill until Harry and that detective with the dog finally left. He crouched along the tall bushes that shielded him from the house and ducked into the stone building where Harry pulled the honey from the hives.

The last time he and Isabella had visited her sister, Harry had asked him to help move barrels of *lampante* into the honey house.

"*Lampante?*" Isabella looked like that stupid RCA dog when she tilted her head and asked the question.

"Yes. A friend sold us oil pressed from the olives picked up off the ground. It's not good for cooking, only for lamp oil or starting fires. We'll probably never use it for anything."

"Why buy something you can't use?" Dom didn't bother to hide his scorn.

"He's a good man who needed to sell it," Harry answered, in that tone that said not to ask any more questions.

They had pushed the *lampante* barrels behind the wine barrels, which were now blocking Dom. He put the package he carried on a table and humped the barrels out of the way.

"*Maneggia la madonna*," he swore when he brushed his trousers against the wall. He had to look right for the going away party. Finally, he managed to reach the last *lampante* barrel.

He held the package, hating to let it go. One more look. The cold blue steel shone in the light from the window. He cleaned the gun all the time, sitting in his kitchen, running the cloth along the six-sided barrel. He'd been figuring out where to hide it for weeks. It had to be where no one would look and where it wouldn't rust. Finally, he remembered the *lampante* barrels.

He slid his palm around the crosshatched wooden grip, slipped his finger through the trigger guard, and pulled back the hammer with his thumb. He thought of his father's hand gripping the gun, shooting Austrian soldiers in the First World War until he died at the Battle of Caporetto. His revolver was all Dom had left of him.

He wrapped leather bootlaces around the oilcloth package, tied them tightly, and watched the gun sink. He'd come back for it when the war was over. No one was taking his gun. Not only because it had been his father's, but because of what had happened in New Jersey. Another reason he and Isabella had to move away from the coast. He didn't want anyone looking too carefully at his papers, at who he was.

19

An Exceptionally Patriotic High

Before the war I would have waited until one in the morning, when the clubs were swinging, and booze had loosened people's tongues. But now it was always one in the morning or eight in the morning, or noon, whatever you needed it to be, whether your shadow lengthened and shortened under the streetlights or hid under your shoe from the sun.

Not only here. Across the bay, streams of soldiers and sailors flowed through the streets, making the most of still being stateside, still being whole and fresh and young, and women crowded the USO, determined to show them a good time. The gaiety and flirting staved off the threat of death, strengthened the pretense that the boys would all come home and the girls would wait.

I parked on a side street and walked up Chesley in the warm April night, making my way through the crowd outside the Club Savoy, where Jimmy McCracklin was playing. Auntie Josephine had agreed to meet me at the Dew Drop Inn and introduce me to some of the girls.

A woman stepped out of a doorway, her hemline at an exceptionally patriotic high.

"Hi, handsome. Got a light?"

She didn't seem like a pro. Probably working for drinks or some extra cash. Hell, there'd be plenty of men willing to give her whatever she wanted.

"Sure." I flipped open my Zippo and spun the wheel. When the woman bent her head to the flame and cupped my hand in hers, I saw a scowling Auntie Josephine. She gestured with her head for me to get over to her and a caramel-colored woman.

She stomped her foot. "You down here shopping or to do some work?"

"Maybe she knows something."

"I bet she knows plenty, but it ain't nothing you need to be finding out."

I offered her friend my hand.

"I'm Oliver Wright."

She set her gloved hand in mine as if she expected me to kiss it. A tiny black hat perched on the front of her head, partially hiding her features behind its net scrim. She must have glued that hat to her skull for it not to slide right down off her slicked-back hair. She wore a black silk jacket over a black-and-white print dress. Not your typical lady of the night.

"Monica."

I didn't know how to ask her if she had been attacked.

"It happened to Monica's friend." Auntie Josephine had read my hesitation. "You can't talk to her friend, 'cause she's gone out of here. That's the reason Monica came. To tell you what happened."

"Why did she leave?"

The women looked at each other and motioned toward the club. Monica led the way, nodded to the bartender, and slid into a booth in the back of the smoky room. I scanned the crowd—all shades of black and brown. No one I would call white.

"We can talk here without any worries. Doesn't matter what the police are saying. We know the man doing this isn't colored."

"How do you know?"

"My friend saw his arm. His shirt slid up for a second. Someone else caught a glimpse of his forehead. Ofay bastard." Monica seemed surprised by her own outburst. "Sorry." She puffed out her cheeks and blew air through her lips and still managed to be alluring.

A waitress set a round of drinks on the table. Whiskey for me and Monica, ginger ale with four cherries for Auntie Josephine.

"I'm sorry. She was my best friend, and now she's gone off with a man who's beat her before and will do it again."

"She left because she was attacked?"

Auntie Josephine bit a cherry off its stem. "He tells them he knows they liked it, so he'll be back to give them more. She believed he was waiting for her. She was afraid to go out. Couldn't work. Finally, she took off for Detroit with a good-for-nothing, draft-dodging womanizer."

I had read the thin files on the assaults. Whoever had taken statements had only noted dates and the women's names. It had probably been Wade, who wouldn't want minor details like the color of the guy's arm to deflect suspicion from his favorite Negro scapegoats. Who was this guy? And did he really believe they *liked* it?

"Have you told the police this? What you're telling me?"

"We tried, but they don't believe us. Keep saying we're wrong, that it's one of those Negro sailors from Mare Island or Port Chicago. We decided to police things ourselves, watch out for each other. Then he got Becky. We had to try to convince the police again."

"Fat lot of good it did us." Auntie Josephine laid her hand on my sleeve. "Till you."

Her bracelet sparkled in the candlelight and reminded me of the missing birthday earring.

"Did Becky have any jewelry go missing when she was attacked?"

Auntie Josephine stopped a cherry halfway to her mouth. "What?"

"She lost one of her favorite barrettes. We thought it came loose in the struggle."

So he might have taken it. "What about before? Were the women missing jewelry then?"

Monica put her hand to her mouth. "You think he's taking souvenirs? How vile."

"Is there anyone else I can talk to? Anyone who knows anything?"

They gave me a few more names of women who would talk to me and where to find them and told me stories about their friend Zora.

Monica rose. "If Zora phones, I'll ask her if she lost any jewelry that night. See if she'll talk to you."

I got up and held out my hand again.

"How can I get in touch with you if I have more questions?"

Monica looked at me from under her long lashes. She started to answer, when Auntie Josephine butted in.

"You know how to reach me. You need anything, I'll set you up."

I bit my lip. Monica might have winked at me through the net. "Okay. Let me see what I can do." *Somehow this is going to have to fall under shipyard crimes.* I nodded to them.

"Oliver?"

I glanced back at Auntie Josephine. "Thank you for coming to our hospital to talk to Becky. Don't think anyone from that station ever walked in there before, 'cept to arrest someone."

"It's my job, Auntie. No need to thank me. Tell Becky hello."

I thought about the missing barrette as I turned down the side street away from the noise of the crowds. A shoe scraped on the pavement, and a violent shove knocked me into two men who appeared out of nowhere. They grabbed me and pulled me into an alley. I got off a yell before one of them punched me in the stomach and knocked all the air out of me. As I gasped for breath, another blow landed near my kidneys. If that was a bare fist, the bastard had hands of steel. I slammed onto the brick road and managed to snap a kick at the shin of the nearest man. Something gave. One down.

I rolled away from the feet about to stomp me and hit the garbage cans. I rolled back the other way and pushed myself to my knees. A kick to the ribs lifted me off the ground, and I fell sideways. One of the men raised a truncheon above his head. I grabbed a lid and tried to get it between me and the club. If that connected, I was as good as dead. The blow didn't come. Someone ran into the alley, swinging a two-by-four that smashed the man with the truncheon across his shoulder and swung back into the face of the other man. My Good Samaritan stood between me and my attackers, brandishing the length of wood like a bat.

One of the men held out a hand in surrender; the other clutched his side. They grabbed their friend under the arms and dragged him away.

"How badly are you hurt? Do you need an ambulance?" It was the Easterner from the café.

I groaned. "Unfortunately, I think I'm going to live."

"When you're ready to get up, let me know." He could barely catch his breath, let alone help me up. We rested. I tried to breathe without expanding my rib cage.

"How did you know I was the good guy?"

"In the movies, the one getting beat up by three other guys is usually the good guy. Not that I put much stock in what I see in the movies." The man tried to brush off his pants; he still wasn't breathing easy. "You were in the Café Avellino. I knew you were a cop." He smiled. "Not that that necessarily makes you one of the good guys, either."

I couldn't argue with him.

"Besides, I saw how you reacted when that asshole Slater came in."

I managed to drag myself up and leaned on a garbage can. "What yard you in? Welder, right?"

"Is that a guess, or are you a modern Sherlock Holmes?"

"Burn marks on your hands, holes in your clothes. Even Nancy Drew could figure it out."

"Guess so. But you shouldn't explain. Ruins the effect."

"I'm Oliver Wright."

"Jonah North."

Jonah walked with me to my car where Harley was trying to squeeze through the wing vent. The inside of the driver's door was a bit worse for the wear, but I couldn't blame my dog. After I had convinced Harley that the danger was over, I asked Jonah if I could buy him a drink.

"No, thanks. If I get this many burns when I'm sober, I'd probably weld myself to the hull with a beer in me."

I laughed, realizing it had been a long time since I had. And it hurt.

"I'd like to buy you dinner. We should make it sooner rather than later because I've reenlisted and I'm not sure how long I'll be here."

"Why not sit it out? Though I think it might be more dangerous for you here than over there." He seemed completely serious.

"I'll be more useful there. Harley, too."

"You're taking the dog?"

"More like he's taking me. We're going to the Marine K9 Corps in North Carolina. When all the dogs and men are trained to work together, we'll go wherever they need us."

"I'd like to write a . . . uh, write to you when you go. Would you mind?"

"It would be great. Nothing like news from home when you're far away. Can you meet at the Hotel Mac at seven on Sunday?"

"Look forward to it, but now I'd better get going. If you're ten minutes late, they treat you like you're part of the Fifth Column."

"Take care, Jonah. Thanks again."

I watched him stride down the street, gathering appreciative glances from the women. I apologized to Harley and promised him that from now on he would go with me wherever I went. No more waiting in the car.

20

Charred by the War

The tiers of candles shimmering at the feet of Our Lady of Mercy failed to comfort Lucy Forgione. She knelt at the altar, wishing she could pray for her sons, but the hatred in her heart consumed her, drove out her faith and her patience. She hated the men who caused the darkening of the pews behind her. Every week another woman appeared at Mass dressed in black, charred by the war.

Sorrow filled the church, yet the women remained faithful. They prayed for the war to end, for the grace to accept God's will, for the souls of the sons they had lost and the protection of the sons they still had. Or thought they had. It was sometimes weeks before they found out the child they had been praying for had already been blown up by a grenade or bayoneted or drowned or burned alive.

They came to the café and she translated the letters the boys had written them, letters that were now their most valued possessions, perhaps their sons' last words. She wrote back for them, ordinary things to keep the boys connected to the life they had been taken from, to keep them from worrying. Their mothers bit their lips and steeled themselves against their tears, afraid they might blur the ink and reveal the truth: everything was not fine.

Lucy leaned on the altar rail and pushed herself to her feet. She had never felt so alone, especially here. As she walked to her pew, she saw Edna Hermit kneeling near the back of the church. She was a hardworking woman. Had been the Wrights' housekeeper since before Zoe was born and still managed to do the Slaters' laundry. Sometimes, when Lucy was helping with dinner in the Buonarottis' kitchen, she noticed her hanging wash in the Slaters' back garden. Edna's son, Nate, had climbed over the Slaters' fence to play with Steve and his sister, Anna Maria, so many times, that Harry had put a gate in the fence that separated the gardens. Lucy hadn't seen Edna since Steve and Nate had left for the army. Everyone had gone to the station to say good-bye, and Anna Maria had startled everyone, including Nate, by kissing him on the cheek.

Before Edna bowed her head, Lucy caught a glimpse of tears, two snail tracks on her mahogany skin. Lucy felt alone surrounded by people she had known all her life and could only imagine how that solitary woman must feel. She felt touched by a fleeting grace—there were many ways to pray.

When the mass ended, Mrs. Hermit picked her way through the women who lingered in the vestibule. Lucy hurried after her, and called her name, but she didn't turn around. Probably wondered why one of them would talk to her now. Lucy touched her arm. She felt like an elf next to the tall woman.

"Mrs. Hermit, I'm Lucy Forgione. Steve Buonarotti's great-aunt." She hurried to explain. "Last time I saw you was when we sent the boys off. Nate's a lovely boy. A man now, I guess."

"Yes. I suppose he is. We haven't heard from him in a while."

"You know what the mail is like. Nothing for weeks, then four letters in the same day. But we still worry. That's why I wanted to talk to you. Would you like to join our rosary group? We meet at my house to pray for the boys."

No one seemed to be looking directly at them, but Lucy could feel their eyes.

"I don't think your friends would like it."

"Don't worry about them." Lucy brushed the air, as if sweeping away any concern about the others. "Please. Our boys are fighting together; surely we can pray together."

"Together? You have any idea how the army treats boys like mine?" Words flew out of Edna's mouth as if they had been bottled up for a long time. "If your son were wounded, God forbid, they'd let him bleed to death before they put a single drop of my son's blood in him. Like it would turn him black. Make him start jumpin' like Bojangles."

Lucy struggled to find words. All she could do was say she was sorry. For them and for the boys. She turned away from Edna and the catty little groups of women mewling about them and headed down the hill toward the cafe, wondering if what Edna said was true.

Lucy watched Edna hesitate outside the cafe. Finally, she pushed through the door and walked up to the counter.

"You have any of that humble pie?"

"I'm afraid we're sold out."

"Fine." She turned back to the door, seemingly satisfied at receiving the rebuff.

Lucy called after her. "I do have some nice crow if you're interested."

"If it's all the same to you, I'd rather have that bun there." Edna pointed to the case. "Those crow feathers tend to stick in my teeth."

Lucy noticed Detective Slater glaring through the window. He did not look pleased. Thank God he kept going down the hill toward the station house. Edna wandered nonchalantly to the back of the café, and Lucy knew she had seen him too. They sat in the back, drank coffee, and talked about their boys, feeling their way to an accord.

Last night, Wade had tried to drink away his anger at The Stop. The guys were supposed to put Wright in the hospital, not end up there themselves. When the chief bellowed his name, he groaned and tried to look as if his head wasn't about to explode.

"Where have you been?" He didn't wait for Wade to sit down. "I'm being pressured about the attacks. Someone's been writing letters to a colored paper back East, saying it's not the Negro sailors."

"Just because we haven't gotten one of them to confess yet doesn't mean we're wrong. We'll find him sooner or later."

It was fun to watch them squirm, see them panic when he wouldn't let them call their outfits to keep from being put on report, especially since he was sure they weren't guilty. Didn't matter. The word should be getting out to avoid his town when they had passes.

"I spent most of the night searching for a girl who'd been attacked, but didn't report it. I guess we aren't looking too good out there. That's my fault, Chief. I know it is." *What an ass—Cavanaugh always falls for a little groveling.*

"Well, Wright's doing your job for you. He turned up someone who seems to know something."

"What's her name?"

"She calls herself Zora."

"I think I know who he's talking about. Chief, it's my case. Tell Wright to stick to those beatings."

"I'm the one who tells people what to do. Not you."

"Sorry, I didn't mean it like that. I'm dead on my feet."

"Find out who's doing this, or I'm putting Wright on it. The last thing we need is a colored newspaper snooping around. Now get to work."

Wade could barely hide his contempt for the chief, especially after a member of the appointment committee had told him *he* should have gotten the chief's job, but they had wanted to send him a message. They suspected his Uncle Sandy had been paying off Chief Anderson and they weren't going to put Wade in a position of trust. Even though he hadn't been involved.

He had finally decided to move to a place where no one knew his family. Then that damned Wright came back to Pt. Richmond and gave him another reason to leave. Now he had to convince Cora—and get to the bottom of that business with the locket.

21

Flour Sacks with Sleeves

Jonah looked up from his writing when Mrs. Forgione asked Mrs. Hermit what grits were.

"Why are you asking about grits?" Mrs. Hermit's lips rolled in as if to keep herself from smiling.

"Two women asked me if the café served grits." Mrs. Forgione leaned over her coffee. "They were wearing dresses that looked like flour sacks with sleeves, much too thin for the weather. Seemed very backward. They must really want grits if they made themselves ask about them. Truthfully, I didn't understand their accent. They seemed so forlorn."

"You don't know grits? I should make you some. It's cornmeal cooked into a cereal, with lard in it."

"Lard?" Mrs. Forgione shuddered. "Maybe I should offer polenta in the morning. It sounds like grits. Without the lard. I wonder why they don't make it themselves."

"Lots of those places where these new people live don't have any kitchens. Lots don't even have bathrooms. Lots are just lots."

Mrs. Hermit looked thoughtful. "If you wanted polenta and I gave you grits, would you be happy? No. Why not give them what they want?"

"I'm too old to start cooking things I never heard of. Especially under-seasoned, overcooked American food."

"I'll do it." She looked as if she had surprised herself. "I could make breakfast for these folks. But you need to think about it. You might be starting something you don't like in the end. These people just keep coming and coming. The ones from the South are ruining things for the rest of us. White people can only take so many of us at a time."

Mrs. Forgione set down her cup and stared at her friend.

"Don't give me that look! White businesses used to let us shop—not try any clothes on, but we could buy things. Now they won't let us in. Won't cash our checks. We can't even get buried in the damned cemetery anymore."

Mrs. Forgione pursed her lips. She looked as if she were converting a recipe by thirds in her head. "The café is named after the town my father came from—Avellino. He told me stories of his journey to England and then America, and how he felt when he was tired and hungry and the restaurants and boardinghouses had signs saying 'No Dogs, No Dagos.' But I love the café the way it is. I don't want my longtime customers to feel like strangers here."

For a moment, as he listened, Jonah felt good. Nothing would change.

Then she went on. "But the world is changing whether people want it to or not. So we'll fix up the storeroom, scrape the paint off the windows and door, make another side to the café, with another entrance. If we don't like what happens, we'll close it. I don't think this side of the café is what the new people want. I think my real friends will still come here and the heck with the rest of them." She thumped on the table. "I think Papa would approve."

Mrs. Hermit opened her pocketbook, took out a notepad and pencil, and licked the tip. "We're going to need some supplies, starting with lard."

Jonah picked up his cup to cover his smile. The friendship between the two women intrigued him. After eavesdropping on them these past few weeks, he had decided they were sisters under the skin—well, obviously *under* the skin. Now they were teaming up to change the café. *His* café.

22

Between Him and a Blowtorch

In the two weeks since I'd been attacked in the alley, Harmon and I had been working dull cases that amounted to a kind of adult babysitting, breaking up brawls and arresting people still holding a bloody knife. I felt like a garbage man instead of a detective. Then a fitter had been found beaten to death. Could have been because of his race, or the labor unions, or both.

It had taken time, but I'd developed some trust with a few workers, colored and white, and my network of informants had grown. Harmon was smart and willing to learn and had become almost a friend when I'd stepped between him and the blowtorch a woman welder pulled when we tried to arrest her for beating on her husband and his lady friend.

I'd rather go through that again than sit through dinner with my father and my brother, but Zoe had begged me to come celebrate her archery win with them.

After dinner, Peter disappeared to answer the phone. I wanted to say good-bye so I could leave, pick up Harmon, and try to get a lead on this newest beating. It was technically a homicide, but it was also a shipyard crime, so I'd pressed the chief until he'd reluctantly let me keep the case.

"Don't worry. I won't tell anyone we talked. When do you get off your shift? I can meet you wherever you say." Peter listened for a moment, said okay, and put the receiver in the cradle.

"Who was that?"

"It's got nothing to do with you."

"I heard you agree to meet someone. If it concerns the shipyard beatings, it has a lot to do with me. Besides, you're a prosecutor, not a cop. Lawyers don't know how to deal with thugs, not until we've done the dirty work and they're handcuffed to the table."

Peter gave me the cold look, the one that reminded me of our father.

"Think I can't meet someone and talk to him without you around?"

Damn. Why did I forget everything I knew about handling people when it came to my brother?

"Let's go together."

"He said to come alone or he wouldn't talk."

"He doesn't have to know I'm there." I played the only card I had. "Think about Jennie and the kids. What if something happened to you?"

"I forgot you're supposed to be a hotshot at interrogation. Is that your gift? Knowing the other person's weak spot?" He nodded toward the door. "Let's go out on the porch. I don't want anyone to hear us."

I followed him, lit a cigarette, and waited for him to start talking.

"I don't know who it was. He said no one was supposed to die."

"When are you meeting him?"

"There's nothing definite yet."

"You said you'd meet him."

"Did you hear me? There's nothing definite yet. He's going to call back."

"Peter, I'm not nine years old anymore. I've sat in on more interrogations than you have and sure as hell can tell when someone's lying to me. Especially you."

"Stay out of it, Oliver. This isn't your fight anymore. You left years ago, remember? And now you're leaving again."

"I'm not exactly going on a pleasure cruise."

"If it weren't the war, you would have found another reason to leave."

"You don't need me here."

"That's right. We don't need you. Our father asked you to do one thing for him, the one thing you're actually supposed to be good at, and you let him down."

He turned back toward the house.

"You've managed to change the subject again, Peter. We were talking about *your* family. About the risks *you're* taking."

He hesitated in the doorway.

"For what? Becoming a judge?"

I watched through the window as he walked into the study. All of it suited him, suited him and the judge both—the Tiffany lamp on the desk, the rows of legal books on the floor-to-ceiling shelves, the chess game on the table by the French doors. Our father sat in a leather wingback chair, a glass of amber liquid at his hand, and beamed when Peter sat beside him. A smile played across Peter's lips and he looked at the window. He knew I had seen.

"Your brother's stubborn, Oliver. He'll never understand."

Jennie's voice came out of the dark. She walked up the porch steps.

"He can't see that the judge was one kind of father to him and an entirely different kind to you. I guess that happens to a lot of children—their parents playing favorites, giving all their love to one child, probably without even knowing they're doing it."

I remembered my father's disappointment in me. For as long as I could remember, I had wondered why. Why my father didn't look at me the way he looked at Peter. I'd been given a chance to change that, and I'd decided to re-enlist. What if the judge had been right about my brother being in danger? What was he getting involved in?

I lit another cigarette, drew on it.

"It doesn't matter anymore, Jennie. His life is here, with you. Mine will be where Charley is. After the war."

"I love having you back. So do Zoe and Theo. Well, I think Theo does. He's invited you into his studio, so he must be happy you're here." She sat on the wooden porch swing. "You know, we've named you their guardian in our will."

"Don't do that! Oh, God. I didn't mean that the way it sounded. I mean you don't *have* to do that. It wouldn't hurt my feelings if you chose someone else, someone married, better suited to take care of children." Peter must have thought that was droll. Finally tying me to the family, from beyond the grave. I was willing to help out, but not to be the one responsible, not forever.

"They're not really children anymore. We don't know anyone we would rather see help them become adults. For all his anger about your leaving, Peter loves you, respects you. Look how fine a man Charley is."

I stared into the darkness. I always credited Elizabeth for Charley.

"What about your sister? She has children."

"It's Theo. He's never going to grow out of whatever it is that—God, I don't want to say *is wrong with him*—makes him different. Wonderful, but different. For some reason, he's closer to you than to anyone else, except me and Zoe."

I caved. I'd do it for Jennie, for Theo. For my niece, whom I adored. Besides, it would probably never happen.

"Peter's a lucky man, Jennie."

I could hear the smile in her voice. "I tell him that all the time."

Summer

1942

23

The Shelter of Compassion

Harley and I climbed almost four hundred feet to the top of Nicholl Nob, just over the tunnel that ran to Garrard Boulevard. I looked toward the Pacific, where, almost six months to the day after the attack on Pearl Harbor, the US Navy had won the battle for the Midway Atoll, Japan's worst naval defeat in 350 years. The tide of the war in the Pacific had turned, and now the Allies had begun a relentless campaign to take back the Pacific islands on their way to invading Japan.

While Harley explored the trails, I listened to the songs of the red-winged blackbirds that swayed on the rushes in the marsh below, their epaulets flashing red in the June sunshine. My orders had finally come through: Harley and I were leaving the next day for Camp Lejeune, North Carolina.

I'd made peace with not knowing when Michael Fiori would be home from Montana; Harry wouldn't give up until the boy was back. It still bothered me that I hadn't been able to connect the Klan to what had happened to the Fleming children, but Peter and my father would be safe as long as Peter didn't uncover new information about the fire. No, it was time for me to leave, and I'd come to say good-bye to Pt. Richmond, the bay, and the Golden Gate.

The trail I had played on as a child was blocked with olive-drab logs pointed at the sky like gun emplacements. Before enemy planes could get this close to the refinery and the shipyards, they would have to evade the ring of forts and camouflaged artillery that protected the headlands. I'd sat in the dining room at the Top of the Mark the night before, surrounded by white linens and candlelight, and listened to the thunder of the guns practicing while searchlights swept the entrance to the bay.

Soon I'd be hearing artillery fire aimed at me. And Harley. At least we would be together. I couldn't have sent Harley to the Corps without me, but people all over the country had done that—volunteered their family dogs to help win the war.

The shepherd loped out of the brush, tongue hanging out one side of his mouth in that goofy smile that made him look like a puppy again.

"Let's go see Mrs. Forgione and get you some water." We raced down the hill, Harley leaping in the air and spinning in circles.

Tonight, dinner with the family; tomorrow, active duty in the Marines. I rubbed Harley's head.

"You and me, boy, off to who knows what. Let's go to the café and finish saying our good-byes."

"Oliver, Oliver!" Mrs. Forgione stood in front of the café, beckoning me to hurry. "Thank God! You have to help the dog. I called Harry. He should be here soon. But they took the dog!"

"Calm down. Tell me what's happened. What dog?"

"Harmonica Man's dog, Emma."

"Who took her?"

"Paul Butler. Wade Slater made him take her to the pound."

"Why?"

"He said the dog attacked him when he arrested Harmonica Man, but she didn't. Mrs. Hermit and I saw it. The dog growled, but she didn't bite him. She tried to get between them, that's all."

"He arrested Roan?" *He must be frantic, locked up and without his dog.*

"He accused him of being an illegal alien and asked for his papers, and when Roan tried to walk away, he grabbed him and they tussled, and then the dog got in the middle."

"Where's Roan?"

"*Madonna mia!* At the police station. I called Harry to come help him. You need to help the dog. They're going to put her to sleep. I think if Mrs. Hermit and I hadn't gotten in the way, Wade would have shot her right there."

"Don't worry, I'll get the dog. But first I have to see Roan."

Harley got up, tongue still hanging out the side of his mouth. I motioned him back down.

"Could Harley have some water? Please. I'll come back for him." I signaled him to stay.

When I ran down the slope beside the fire station to the back door of the jail, I heard yelling and swearing and high-pitched keening. I pulled open the door and stopped.

A flurry of brightly colored rags and ribbons engulfed Wade. Bells jingled as Harmonica Man tried to free himself from the police holding him down.

"Stop! Roan, stop struggling! I have Emma."

"E-m-m-m-m-ma?"

"Yes. I have her. Calm down."

"Stay out of this, Wright! I thought you were g-g-g-gone!" Wade mocked Roan and swung around on me.

"I'm not gone yet, and I'll be back."

He got in my face. "Maybe you'll be back and maybe you won't. But *if* you come back, make sure you're in one piece. There's no room on the force for cripples."

His words stunned me, but I shook them off. "Why in God's name did you arrest Roan?"

"For all I know, he's an illegal alien. He doesn't have any papers. He roams around the Point, spying on people, sitting on the hills, watching the bay, playing that damned harmonica. It would be the perfect cover for a spy."

"You know he's not an enemy alien, and he's not a vagrant." I wasn't sure how long Roan had lived in Pt. Richmond, but when I'd come home to visit my mother, I'd caught glimpses of him walking the hills. "He lives in Mrs. Dunn's boardinghouse. You know that. What the hell is wrong with you?"

"Doesn't matter. He resisted arrest. He's staying here." Wade became conciliatory. "Why don't you fill out a report on his background, and we'll see what's what?"

Roan wailed again, and I realized Wade was deliberately delaying me.

"Don't worry, Roan. And don't resist. I've got her!"

As I ran out the door, I bumped into Harry.

"I'm going for the dog. Tell him that Emma is safe."

I hoped that was true. I whistled for Harley, then we jumped in the car and sped past the Indian statue to the veterinarian's office. I ran inside and cautiously poked my head into the treatment room, where Andrew was examining a dog's ear.

"Sorry to interrupt, Andrew, but it's an emergency."

"What is it?"

"Emma's at the pound, about to be put down!"

"Emma?" Andrew frowned, as if he didn't know the dog.

"Roan's dog, Emma!"

"But why?"

"I'll explain on the way. Come on."

"God, she must be terrified. She and Harmonica Man are never apart. Let me get some supplies."

"Hurry up! We could be too late."

Butler turned around when our car squealed to a stop. He hooked his thumbs on his gun belt and smiled when we jumped out of the car.

"No point in working up a sweat—she's already in the chamber. Wanna watch?"

I pushed him aside and followed Andrew.

"I've tried to convince the pound to stop gassing the animals, but they argued dollars and cents and wouldn't listen." The vet shook his head. "You don't ever want to see what happens inside them."

"Too late for that, Doc." I would never forget what I'd learned when I'd gone to interview an animal control officer about a burglary.

Andrew, white-faced with fury, grabbed the chamber operator by the arm.

"Shut off the gas and open the door!"

"I can't. The gas will escape."

"Get out." He shoved the man aside, shut off the gas, and grabbed the door latch. "Oliver, when I open this door, hold your breath and help me carry her outside."

"Got it."

Emma's orange-and-white paws twitched on the metal floor. Andrew took a deep breath, then dove into the chamber, grasped her shoulders, and pulled her through the opening.

I caught her back end as it slid by and helped rush her outside.

We laid the limp dog on the ground by the car. "Good girl, Emma," her eyelids flickered.

"She needs oxygen. She's drowsy but responsive." He sent me for his bag while he checked her gums and lips. "The oxygen should stop any damage to her heart and brain." He fit one end of a tube to a bottle and the other end to a metal funnel. "I don't know if this will work. Hold the bottle while I press the funnel against her muzzle."

I stroked her with one hand and held the green-and-black bottle with the other. "What is this?"

"A bailout bottle. I have a college buddy in the Army Air Forces who's working to develop a better system for pilots who ditch. He brought me a couple of bottles to see if I could figure out a way to rig them up with canine gas masks. Unfortunately, I've been too busy to work on it."

He checked her eyes and tried to take her pulse while holding the funnel tight. "The bottle holds about eight to ten minutes of oxygen. The tricky part is that there's no regulator, but with all the play in the funnel, I'm sure she's not getting too much at once. If anything, it will be too little."

We soothed the dog and waited. Harley lay nearby, his head on his paws, watching. Soon I heard a *thump, thump, thump*. It took a second to realize it was Emma's tail striking the packed earth. She tried to raise her head.

"Let's get her back to the office. She needs fluids. We want to make sure she doesn't have any long-term effects from this."

Harley gave Emma a sniff and hopped in the front seat. Andrew sat in the back, stroking her head.

I asked what kind of a dog she was.

"I can't figure her out." I watched him in the rearview mirror. "She could be a golden retriever crossed with a bull terrier; or an Australian shepherd crossed with a corgi or terrier; or maybe boxer, collie, and something else short. Hard to say."

"Maybe Harley knows."

"Wouldn't doubt it."

The shepherd, who sat square on the front seat as if he were the navigator, looked over his shoulder when Emma whimpered.

"There is a plaque in our office." Andrew stroked the golden dog's head. "I've read it a thousand times—since I was a young boy. On it are the words of St. Francis of Assisi: 'If you have men who will exclude any of God's creatures from the shelter of compassion and pity, you will have men who will deal likewise with their fellow men.'"

I thought about war, about pointless cruelty.

"That Slater has a lot to answer for."

24

A Plane of Pure Being

It was almost closing time when I finally made it to the Café Avellino.

"Oliver, what happened? How are they?" Edna Hermit called to me from behind the counter.

"Andrew thinks Emma will be as good as new. After Harry got Roan out of jail, he took him to Andrew's office to wait for us. Paul Butler had gone back to the station and told everyone what we were doing at the pound. Everything is good. Charges dropped, Emma safe. She was woo-woo-wooing to Roan when she wasn't licking his tears. Harry had a time keeping Roan under control until he knew she was safe."

"Too bad he wasn't there when Wade was waving that gun in Mrs. Forgione's face. I'd like to have seen what Harry would have done then. He'd have taken him down a peg or two." Edna smiled.

Mrs. Forgione told me what I wanted to eat, then set about making it. "That Wade. He was a mean one, but he seemed to change after he married Cora. Now I don't know. Seems he's back to hating anyone who's happy." She layered ham, fontina, roasted peppers, and caramelized onions on ciabatta. A squirt of olive oil and a dash of vinegar finished it off. "I think he can't stand how much Harmonica Man and Emma love each other. As if he has to smash the love." She handed me the sandwich.

"What did you think of him? When he was a boy?" I leaned on the marble top.

"He was hard to figure out. Sometimes he seemed anxious to please, could be a real charmer. Other times he looked right through you. I've seen him throw mud on a girl's new dress or knock a bird's nest out of a tree. As if he had to spoil what other people had. Maybe because he had precious little himself." She shrugged. "Let's hope whatever has brought back that anger goes away soon."

Edna muttered something.

"What did you say, Mrs. Hermit?"

"That I hear you're going away tomorrow. I wish you well, Oliver."

"Penny for your thoughts, Edna." Mrs. Forgione started to chop the greens.

"I was thinking about Cora and Wade, how he seemed to be a different person there for a while."

"He had a hard life. I often wondered what might have happened if Phyllis Brennan hadn't died. Cora's probably the first person to be kind to him since then."

"Phyllis Brennan?" Edna looked up.

"A local girl he'd been sweet on since high school."

"What happened?"

"They found her on Keller's beach. No one ever knew what happened. There was a rumor she might have been pregnant, but I'd have been surprised if that were true."

IN THE SHADOW OF LIES

"Pregnant young girls." Edna set her knife down. "Not an easy life. Was there anyone for him after her?"

"A parade of blondes, but no one for long."

"He surely charmed Cora, but I don't know. He seemed to make her happy, but now, when I go to do the laundry, she's different. It's as if a light's gone out in her."

I sipped my cappuccino and bit into the warm sandwich. Sometimes I felt like a barbarian when I ate in the café. Most of the Italian men cut their sandwiches with a knife and fork. They didn't know the feeling of warm bread in their hands, of biting through the layers, of wiping juice off their chins. They tried to blend in because of the war, but they had no idea how many things made them stand out as "not American."

I took a little package out of my pocket and opened it again. The bundle looked like Roan: red and yellow ribbons woven together to make a scrap of cloth, much like the streamers Roan decorated himself and Emma with. You could barely see his face through the strips of fabric and feathers he had sewn into his cap.

He wandered with Emma up and down the hills of the Point, pushing his bicycle or fussing with the bundles he had lashed to it. He had a room, so why did he carry so much stuff with him? Maybe he was afraid someone would take his strips of cloth. Some were from Guatemala, some from Peru and Mexico. Roan would explain the embroidery and say where things were from, but he wouldn't tell how he got them. Sometimes I heard his plaintive harmonica before they appeared: three dots on a hillside, Emma out in front, leading the way, her magnificent feathered tail like a drum major's baton, Roan pushing the bicycle, all three festooned like Christmas trees.

The cloth in my hand contained a small tin heart, concave on one side and convex on the other. A *milagro*.

Roan had still looked shaken when he'd handed me the bundle. Then he raised his head and looked me directly in the eyes, and I saw him, saw into him. Something passed between us in that moment. Something beyond two people, beyond ordinary life, as if our souls had become one, on a plane of pure being. It passed, and I was left looking back into Roan's eyes, at deep intelligence and pain, at earnestness. I dropped my eyes, overwhelmed by the beauty of the other man's unguarded emotion. *He saves people from seeing this, with his camouflage of color and pattern, with his lowered gaze and odyssey through the hills. He's just Harmonica Man, labeled and dismissed.*

"Thank you." Roan stumbled over the words. Partly not used to talking and partly not able to.

"You're welcome, Roan."

He hesitated, opened his mouth, and struggled to form the words he wanted to say. I struggled, too—to keep my mouth shut and not try to guess what he wanted to tell me. Finally, I heard, "Will you be Em-Em-Em-ma's . . ." He stopped, defeated. "Will you t-t-t-take care of her if anything happens t-t-t-to me?"

It was more likely something would happen to me than to him, but given the events of the day, maybe he needed reassurance.

"I'd be proud to be Emma's guardian. And I'll tell Theo and Zoe that if you and Emma ever need anything, they're to help you. Go to them or Mrs. Forgione. She'll know what to do."

Roan had tapped his chest twice to thank me, then gestured to me with those fingers, as if he were making me a promise.

I rubbed the little silver heart, wondering where Roan had gotten it and what it meant to him. I slipped it into my pocket. *Every warrior needs a talisman.*

Autumn

1942

25

In Time for Columbus Day

Jonah sat outside the Café Avellino, enjoying the warm, dusty smell of autumn. He felt guilty sitting in the sun, having a cappuccino. He always felt guilty when he wrote to Oliver.

Dear Oliver,

Mrs. Forgione says hello. Yes, I am once again at the café, indulging myself. I won't tell you what I am having. You can probably guess.

She is having a quiet celebration about the restrictions having been lifted from Italians. In time for Columbus Day and the November elections, not to be too cynical about it. The Democrats need the Italian vote to maintain control of Congress. They have not, however, returned the fishermen's boats to them.

It's hard to believe you've been gone four months. Especially since I thought you would have won the war by now.

We've had our own little war here. Someone decided Pt. Richmond would be a good place to open a Negro USO. Even found a perfect empty building. But the good citizens did not agree. Guess who won?

Despite my shortcomings and tendency toward self-immolation, I'm head of a welding crew now. I'm lucky to have easygoing folks who just want to get the job done. The women make pretty good welders and fit into some of the smaller spaces. Sometimes there's tension when a couple guys decide they like the same girl, but if they weren't fighting over women, they'd be fighting over something else.

How is that handsome Harley doing? Making friends? My landlady took in a stray. Don't know where she came from, but I suggested we not let her go out and bring the rest of the street dogs home with her.

I ran into a friend of yours—Auntie Josephine. She says hello. Wanted you to know nothing has changed. I told her there wasn't much you could do about it from North Carolina. She snorted. But I think she likes you.

Mrs. Forgione asked me to tell you that Michael Fiori is home, and if the Marines will take him he's joining up. As you can see, I'm running out of room. Keep safe, Oliver.

Your friend,

Jonah

Wonder what he's doing right now. I should have told him a woman named Monica asked after him, too. Next time.

He looked down the street toward the police station. The Indian statue had collapsed, its pieces used for scrap in the war effort. A golden glow touched the tops of the eucalyptus trees.

They bent in the wind as the sky flared red, then orange, and the sun slid behind the hills.

November

1943

26

North Carolina

Bitter Ashes

I t had been a year, five months, and a bit over two weeks since I had arrived at Camp Lejeune. But who was counting? I sat in the November heat against the trunk of a poplar tree, aware of how they had been used throughout the South. Whenever I looked at them, I heard Billie Holiday's haunting indictment of white America. Strange fruit, indeed.

Harley dug down to cooler earth and stretched out, panting. I unfolded another letter from Jonah who had been writing faithfully for more than a year now.

As I write this, Oliver, the wind sweeps across a blackened hill, swirling bitter ashes down on the Point, the street, this letter.

The town is up in arms. Everyone says it's like the fire that killed two children before the war. You must remember. They were trapped when a cross burning set the same meadow on fire and spread around the hill. Sammy and Ellie Fleming. Don't know if you knew the family.

No one can believe the stupid bastards who burned the cross then were willing to take the chance of burning one again. They had to have known it was too windy and too dry, but they went ahead anyway, so intent on intimidating an uppity minister that they didn't care who else got hurt.

It was more than a coincidence that they picked the spot where the minister had started to hold sunrise services. The same minister who was renting a house in a white neighborhood.

Apparently, he mistook tolerance for acceptance. Tolerance—an ugly word, don't you think? The inherent judgment and superiority oozing from the syllables.

Everyone thinks they know who did it, but no one can prove it. Just like before, the likely suspects were all conveniently playing cards together, and the police can't shake their stories. Wish you were here to get to the bottom of this. (Now I sound like Auntie Josephine.)

Everyone says it's the Klan again and that the Slaters and the Butlers must be involved because their families have been longtime Klan members. Have to wonder. That kind of hatred can run deep in families. Slater is investigating, along with his pal Butler. Talk about the fox and the henhouse.

If they leave it up to Slater, he'll find a way to blame it on the Negro servicemen.

Take care, Oliver.

Your friend,

Jonah

I looked up at the flag hanging limply in the still heat. *The Klan. Wonder why they picked the hill again instead of the house the minister wanted to rent. The whole thing feels off. Peter will see this as another chance to find out whether the Klan was involved in the Fleming deaths. No point in writing to him, telling him to be careful.*

Maybe Harry will be able to talk some sense into him.

27

He Thinks He's Invincible

Drops of rain silvered the window behind Harry's desk. He had swiveled toward it to compose himself. He knew running back and forth between his JAG duties and the district attorney's office was exhausting the little patience he had. On top of that, after his son had told him how Negro soldiers were being treated in the South, he had put a lot of time into developing a training program for Negro MPs. Now Nate Hermit was an MP assigned to JAG.

The two days he was spending at the district attorney's office were barely enough to keep up with crime in Richmond. He had been letting most of the work fall on the shoulders of his staff and needed to appoint someone as acting district attorney for the rest of the war. In all fairness, that person should be the man sitting on the other side of his desk. Peter Wright. Harry turned away from the window and leaned toward his eager assistant.

"You're not a one-man band, Peter. You have to keep me informed about what you're doing."

"I didn't want word leaking out about my investigation."

"If you didn't need my approval to give this informant immunity, you probably wouldn't be telling me even this much!" Harry breathed on his glasses, rubbed them with a handkerchief. "Tell me everything."

"There's not much to tell. A few days ago, I got a call at home from a man who had been at the cross burning in 1941. He said he had photographs of the other men who had been there." He leaned forward, and a kind of naïveté made him seem younger. "It's hard to believe, but I once saw a souvenir postcard of a lynching. There were even children in the crowd of smiling people."

Harry swallowed in disgust. He had seen similar things. He couldn't think about what it meant to enjoy the torture of another human being. To celebrate it, to want a remembrance of it.

"When are you meeting?"

"This weekend. Somewhere outside Richmond—he doesn't want to be seen talking to me. He hinted there was more to the '41 fire than merely intimidating the professor and he knew who was behind it."

Peter quivered with energy. Keeping a rein on this bright, ambitious man who wanted to become a judge like his father was exhausting. This could be his breakthrough case.

"Why would he risk his life informing? What does he think will happen if his *friends* decide to inform on him?"

"He doesn't want to testify. I'll talk to him, but he seemed pretty sure he could survive this as long as he wasn't indicted."

"Peter, how can we make a case without his testimony?"

"He says we'll have all the proof we need without it."

"Has it occurred to you that the people involved in this might have heard more about your progress in the investigation than I have? You haven't stopped nosing around, asking questions. Maybe they think you are getting too close. This could be a trap." He raised his hand to stop Peter's protest. "Think about it. How did he know to call you, not me or someone else in the department? Or the police. And why two years later?"

"I think he called me after that beating on Cutting Boulevard where the Negro shipyard worker died, but then he must have gotten cold feet. I think the second hill fire has something to do with him calling again."

"Perhaps. But no one was hurt this time." Harry thought for a moment. "Maybe he'll change his mind again."

"I don't think so. He choked up when he talked about the Fleming kids. Mentioned their names, as if he knew them."

Harry waved a secretary away from the door to his office. She could see him through the glass window, but she ignored him and poked her head in.

"I told you no interruptions. Whatever you have can wait."

"But—"

"Go!"

She stammered and apologized a few times before she finally left.

Peter slipped the grant of immunity forms into his briefcase. "Where were we?"

"Worried about you. The men who did this have a lot to lose. Once they were tolerated, even admired, but the whole city would still like to see them punished for killing the Fleming children. I don't need to tell you to be careful."

"Yes, boss." Peter grabbed his briefcase and headed out the door.

Harry shook his head. *He thinks he's invincible.*

The next morning, Peter wished he had stayed in bed. Four o'clock was an ungodly hour to meet anyone. He stood in the drizzle behind an all-night diner in Berkeley—the informant's choice. Vagrants slept on soggy newspapers that tore when the men stirred in their sleep. Dreaming of what? The past? Their mistakes? Maybe their next drink?

He skirted the iridescent puddles and unidentified patches between him and the back door of the diner. The men didn't seem to go far from their beds to relieve themselves. He clenched a gloved hand over his nose and mouth and picked his way to a half-open door. Something dark skittered into the shadows between the garbage bins. Glass clinked.

He nudged the door open with a corner of his briefcase and stepped onto checkerboard tiles that stretched down a narrow hallway. A man motioned from a doorway. He was halfway there when he felt pressure against his back. He froze.

"Oh dear. Are you all right? I'm so sorry. My fault. I didn't know anyone was here. Let me wipe that off."

A woman who looked like she hadn't gotten enough to eat growing up, or since, pulled out a gray rag and dabbed at his shoes. She had backed out of an office with her mop handle sticking out of the bucket.

"You stupid woman!" He had almost fainted when he'd felt the pressure between his shoulder blades. "It's fine. Stop. It's fine."

He waved her off and continued down the hallway to the man who had beckoned.

"I'm Peter." He held out his hand.

The man reached for it as if he knew touching it would mean there was no going back. He pumped it once and dropped it.

"I need to know your name."

"Regis. Regis Simmons."

He had one of those squared-off heads, the chin as wide as the forehead, blunt, and looked to be in his late twenties, maybe early thirties.

"Good. Let's sit down. You picked this pace, so I assume it's safe."

He nodded once. Nodded again as if reassuring himself.

"Why don't you tell me what happened, Regis? Take your time. I'm going to take some notes. Okay? Let's start with the fire in 1941."

"Look, no one was supposed to get hurt. That's why we burned the cross on the hill instead of in the neighborhood." It was more a plea than a statement.

"Why did you burn the cross at all?"

"To put that uppity colored teacher in his place. They said the war would bring more and more of them in, and if we didn't show them we meant business, we'd be overrun with them, like rats." He frowned, as if unable to believe what he was saying. "Anyway, we never meant for anyone to get killed, not then and not—"

"Not . . .?"

"Nothing. A fight got out of hand. Most of the men involved are in the service now."

"But not all of them."

"No." He looked down at his hands.

"Did you call me after that fight? And then not show up?"

"I don't want to talk about that right now."

"Okay. Tell me about the fire in 1941. What happened?"

"The hill was so dry. We cleared an area, but the winds kicked up instead of dying down like they should've. I told him! I told him we should wait, that the wind could carry that fire anywhere. But he said it was too late to wait. They had found out someone was going to sell to that teacher, and if we didn't move soon, no telling what would happen."

"But you tried to stop it. That says a lot about you, about your character."

Regis looked away, then back. "It might be hard for you to understand, but when I was invited to join the group, I thought it was about being American, about fighting for what you believed in."

"And something happened to change your mind?"

"The night we got back from the fire, I heard the head guy talking on the phone. It sounded as if he had been paid to set the fire, but then I thought I must have misunderstood. And then I forgot about it."

"But now?"

"We were being used. For someone else to make money. Now I'm sure of it."

Peter tried to ask why he was sure, but Regis went on talking.

"I feel so bad about Sammy and Ellie. And Joe. We thought he was finally getting over it, and then this last fire stirred everything up again. He goes to that meadow every day and just sits. Maude can't get him to do anything. He won't eat, can't sleep." He muffled a sob. "It would have been better if he had died in the fire!"

"How do you know the Flemings?"

"Maude's my sister. I had to help carry their little coffins. Hold her hand while she cursed God and asked how someone could do that to her babies. Now she wants Joe to live with me until they move. She can't bear living by those woods anymore."

"Where are they moving?" *Where in the world could they go to escape the memory of the fire?*

"Up north. Maybe Sebastopol. As soon as they can find a place."

"Tell me, who else was at the fire?"

"First you have to promise my name won't get out."

"We can protect you from anyone. Even the Klan."

"You can't protect me from my sister hating me if she ever finds out. If I tell you, you *have* to keep me out of it."

"Why tell me at all?"

He looked up, his eyes still haunted by what he had done. He didn't have to explain.

"One of the others might tell the police. I can't save you from that."

"I'm willing to take that chance. Besides, I'm only giving you some of them. That way I won't be the only one who isn't picked up. If you get the leader, that should break them up and send a warning."

"Why didn't you send me an anonymous letter if you don't want to testify?"

"It wouldn't be enough. You already suspect some of them, and they're still running around. Besides, if I help you, you can make sure I'm not prosecuted."

"You told me you had photos."

"Negatives. Of *upstanding citizens*. Some of them are so arrogant, they pose for photos without their hoods."

"Some?"

"Some of us are smarter than that."

28

It Could Wait

As soon as Peter pulled up to his house, Theo ran down to say good-bye, stopping a good foot away from his dad's window. Peter thanked him for the drawing he had found in his briefcase that morning, a portrait of Brio, their marmalade cat, crouched at the edge of the grass, waiting for his prey. Theo nodded, and Peter detected the faintest smile.

Edna Hermit shooed Jennie out the door, telling her to go—everything would be fine. Peter wished he could cancel the trip to Sacramento and set the case in motion, but he had disappointed Jennie so many times, and once this case began, he would have no time for her at all. Too bad his father was in Los Angeles at a conference. He could hardly wait to tell him he'd gotten evidence that would tie the Klan to the Fleming deaths. Something Oliver hadn't been able to do.

He drummed his fingers on the steering wheel. He should call Harry, but either he'd want Peter to work on it right away, or he'd assign the case to someone else. It was cancel the trip or wait until Monday. Maybe he'd cover all his bases and call Harry tomorrow when he'd be at church. Leave a message. The bad guys weren't going anywhere before Monday. It could wait.

He debated whether to go in and change his shoes, but they weren't wet now, merely a little spotted. He yawned. He wanted to get to the hotel and take a nap.

The tires sizzled along the wet pavement as they headed home, vacation behind them. Peter had managed to forget about work for almost a day, and he and Jennie had been reminded of what life had been like before work and family had overwhelmed them. He glanced at her. She had rolled down her window and closed her eyes. The scent of eucalyptus trees filled the car and reminded him of their being children together—the boys swinging on a tow rope from the tree branches while the girls gathered the dimpled nuts and strung them on cords. He remembered her tumbling off their cardboard toboggan when they shot down the long, dried grasses that were as slippery as ice. The fun had lasted barely a week before the firemen found out what they were doing and burned the dry hillside.

Lights came up behind them, high off the road.

The guy could flash his beams all day, but there was no place to pull over so he could pass. The truck loomed in the rearview mirror, getting closer and not slowing down. It tapped their bumper. The car lurched, began to slide out on the slick pavement. *What the hell?* He braked as they came into a curve, but the truck rode his bumper and pushed them down the road. Jennie braced herself against the dash. The truck dropped back, and Peter struggled to control the fishtailing car. He straightened out as they headed into another curve. The truck sped up and rammed them. Jennie screamed his name while he fought to steer a car that was airborne.

And then the crash, the rolling, the sound of glass breaking. Then nothing.

29

Just Out of Reach

The shipyard glowed at night. Sometimes when the lights on the cranes blinked against the black sky, Jonah felt a yearning for something just out of reach. Fog floated on the water and muted the noises of men and women working fast and hard to finish another ship, to draw the end of the war closer for themselves and the men fighting it. He thought his crew transcended their fear and fatigue the way combat units did. Helping each other, encouraging newcomers, never giving in. They had to win. Anything less was unthinkable. The black-marketeers and people profiting from the war didn't matter to his crew, who worked as if the war were theirs to win single-handedly.

He spotted Regis Simmons squeaking in under the whistle. He'd transferred to Jonah's crew and had begun to seek him out at break time. He was a good welder, but the week before he had seemed to be in a trance. His tacks had needed to be chipped off, and he had lifted his hood absently and gotten a flash burn to his eyes. Physically he was fine, but his distraction put other people at risk. Jonah had told him to take a few days off.

"Hey, Regis. How you doing? How was the weekend off?"

"Good." His smile was forced.

"Be careful today. I don't want you or anyone else hurt." Jonah patted him on the shoulder, dragged his own lines across the platform, and set to work.

Regis had gone to work as usual, even though he could barely concentrate. Something would happen soon, but until it did, he had to lay low. He had spent his time off in Marin, making sure he didn't run into any of the men he had ratted on. Once they were arrested, the other men from the fire would make sure to keep away from each other.

He tried to pull himself together, to act normal. He took a deep breath. *Focus. Do your job.* He lowered his hood and tried to concentrate. When he finally set down his torch, someone tapped him on the shoulder. His heart lurched.

"Break time."

Another welder nodded toward the pier where the crew usually gathered. He grabbed his lunch box and followed but stopped cold when he saw a flanger reading a newspaper in a pool of light.

ACCIDENT CLAIMS LOCAL DA.

He snatched the paper and scanned the article, ignoring the flanger's cussing. The pier moved under his feet. How could they have known? *Was* it an accident?

He dropped his lunch box and hurried to the inner hull, where Jonah would be checking the work. He tripped over a wrench, and Jonah turned toward the clanging. Regis opened his mouth but couldn't speak.

"What is it? Is someone hurt?" Jonah moved toward the exit.

"No. No. I. Oh, God."

"What?"

"I'm in trouble."

"What can I do?"

He hesitated. What if he made it out of this? He'd be a fool to confess and then wish he hadn't.

30

The Son Who Survived

Harley inched closer and closer to me along the belly of the plane, until he lay across my thighs, pinning me to the floor. When my hand found his ruff and tightened into a fist, he closed his eyes and pressed even closer against me, as if he wanted to absorb my pain.

My eyes were closed, too; my aching jaw clenched. I wanted to bury my face in his fur and release the grief and anger that had been growing in me since the chaplain had walked onto the obstacle course looking for me.

Not again. Not that look of sadness and regret. *Not Charley. Please, God, not Charley.* To my shame, I had felt a moment of relief when the chaplain said it was about Peter. My brother had been in an accident.

Now I was on my way home—home to another funeral and more grieving children.

It had been a week since Peter's funeral. They still didn't know how it had happened. Jennie couldn't remember anything, not even how she had made it to the road, where some hunters had found her dazed and cradling her arm. She had begged them to help her husband, but there had been nothing they could do. At night, I sat with her on the porch after the children were asleep and held her while she cried.

Later that day, I'd be going back to Camp Lejeune. My leave was up, but the truth was I'd had enough of my father.

Edna had said she wasn't sure they could manage without me and had made my favorite food, hoping I'd do more than push it around my plate and drop pieces to Harley when I thought no one was looking.

I passed the mashed potatoes and gravy, happy to see Zoe smiling again. Edna had told me she thought her heart would break holding that girl while she sobbed after the accident. When I came home, Zoe clung to me, and Theo seemed to fret less. He'd sit stroking Harley's fur until I thought he'd rub the dog bald like a favorite teddy bear.

When one of the assistant DAs brought Peter's briefcase by after the inquest, Theo had grabbed it and run to his studio. Now he carried it everywhere he went. At first, Jenny thought we should take it away from him, but we'd decided to let him have it. If it gave him some comfort, what harm could it do?

My homecoming had given me more to grieve than just my brother's death. I couldn't forget the look on my father's face when I dropped my duffel bag and reached out for him. He had turned away as if he couldn't stand the sight of me, the son who survived.

I knocked on Harry's door, then turned and watched the bark of the trees turn copper in the golden light. A layer of fog crept under the maroon clouds that streaked the pale-pink sky, and within seconds a purple-gray wash muted the colors and the sun disappeared.

The door opened.

"Harry."

"Come in. I'm glad you're here." He had grown thin. His cheeks were sunken, and the lines between his nose and mouth had deepened.

I shook my head *no* when he offered me coffee and food. I hadn't been hungry since the chaplain had told me about Peter. All I'd thought since was that I shouldn't have enlisted—I should have stayed, been there. Even the regret felt familiar. I wasn't where I should have been, and now someone I cared about was dead.

"Tell me how this happened." I didn't have to elaborate. Harry would know I'd come only to find out everything I could about Peter's death.

He motioned me to a chair by the fireplace and sat facing me.

"Peter was supposed to meet an informant that weekend, someone who said he had photographs of the '41 cross burning. I tried to warn him, but you know what he was like." He held up a hand. "I'm not saying it was his fault; I'm simply telling you how it was."

I nodded. "If he met an informant, wouldn't he have called you?" Even as I asked the question, I realized Peter might have kept it to himself for his own reasons.

"I expected him to, but . . . I think he wanted to make sure I didn't give the case to someone else." He shook his head as if he would never understand it. "Jennie said he met someone that Saturday morning. He told her they had to make the most of their trip because once he came home, he would be working day and night. He called here Sunday morning and left a message that he'd call when he got home."

"Did he tell Jennie who he met with?"

"No, and I think the case would've been the last thing on his mind when he was struggling with the car, and afterward. Well . . ."

He described the scene. How he and Doc Pritchard had noticed crushed stems leading to the center of a stand of giant ferns. It looked as if Jennie had been thrown from the car and landed among them. The fronds had cushioned her fall and saved her life, but if she hadn't crawled out of them, no one would have thought of looking for her there. He had made sure everyone in Richmond knew she didn't remember anything. Just in case.

"You think it wasn't an accident. That somehow the people who set the fire knew about the informant. But how?"

"Nobody else knew. At least from our end."

"Don't you have any idea who the informant was?" I couldn't hide my frustration even though I knew Peter's death wasn't Harry's fault.

"The day after Peter's death made headlines, Maude Fleming's brother didn't show up to take his nephew to the movies. She found him hanging in his garage. I think he might have been Peter's informant."

"Suicide?"

"That's how the police treated it. By the time Doc Pritchard arrived, Simmons had been cut down. According to Slater, they did it to spare Maude."

Slater again. Perhaps he *had* thought it was a suicide. I wished I knew which side he was on.

"Like your brother's death, it was too coincidental. If Simmons was the informant, I wish he had come to me. Peter's death must have terrified him." He raised his finger. "One odd thing: Doc Pritchard said the piece of rope left hanging from the beam was braided—like a dock line or anchor line. It would have been more painful than a thicker, softer line, but if you're going to kill yourself . . ."

"And?"

"Later, Doc asked Maude if her brother sailed. She told him he was afraid of the water, that even working near it at the shipyard was hard for him. I know that's not dispositive, but it gives us more reason to question his death. And your brother's."

For a few moments, we sat quietly, lost in thought, then Harry offered me a drink. I refused as politely as I could.

I wanted out of there—out of that house and out of Richmond, back to the war, where at least I knew who the enemy was. But when the war was over, I'd be back. I'd find out who had killed my brother.

Winter

1944

31

It Went Off by Accident

The war had reversed the natural order of things. American soldiers were in Italy, fighting to liberate the country from the fascists and the Nazis, and Italian soldiers were in America, collecting garbage and working in the fields. Harry was an attorney—he had no illusions about life being fair or justice existing in the world, but there had to be limits to unfairness. He had tried to explain that to Paola when she'd asked if he would mind having two Italian prisoners of war to dinner on New Year's Day.

He had reminded her they were *prisoners* of the country, not guests, and they could well have killed American soldiers. Soldiers like their son. He empathized with the angry parents of American boys who were dying overseas while the Italian POWs were safe, dancing and drinking wine in the States, walking the streets of San Francisco in surplus army uniforms. Except for the plastic buttons and ITALY patches on their shoulders and caps, they could have been American soldiers home on leave.

The POWs helped with the manpower shortage, but working shouldn't entitle them to extra privileges. It should be privilege enough that they were not sitting idle behind barbed wire.

But they're Dom's sons, Paola explained. Her sister Isabella had begged her to invite them for dinner so they could see Dom.

When did he get sons? Harry asked, and how did he know they were POWs?

Dom's friend delivered supplies on Angel Island and knew as soon as he looked at Cesare that he had to be Dom's son. She explained that when the boys' mother died, Dom had left them in Italy with their grandmother, and had come to America to make money so he could send for them.

Apparently, that hadn't happened. Harry ducked his head and looked up at her.

No. No, she didn't know why, but he ended up in California, and married Isabella, and, well . . . She had run out of steam.

Why couldn't they go to Dom and Isabella's house? he had asked, only to be told they couldn't make the trip and be back in time for curfew.

Paola had put her hand on his arm, reminded him it could be their son, God forbid, who was a prisoner. What would Harry want for him?

He had embraced her, grateful once again for her beautiful soul, the soul that asked for the best in all of them.

Fine, he had said. Fine.

He had been unable to say no to Paola, and now two Italian POWs were at his table.

"That was pretty good. Almost as good as my mother used to make." Dom tipped the dining room chair onto its back legs and rubbed his stomach.

"Would that be the boys' grandmother who is still in Italy? In the middle of a war? I see how you value her." Most of the evening's conversation had been in Italian, for the benefit of the boys, but now Harry spoke to Dom in English.

Paola rose to clear the table, giving him a *be nice* look as she turned her back to Dom, but Harry knew if she weren't so fond of her mother's dining chairs, she would wish Dom would fall over, hit his head, and forget he had ever known them.

Dom blustered about how he had worked and worked so he could send for the boys and their grandmother, and then the war had broken out.

Harry and his wife exchanged a look but said nothing. Dom didn't seem to notice.

Dom led the boys to the table under the arbor.

"Why didn't you send for us and Grandmother *before* the war? Who knows what is happening to her now? And why did you tell us not to tell anyone we were seeing you?" Tomaso spoke to his father in English. He had understood Harry's question.

"So, your English is pretty good. Think you're smart." Dom switched to Italian. "It's a long story. I couldn't come back to Italy for you."

"Oh, the new wife doesn't have anything to do with it?"

Dom stared at Tomaso making his eyes as cold as he could. The boy had to learn not to talk back to him.

Cesare broke in: "I want to hear what happened."

"When I left Italy, I ended up on the East Coast. Some *paisani* had a business there. I worked for them."

"Doing what?"

"It was Prohibition." He smiled, as if to say, *what do you think we did?* "We brought liquor in from Canada. Things were bad for Italians. The Americans looked at us like we were animals. When Sacco and Vanzetti were arrested, things got even worse. People hated us, attacked us. We decided to fight back." He broke off a branch of rosemary, stripped the needles. "One day we were ambushed. I got knocked down, and another man grabbed my gun. It went off by accident and hit a policeman." Dom shrugged, implying, *these things happen.*

"Oh my God." Cesare's eyes shone.

"I had to leave New Jersey. I grabbed the gun, because it was my father's, and ran. I ran as far away as I could, all the way to the Pacific Ocean."

Dom could see Cesare believed every word.

"Do you still have the gun?"

"It's in a safe place." He glanced at the honey house.

"Why can't we tell that we saw you?" Cesare frowned, not understanding.

"Because Nic Criscilla disappeared. My friends let it get around that I was dead. No one can know I'm alive."

"If it was an accident, no one would blame you."

Dom looked at Cesare as if couldn't believe how stupid the boy was. "Of course, they'd blame me. You think they'd believe a dirty dago?"

"Fine, Papa. We will not tell anyone." Cesare gave his father a hug, but Tomaso held back. Only when Dom threw an arm out for him did he reluctantly accept the embrace.

He glanced at the house. "It was good of Uncle Harry to invite us."

Dom spat on the path. "It's easy for him. He's always had everything handed to him. Not like me."

"I think Tomaso likes Cousin Anna Maria," Cesare teased.

"She's not our blood cousin." Tomaso pretended to poke at his brother, who danced away.

Dom handed Tomaso a crumpled piece of paper. "You have to leave soon. You can reach me at this number, but remember—no one can know I'm here."

Harry gazed into the winter garden and watched Dom talking to the boys, Italian soldiers safe under the bare wisteria vines. Did they know how fortunate they were not to be Italy? His Aunt Lucy's son Nicky was in Naples, not far from the village of her father. In retaliation for Italy's joining the Allies, the Germans had nearly destroyed Naples before the starving Napolitanos had managed to drive them out.

No one in Italy was safe from the vengeance of the fascists and the Germans. Civilians in the north were savagely murdered for suspected resistance or for harboring escaped prisoners of war struggling to join the Allies in the south. The country, the people, were being destroyed.

Once again, the blameless will suffer: the children, the dumb animals. The war will destroy what gives life to the body and spirit, gives shelter for the living. Again, the fields will be scarred and the trees bare, the olive groves splintered, and the orchards turned to charcoal. When the fighting ends, the women and old men will harvest only bones and mines, and the want and hunger will continue for years. Where will the people find the strength to survive?

July

1944

32

Everything Disappeared

Jonah sat in the Café Avellino and listened to the chatter about the explosion that had rocked the Bay Area the night before. It had been hours before they found out it wasn't an enemy attack, that the explosion had been at Port Chicago, thirty miles northeast of Richmond.

Dear Oliver,

Last night the munitions port on Suisun Bay exploded. Bombs being loaded into a Victory ship set off almost five thousand tons of high explosives and ammunition in a ship docked next to it. It blew house-size pieces of ships more than three thousand feet in the air and created a twenty- to thirty-foot tidal wave.

Everything disappeared: the pier, the locomotive carrying the explosives, the railroad tracks, and three hundred men, most of them Negro. Sailors spent the night picking up pieces of their comrades and putting them in baskets.

Mrs. Hermit's nephew is unaccounted for. No one knows whether he was on duty last night, but he hasn't called.

I wish I had something good to tell you. Maybe I shouldn't be telling you this. You probably have troubles of your own.

Give that Harley a hug for me. And take care of yourself, Oliver.

Your friend,

Jonah

Mrs. Forgione greeted Jonah, then went into the kitchen to take off her hat and put on her apron. She hoped work would help, but it was harder and harder to keep going. The war ground everyone down. It had been more than two years since Midway, since everyone said the tide of the war in the Pacific was turning. Since they were supposed to be gaining ground in Europe. But it kept going on and on.

People jumped when the phone rang. They peeked around curtains to watch the Western Union car travel through the streets, relieved when it passed their houses, but ashamed, knowing the bad news would stop somewhere. The longer the war went on, the more chances there were that her boys would die. That was what ate at her—the fear and the waiting.

33

Guam

It's Your Turn

" Die, Marine, die!"

The words drifted through the dark July night. They came from nowhere and everywhere in the lulls between artillery fire. Harley's ears swiveled forward—listening but not alerting. The Japanese were out there on the rain-soaked plateau, so close even I could smell them.

I pulled my poncho around Harley, more to comfort myself than to keep him dry. Daylight had almost faded by the time we had blasted and burned our way through the enemy cave defenses, and now, exhausted, we made do with what we had: we deepened depressions created by our own shelling and hunkered down.

Something was brewing. The Japanese had been laying down intense artillery and mortar fire along our lines, making it impossible to hear enemy movement or judge its strength. More than a thousand Americans had died taking the hill, and what was left of my division had to hold a front of some five miles on the Fonte Hill above Asan Beach. It was more a series of strong points than a frontline. While we had been capturing the ridge, the reserve Japanese had gathered and planned their counterattack, one huge offensive meant to sweep us back to the sea.

We were quiet. During breaks in the artillery fire, we heard the enemy clinking bottles, laughing and singing. Any movement or sound from our line drew gunfire. Around midnight, the gunfire became more regular, as if they had begun to fire along the line, looking for weak spots where there were no Marines to return their fire.

I remembered the advice of a Pacific-seasoned gunny: "A lot of the Japs speak English. Don't shout your names to one another; one of them will shout the same name later, and the Marine who sticks his head up will lose it. If they scream to get you to shoot, don't. If you do, they'll know where your automatic weapons are. Don't take the bait. And stay loose if you face a banzai charge; don't fire till you see their buckteeth!"

Buckteeth? What had happened to me? I used to hate those propaganda depictions of the Japanese as a race of nearsighted, bucktoothed devils. Now it was the Japanese I hated. The truth was, they were extraordinary fighters who showed no mercy to civilians or prisoners, to anyone in their way.

The stories of Japanese atrocities traveled through the Allied forces. The unwritten rule in the Pacific had been to take no prisoners, even before Allied soldiers heard what had happened on the India–Burma border. Two dogs on patrol had led their handlers to a clearing where seven heads stuck out of the ground, talking to one another: Americans, buried by the Japanese in neck-high foxholes, peed on, hit with rifle butts, and abandoned to die.

Quit thinking and stay loose. I wished my men could do what they always did: joke and tease to keep each other going, to hide their fear. I could feel their nerves strung tight in the silence of waiting, in the heaviness of the black night. Fighting was easier than anticipating. There was too much time to think.

I waited, the men waited, while our enemy built up the courage to die taking back the island. I closed my eyes and scratched Harley's ears. We had landed on Guam on July 21. Four days ago. Four days that seemed like four weeks.

We had watched from our transport while US bombs and artillery lit up the island that had been taking a pounding for more than three weeks. Someone joked that it should have sunk by now under the sheer weight of the artillery piling up on it.

Hundreds of Corsairs and Hellcats dropped bombs and napalm, then rolled over and strafed the beach and the surrounding cliffs. Red tracer bullets and small fires sparked on land; the hill exploded in bursts when shells from the battleships' sixteen-inch guns jammed home. Earlier, the Japanese planes in the area had been destroyed. From our ship, it looked like the enemy was being annihilated. Should have been a piece of cake.

But when we waded ashore in hip-deep water, our dogs swimming beside us, we emerged on a beach circled on three sides like an amphitheater. Machine-gun bullets and mortar shells came down at us from all sides. Amphibious landing craft disappeared in sprays of water and blood. The Japanese were still being bombed and strafed, but their defenses were so cleverly and securely placed that our planes and ships couldn't reach them.

I urged my men through a blood field of the dead and dying, herded them across the sand and coral to the scant safety at the base of the cliff. The dogs' training held. They followed their handlers without question, unflinching as artillery shells exploded around them and mortars burst, sending showers of sand and chunks of bodies through the air. The men ran through the screams of the falling and fallen, dragged wounded comrades as they went, left the dead for later.

There was no background movie score to romanticize the killing, no triumphant crescendo of strings to signal victory—only a relentless battering of the senses, the smell of blood, the stench of urine, the whimpers of grown men knowing they'd never see their mothers again. At the base of the cliff, we regrouped, with me yelling, "Dig in! Dig in!" to Marines who needed no urging; we dug frantically, looking for cover for ourselves and our dogs.

I scuttled along the line of men, counting them off, steeling myself for losses. Miraculously, every soul in my group—man and dog—had made it.

Sergeant Hirsch ran to me in a crouch.

"Don't look now, Lieutenant, but I think we're surrounded."

"Like shooting fish in a barrel." Thank God "Hershey" had made it. I'd have been lost without his combat experience and good sense.

"The fuckin' Japs knew where we'd have to land. They built themselves some concrete bunkers and registered each damned gun to chew up as many of us as they could."

"We need these islands to get to Japan, Sarge. They knew we'd be back."

"Yeah, they're not stupid. Just evil sons of bitches!"

"Did everyone in your group make it?"

"Adams has his ticket home. He got hit in the leg, but his dog's fine."

While the sergeant rambled on as comfortably as if we had been chatting over coffee in the mess, I pulled out our map. Our orders were to go to the command post. I studied it, then handed it to Hershey.

"What do you think?"

"What do I think? I think this is a map of some other damned island! Shit, this don't look nothin' like where we are."

"I thought it was just me." I scanned the beach. We needed to move. Somewhere.

"What else we got, Lieutenant?"

I took out the recon photos, and we examined our position, trying to make sense of where we were.

We scouted the area around the command post. Glints on the hills above us confirmed that the Japanese were doing what we would have done: watch the enemy below and wait to see where they dug in for the night. The Japanese counterattacks would come at nightfall, while the drone of the American planes faded away, using the last light to make their way back to their carriers.

"Come on, Sarge, let's get our people out of here."

The next day, and the next, and the next, we fought for the hills where Japanese mortar and machine guns punished us and kept us pinned to the beach. Our orders had been as old as warfare itself: take the high ground and hold it. Marines climbed the slopes and limestone cliffs with rifles slung on their backs, defenseless, searching for a handhold, a foothold, perhaps a clump of grass to grab on to, while Japanese soldiers emerged from holes dug into the cliff, picked off a soldier, then disappeared. Men with nowhere to hide clung to the side of the cliff and watched hand grenades roll toward them, but they kept climbing. Machine-gun fire tore up whole companies in the struggle to take the hill.

The dogs were of no use in that kind of fighting, so Harley and I and the other dog teams spent the days taking point on patrols through the deep saw grass. We searched for enemy soldiers who had survived the bombardment and hid, waiting to take out our exposed patrols.

Harley worked off-leash in front of me. The heat punished the dogs, and the humidity and mosquitoes drained the men, bringing with them the threat of malaria and dengue fever. Patrols passed dead Japanese soldiers propped against trees, their bodies swelling in the jungle heat until they burst. The dogs ignored the corpses, but the stench clung to the men and followed them for days. As the bombardment wore on, parts of bodies hung from trees; the ditches filled with bloated corpses writhing with maggots. A rotten miasma filled the Marines' mouths and noses. And then more flies emerged. And more mosquitoes.

The night brought no relief. The dogs lay at the edge of foxholes, on guard, protecting us. We all slept easier with the dogs nearby, especially after the night a dog nudged his handler and pointed his nose toward a tree at the edge of camp. At first light, a Marine sharpshooter blasted the Jap sniper out of the tree before he got off a shot.

Die, Marine.

I closed my eyes and felt inside my shirt for the letter from Theo that had caught up with me on Guadalcanal. More drawings than words. Since I'd shipped out, I'd found myself touched by any news from home. But when I opened a letter from Charley or Jennie or the kids, I could barely swallow the welling of emotion that filled my body. I'd turn away and hold my breath to keep the tears from spilling.

Harley stirred under my hand, rose, and pointed his nose toward Mt. Tenjo. I keyed my handset: "Alert down the line. They're coming."

Orange flares stained the sky, silhouetting clumps of grass and dead bodies. Hundreds of Japs screaming, "Banzai!" flickered in the orange light and charged our ragged line with rifles and hand grenades. We alerted the battleships, and they lit up the plateau with bursts of white star shells. I told Harley to stay and thought of my fellow Marines, ready to die for one another and for the families we had left behind.

I shouldered my rifle. "There are already too many fucking dead Marines. It's your turn."

Tuesday

October 24, 1944

34

Point Richmond

Eighty Minutes

L ucy wiped the counter and glanced at the door of the café again, willing her friend Edna to rush in wearing that smile that made you feel like it was good to be alive, the smile that had been absent for the past six weeks while the trial of the Negro munitions workers from Port Chicago dragged on. Now the trial had ended, and the naval court was deliberating. Soon the men would hear the verdict.

Edna's nephew was one of the men on trial. A pass to Oakland had saved his life, but he had come back to find most of the men in his unit dead or missing. For days, he and the rest of the munitions workers had shoveled up pieces of their friends' flesh and put them into baskets. When they had been asked to load explosives at a newly built pier in Vallejo, they had refused.

They were plain scared. They had always been told that the munitions weren't armed and couldn't explode. Until they did.

The men asked for other duty. Asked to be sent into combat, where at least they would have a fighting chance. But instead, when they resisted loading the ships, they were arrested. No one understood why they were charged with mutiny instead of insubordination. Most people believed the Navy wanted to frighten the troops and stop any protests against the way Negro servicemen were used.

Although she had cooking to do, she couldn't bear to be in the kitchen. She expected Edna to walk in any minute, so she stayed out front and stacked and restacked the boxes of nougat candy she gave to her customers. She heard the bell: Edna stood in the doorway, her face ashen.

Lucy's hand went to her heart. "No."

"Guilty." She shook her head. "All of them. The trial took six weeks, but those judges made up their minds in eighty minutes. He could get five to fifteen years' hard labor and a dishonorable discharge."

Wednesday

October 25, 1944

35

Drowning in Unshed Tears

I opened my eyes and shivered. It was the same dream. In it, I dug a grave. When I finished, I stood up and wiped my forehead. All around me, fields of graves marked with helmets dangling on rifles stretched as far as I could see.

The doctors had told me all I needed was time to recuperate, to put it behind me. I told myself it was only a dream—had been telling myself over and over, morning after morning.

I was back in Pt. Richmond, but Guam was only as far away as the next night's sleep. It wasn't the memory of fighting, of being wounded, that tortured me. It was walking away from the endless graves, from the rifles stuck bayonet-down in freshly turned dirt. My men had buried too many friends, friends who had died beside them, sometimes quickly, sometimes so slowly they had begged their buddies to finish them off.

Then the living had moved on—on to more killing. The war allowed no time to mourn, to grieve, to honor the death of a man they might have loved as deeply as they would ever love anyone. They moved on, they fought, they buried more men, they moved on—and no one could see that they were drowning in unshed tears.

I had hidden my face when the hospital plane taxied down the runway on Guam. The medics expected me to be grateful that I was leaving the fighting, but grief filled my heart. I was leaving behind friends willing to sacrifice their own lives for each other and for their dogs. It was why they fought. Forget the pretty speeches about preserving democracy and freedom—they died for each other, killing and being killed to end the endless killing.

Back in Richmond after weeks in the naval hospital, I fought sleep until I was exhausted. Some nights I found peace in the blues clubs, where I stayed late into the night after the crowd left and the musicians played for themselves, driving deeper and deeper into a world of their own making. The plaintive tones of the sax, the indescribable sadness of the clarinet, comforted me, took me to another country. No, not another country—a place with no countries, a place with no lines to defend or hills to take. No graves to dig. I loved the music, but it had been the voices that had drawn me into the dark club that first afternoon.

They were like the first tones I'd heard when I regained consciousness on Guam's bloody ground. Slow and deep, conversational, soothing my dog.

"Easy. You be awright, fella. Lemme help you. Tha's a boy. Good dog." The sound of a man knowing how to talk to animals.

"His name's Harley." I couldn't believe he was still alive enough to try to guard me. "How bad is he?"

"I's not a vet, but it look like that bullet done gone through his neck. They's a lot of blood, but if he gonna die from it, he be dead by now."

I faded away and woke up in the field hospital. I remembered surviving the first two waves of banzai attacks, and then nothing until that voice.

"Hey. How you doing?" Hershey stood by my cot, holding a canteen of water.

"Where's Harley?"

"At the vet hospital. I'll bring him by later. He's going to be fine."

"What happened?"

"You were shot in the knee. Your days on patrol are over." He tried to lighten the mood. "Seems I won't have to keep saving your ass. Leave me time to end this blasted war, now I don't have to babysit you."

I swiped at my chin where the water had dribbled down. "Harley needs to go home with me."

Hershey sucked his teeth. "I don't think they're going to allow him on the plane to Hawaii."

"We need to figure something out, Hersh. He never enlisted. He still belongs to me, not the Marines. He is a Marine, but he doesn't belong to the government."

"After what you two did last night, I think we should be able to wrangle something."

"What we did?"

"You don't remember? Holy shit!"

I shook my head and winced. "Please, just tell me."

"Harley alerted behind us between banzai attacks. We crept out and spied some Japs sneakin' along the gully that runs toward the field hospital."

"And then?"

"We called to warn the field hospital, then picked up some men and headed down after the Japs, but when we tried to cross a gap between the gullies, we started taking machine-gun fire. Figured there was a nest behind a clump of saw grass above us. We were pinned down. Couldn't get to the field hospital, so you and Harley flanked the nest, came down behind them, and took out the machine gun."

"Is that when I got shot?"

"No. You caught up to us, and we tore down the hill to the medic tents that were under fire from the Japs. You should have seen it. Well, you did see it, I guess. The warning we called in gave the docs and the walking wounded time to drag and carry the guys who couldn't walk down to the beaches. Cooks, medics, the docs, mechanics, Marines with head bandages and crutches—half undressed and armed just with the rifles they came in with—held off those Japs until we showed up."

"I remember someone talking to Harley. Helping him."

"That was Luther, a cook from the colored mess unit. He told me what happened after you and I got separated. He saw you get shot in the leg and fall. A Jap was about to finish you with his bayonet, but Harley broke cover and flew at his throat. You know the dogs aren't supposed to do that, don't you?" Hershey winked. "You shot at another Jap who was aiming at Harley. You missed, and he shot at you instead. You distracted the bastard aiming at Harley long enough for Luther to cold-cock him. With a friggin' fryin' pan. Harley got hit somehow while he was guarding you in the middle of the fight."

"And I missed the whole damn thing."

"The docs say it'll come back to you bit by bit. The second bullet barely grazed your head, but you probably have a concussion."

"And Luther?"

"Back to mess duty." Hershey looked hard at me. "You might not want this next part getting around, specially if you're planning on taking Harley home with you. Luther's not talking about it. But you oughta know."

"Know what?"

"Harley killed that bastard who charged you. Tore out his throat."

I turned my head away. "He *is* a Marine."

"Damn straight!"

I'd had no trouble getting him on the plane after word had spread that he was the dog who'd caught the enemy sneaking down to the field hospital. Now Harley was resting his head on my rumpled bed, snuffling at me to get up and let him out. I wondered if he ever dreamed about Guam.

"They were going after the halt and the lame, Harley. What kind of people are they?" I sucked in my breath as I hobbled over to the door. "Talk about the halt and the lame."

Chief Cavanaugh waved me to a chair and grimaced at the telephone he held away from his ear. When he had become chief, Richmond had been a sleepy backwater, but the war industry had quadrupled its population, and although the city could pay for more cops, it hadn't been able to compete with the salaries men made in the defense industry. The war effort was winding down, and the shipyard was letting people go, but not many folks seemed to be leaving town. Richmond might not have treated them too kindly, but people had more opportunities for a good life here than in the places they had left.

He hung up the phone and got right to it.

"I asked you to come in because the Army needs help with a sensitive investigation. A death on Angel Island. The colored troops heard about the verdict in the Port Chicago trial last night and took it out on the Italian prisoners. The MPs thought they had things under control, but this morning they found a dead POW."

A murder case. Maybe that would help me sleep.

"JAG wants an experienced homicide detective to oversee the investigation. Someone able to work with the military but be as impartial as possible. Because of the verdicts in the mutiny trial, this whole investigation will be scrutinized for any kind of discrimination. Harry Buonarotti knows we're understaffed and suggested I ask you. He'll provide you with an assistant."

I realized the chief was assessing me and I sat with one leg outstretched, hoping to appear casual.

"If you need more time to recover from your wounds, you don't have to do this. You *are* still on medical leave."

"I'm fine, sir. When do I start?"

"Now. Do you need a driver? With your leg?"

"I can manage, sir. It's merely an annoyance."

"Right." He looked skeptical, but let it go. "I see you have a weapon."

"Yes, sir." I touched the holster on my hip.

"Take these. You might need them." He pushed a cuff set, a badge, and a Richmond Police Department ID across the desk. "Take the coast guard ferry to the island where an MP will meet you. See what's going on. You'll report to Captain Buonarotti."

"Chief, if the Marines release me, I'd like my job back."

He looked away. "Let's see how things go on Angel Island. See if your leg holds up."

36

Angel Island

Returning to Shore

When the last of his men had boarded the ferry to take them back to Angel Island, Luca Respighi walked on behind them. The Italian POWs huddled together in the shelter of the upper deck and began a game of *morra*, keeping their voices low as they called out numbers, betting the small wages they earned from emptying garbage cans in Oakland.

Luca stood at the rail, feeling the sunshine on his face and the vibration of the ferry engines beneath his feet. They were early coming back today. The fog crouched out in the Pacific, not yet ready to obliterate everything more than a few yards away. In this light, the ocher hills edging the bay were the hills of Sicily—even the water gleamed like golden silk behind them. If he closed his eyes, he could almost pretend he was crossing the Strait of Messina. Almost. The shrill sound of the gulls and the smell of fish and salt were the same, but not this piercing cold that blew in from the Pacific.

Still, it was infinitely better than the heat of the African desert where he and his men had surrendered. Or been captured. He wasn't sure what to call it. The British, the French, and the Americans had surrounded them. The men were hungry and dehydrated, sunburned and exhausted, plagued by lice, and, more to the point, had no ammunition left to fight with. Leaflets from the Americans fluttered down on them, advising them to retreat, and they did, until they could go nowhere but into the sea. He concealed his men from the British and French and waited for an American patrol to reach them. Then they surrendered.

Americans were supposed to treat their prisoners well, but he had begun to think waiting for them had been a mistake when his men were packed into a boxcar like sardines. For ten days, they suffered inside the car as the desert sun baked them and the night air chilled them. They had little food and water and could lie down to sleep only if other men lay down under them. They had dug a hole in the floor of the car to use as a latrine, but soon every breath carried the taste of air filled with the stench of bodies and illness.

But when the train finally stopped, an American soldier marched the dazed prisoners to barracks where they were given soap and water and clean clothes. They ate canned chicken and were even given cigarettes, while the prisoners of the French were thrown into an unshaded wire enclosure and abused by their Moroccan guards.

The voices of children penetrated Luca's thoughts of the desert. Several women with young children clustered around the aft deck, throwing bread to the seagulls that strafed the wake of the ferry. Must be families of the officers on the island going for some special event. Whatever happened the night before must be over, or they wouldn't have allowed families to visit today.

He walked back to check on the men. A dog sat beside a Marine with sallow skin and the pinched look of someone in pain. He reached down often to touch the dog, as if to reassure it, or perhaps to reassure himself. Not Luca's favorite breed. Too many memories of the way the dogs menaced the villagers, frothing and straining at their leashes while the German soldiers smiled.

The dog tensed and looked past Luca, who turned to see what had captured its attention. A red object bobbed in the wake of the ferry. It took him a moment to realize that a little girl had fallen overboard. The dog flew past him and barked at the water.

"*Madonna mia!*" Luca tore off his coat and boots and dove over the rail, leaving the shepherd barking behind him.

"Stop, or I'll shoot!"

A soldier raised his pistol and searched the water.

The POW broke the surface ten feet away from the ferry. The soldier fired at the bobbing head, then aimed again. I struck his arm with my cane.

"Stand down, soldier!" I stumbled against him. "Can't you see what's happening?"

"Oh, I get it." The guard smiled and lowered the gun. "Why waste the ammo? That dago won't last ten minutes out there."

Something flew past our heads once, then again, and I turned to see an MP throwing life preservers into the bay. Harley trembled at the rail and barked sharply at me. He flew into the air and over the side as soon as I nodded.

The MP saluted. "My people don't much take after Johnny Weissmuller, but we do have a talent for throwing. Corporal Nate Hermit, sir."

Our hasty introductions were drowned in shouts and cries.

"Man overboard! Come about, come about!"

The ferry shuddered as the engines slammed into reverse. A woman shrieked, and soldiers and prisoners rushed to her side.

Another group of POWs raced toward a motorized skiff lashed to the rail. The MP took off after them. The boat swung out and back against the side of the ferry while the POWs strained to lower it and the weight of two of their compatriots. The MP launched himself into the skiff, knocked down one of the POWs, and almost wrenched the lines free.

"Sorry. If I don't come with you, that cracker with the pistol will sink you before you can help that little girl—and your captain." He righted himself and looked toward the water and muttered, "Then again, he would just as happily sink me, too."

The POWs looked for a moment as if they were going to pitch him out of the skiff, then shrugged and focused on the men on deck, who gestured and shouted, directing them to the swimmer.

Luca hit the water hard. It didn't yield to his body as the soft, warm water of his home did. He surfaced, gasping from the impact and the shock of the cold. His trousers weighed him down, but he swam, lifted one arm after the other, kicked, pulled, and pushed himself toward the place he thought the child might be. He had gone into the water almost immediately after she had fallen, so he must be close to her, but he did not know these waters and could only hope the current would not take her away from him faster than he could follow.

The frigid water numbed his skin; he dove and forced open his stinging eyes. The sun lit a path that glowed under the chop. He surfaced and lined up on the spot where he thought she had gone in and dove again. *Eccola*—there was her red coat, billowing like a scarlet jellyfish, the trapped air suspending it below the surface. He pushed and kicked himself toward her, his body growing heavier and heavier, but he wasn't giving up. He lost sight of her for a moment, dove again, and saw her sinking in front of him. He grabbed the red coat and pushed for the surface, broke through the water, and pulled cold air into his lungs.

He rested on his back, holding the child on his chest. Something bumped him from behind. As the word *shark* formed in his brain, something white flashed to his left. He spun. A life preserver appeared out of nowhere, bobbing and dipping. He reached toward it, slapped it, but it slid out from under his numb hand. He didn't have the strength to chase it around the bay. And then it came back to him gripped by the shepherd, just head and rudder-like tail above the water as it struggled toward him. The dog nudged the ring tight against Luca, who held the limp girl in the crook of his arm. He tipped the ring on an edge toward him and tried to flip it over the girl. It slipped away, and the dog pushed it back. Again. And again. And then it happened. Luca wedged her inside the canvas circle as best he could. She was safe now, as safe as he could make her until help came, but she was cold, too, and so tiny. He tried to think how long they had been in the bay, even as he began to drift to sun-warmed waters.

The waves of the bay of his home rocked him gently, and he listened to the sounds of fishermen returning to shore.

37

As Usual

I sat beside the bed and willed Captain Respighi to wake up. The doctor had said he'd be fine—if he didn't get pneumonia. The Italian POW had ordinary, even features, a deep bow in the center of the upper lip, a forehead that might have been high even before the baldness. In the movies, it could be the face of a hero or a villain.

Someone coughed behind me. The MP. He had cleaned up after helping the Italians get Luca, the girl, and Harley out of the water.

"Corporal Hermit, sir."

"Are you related to Edna Hermit?"

"How do you know my mother?"

I explained. "She must be relieved to have you close to home."

A shadow passed over his face, but I didn't have a chance to find out why, because he nodded at the bed.

I turned around. The captain had the eyes of a leading man, the man who always gets the girl. They were dark, concerned.

"The little girl, is she alive?"

"She's fine. Thanks to you."

"Not me. *I* did not get her out of the water."

"True, your men did, but only after you risked your own neck to save her."

"I seem to remember a dog. Could that be right?"

"You weren't hallucinating. That was Harley, my dog. He likes to help out when he can."

"Well, thank him for me."

"You can thank him yourself, and Corporal Hermit here, who threw in the life preservers and probably kept that idiot guard from shooting your men."

Nate shook his head. "Don't bother thanking me. I was only concerned about the girl. Believe me." There was an undercurrent in his voice that didn't bode well for what I intended, but I plunged ahead.

"I don't know how much you know about what's been happening on the island, Captain."

"We left this morning before we learned anything."

"One of your men was found dead. Carlo Fusco. Did you know him?"

"He is not one of mine, but I know of him. He's a fascist, and I have as little as possible to do with them. Your government was supposed to have sent them to another camp by now. All they do is cause trouble, harass my men." He rubbed his head. "Is this an interrogation?"

"Good Lord, no. I do need to know where you were last night, but we're here to ask for your help."

"What kind of help?"

"We need someone we can trust to translate for us. I think your men will feel more comfortable talking with you than with an American translator. After what you did today, well, you captured our attention."

"First, please tell me more about what happened."

"There was a fight last night. The colored soldiers heard about the verdict in the Port Chicago Mutiny trial and attacked one of the POW barracks. This morning, they found Fusco's body. You can guess what the logical conclusion is."

"The Negro soldiers are going to be blamed for his death." He glanced at Nate with sympathy.

Nate's only response was a bitter, *as usual.*

I ignored him. "If they did it, that's one thing, but if they didn't, we would like to find out who did."

"And you want me to help you perhaps incriminate one of my own men." The captain seemed more amused than concerned.

"Perhaps. But only if he's guilty."

He smiled, as if he knew I had taken his measure.

"*Bene.* I will be happy to help, but I think I will need some clothes." His arms went out to his sides, and he shrugged, as if to say, *I can't go like this.*

"May I?" Luca gestured toward the pole where the body had been found.

I nodded and walked beside him. "The commander said it stopped raining last night sometime after two a.m." I motioned to Nate to keep up.

Luca canted his head, looked at the ground from different angles. "You say he was beaten, then hanged?"

"That's what the men who found him thought."

"There is no blood on the ground. And it is not very disturbed."

"Yes, I noticed that." I decided to see if he came to the same conclusion I had. "What does that tell you?"

"That they hanged a dead man. The beating did not occur at this spot."

"They hanged him to make it look like we did it." Nate thrust his chin forward, narrowed his deep-set hazel eyes. "The colored troops waiting to ship out."

Luca looked confused.

"It's what happened at Fort Lawton. Your people got away with murder there, and my people got blamed. As usual. Worked once—why not try it again?"

"You're saying whoever did this figured we wouldn't look any farther than the rioting soldiers." I considered the idea.

"I do not know what happened at Fort Lawton." Luca's tone was matter of fact. "We heard only about the death of one of us. It was understandable that a soldier could have killed him. There have been other incidents between the POWs and the soldiers."

"The Negro soldiers," Nate said.

"Yes. There is much hostility. I cannot blame you for that. Your government treats us prisoners better than it treats you— something my men and I do not comprehend." Luca squatted on the ground by the pole.

Nate ignored him and spoke to me. I had grasped the pole and bent forward as far as I could.

"Can you tell how many different boot prints there are, Lieutenant?"

"Do I look like an Indian scout, *kemosabe*?" I tried to lessen the tension between my helpers.

Luca tilted his head and glanced up at me. I waved his unspoken question away. He rose to his feet. "There is not a great deal here to examine. There should be more disturbance, signs of a struggle."

"Even if you find prints, it doesn't help us much." Nate pointed at Luca's boots. "You POWs wear government issue. The boots could belong to you, us, anyone on the island."

Luca wandered toward the incline that bordered the exercise area.

"Look here." Some distance away from the pole, there was a clear imprint of a boot that was not government issue. "This looks like the boot a fisherman would wear. The toe is rounded, the heel not well defined. The outline is soft."

"It had to have been made after the rain stopped last night, or it would have been washed away." Nate pointed to the print. "This proves the soldiers didn't do it."

"Until we know when Fusco died, this boot print only tells us that after the rain stopped, someone might have been on the island who didn't belong here." I wondered if Nate had been the right choice for this job.

I stretched my back and shifted my weight. "Let's cast it, Nate. And take a few photos in case the MPs missed it earlier. Better hurry, before it gets dark. Then you go talk to some of the men who were not involved in the fighting last night. Try to get us a direction for further questioning: who was missing from the barracks, who might have started it, whether anyone had trouble with Fusco. Whether anyone was outside after the rain stopped. Luca and I will go talk to the POWs. Then we'll meet and decide our next step.

Luca and I headed for the barracks where the Italian Service Unit POWs were housed, separate from the fascist POWs, who refused to work for us, the enemy.

I knew what I'd think of any American POWs who worked to help the Japanese win their war, whether the United States had surrendered or not. "Why *are* you helping us? I know Italy is on our side now, but still. It wasn't that long ago that we were killing each other."

Luca stopped and looked across the bay. "To fully explain, I would have to recount twenty years of Italian history. In brief, most Italians opposed Mussolini, but he silenced them and took over the country. His alliance with Germany, our traditional enemy, alarmed many people. Soon he was shining Hitler's boots. Since the armistice with the United States in '43, there has been civil war in Italy. Italians are now fighting to liberate the country from the fascists *and* the Germans."

He started walking again. "To answer your question, we are weary of war and death. We simply want to go home, find our families, rebuild our country. Again. We do what we have to do to end this war." He turned to me. "We wish your country would send us home now, so we can help fight, help liberate Italy. We are your allies now."

"Some of you are. Not all." I moved forward, changed the subject. "Have you done this before? Investigated crimes in Italy?"

"Why do you ask?"

"Have you?"

"We could go on answering each other's questions with more questions all day, so I will capitulate and answer you. I have a close friend who is a detective in Sicily. Sometimes he asked me to accompany him to crime scenes, consult on interesting cases."

"What did you do . . . before the war?"

"I was a psychiatrist—hence my ability to not answer questions. I suppose I still am—I listen to my men and help them to face their fears."

"And your greatest fear?"

"During wartime? What we all fear: first, death, for ourselves and the people we love, but, in the end, the most destructive thing of all: becoming like the enemy."

38

Between Scylla and Charybdis

I looked around the POW barracks. Some men read books from the YMCA; others played cards or wrote letters. One man held on to a towel tied to a pole and leaned back, waving one hand in the air to invisible music. When I nodded toward him, Luca explained that he was probably practicing for the dance the men were holding in San Francisco.

He told me that when we formed the Service Units, many POWs had leaped at the chance to escape boredom and leave the base, but then the beatings had started. The doctor in the infirmary must have thought the Italians were accident prone as they showed up one after the other with black eyes and bruises.

Finally, the Army figured out that the fascists punished anyone who volunteered for the units, so they put the volunteers in separate barracks. But the Army could not do anything to stop the fascists in Italy from retaliating against the volunteers' families.

Three things kept POWs from volunteering: fear of the fascists, loyalty to Italy, and fear of being sent as support personnel to the Pacific front with its heat and mosquitoes and artillery. When the carrot of privileges had not worked, the United States had threatened to send the men to camps where they would not be so comfortable, the camps where the fascists were going.

They had been caught between Scylla and Charybdis, and most had decided to volunteer. Now they went on picnics and suppers with American Italians who sought them out, invited them to church activities, and welcomed them like family. In many cases they were related, if not by blood, then by village.

He gestured toward me and talked to his men. A few of them exchanged looks, shrugs, seemed to come to a decision. One of them spoke up. In Italian. Luca listened, then turned to me.

"Carlo Fusco was not well liked. The men say a number of people wanted him dead."

"Who in particular?"

"He fought with one of the colored soldiers. Larry Kimballs."

"About?"

"Fusco had to pass the colored barracks on his way to his job in the kitchen. He came upon a group of soldiers looking at a photo of a young woman and made a rude gesture—like he wanted to, *ehhhh* . . ." Luca trailed off. I understood. "It was a photo of Kimballs's sister. He hit Fusco, who hit him back, and then an MP came by and broke it up."

"Did he report it?"

"No. The MP was Negro. Both men could walk away. Nobody wanted the trouble." Luca took off his cap and rubbed his head. "The men try to settle things among themselves. We have heard a Negro soldier put on report for fighting can be punished severely. That only makes things worse for everyone."

"Maybe Kimballs decided to even the score later."

"Maybe."

"What else did they say?"

"To talk to the fascists. Fusco had some trouble with one of them."

"He seems to have had a lot of trouble."

"There are a couple of men in with the fascists who would like to join our units, but they are afraid of reprisals. Also, they heard the Army is sending them to a segregation camp in Texas that is supposed to be an unpleasant place."

"So?"

"They would know more about Fusco. I think we could get them to talk to us if we could protect them."

I was getting tired of not being able to ask questions myself, and of not understanding what people were saying. I could have been at the opera. High drama, hands in the air, arms out to the side, interruptions, shrugs, walking away. I thought the Service Unit POWs were required to take English classes. They didn't seem to have done this group much good.

Luca took the men aside to promise that the people who talked to us would be kept separate from the fascists.

Finally, he and one of the prisoners approached me.

"This man speaks a little English. He will talk to us. But he wants us to take his friend, also."

"Agreed." I motioned for the man to sit. "So, what do you have to tell us?"

"Fusco, he not a good man. Always say know America. Live here before. Before the war."

"Did he say where?"

He gestured over his shoulder. "East. Maybe New York? New Jersey?"

"Did he say when?"

"Sacco *e* Vanzetti time."

"Around 1929. But if he lived in the US, how did he end up in the Italian army?"

Luca shrugged. "He must have gone back to Italy at some point. What else did Fusco say?"

"Money." He rubbed his thumb and finger together. "He get lotsa money soon."

"How?"

The POW rattled on in Italian; then Luca translated: "He says Fusco always had a scheme going. Even when they were fighting in Italy, he knew how to get things, to make money. Must have been a genius if he could find money in Italy during the war. He also says Fusco was looking for someone to help him."

Fusco's effects were little different from what I would have found in any Italian POW's barracks bag: socks, handkerchief, underwear, garrison cap and field hat, pants, all secondhand US Army issue.

I shook the canteen—nothing inside. Luca carefully set aside a rosary with black beads and told me that carrying it could be more a sign of superstition than one of devotion, maybe a reminder of the mother or girlfriend who had spent hours running the beads through her fingers.

I found a few photos inside a waterproof cloth. An old woman standing before a pump in a village, the forbidding face of a man, and a photo of a beautiful woman kneeling in the sand, an art deco building in the background. "I know that building. That's Atlantic City."

"*Dov'e?* Where is it?"

"New Jersey. I think we've got us a clue, Luca. Fusco could have been a tourist, but maybe he lived there, and if he did, he sounds like the kind of guy the police might have had dealings with. Let's get to a phone." I thought for a moment. "Let's try Newark. A lot of Italians live there."

I called the Newark Police Department and asked if anyone there might remember a Carlo Fusco from about the time of the Sacco-Vanzetti trial.

"I'm pretty new here, but I can pass on the information. Sergeant Doran will be back from vacation tomorrow. He might know. Been here longer than God."

"What time should I call?"

"He'll be in by seven, but you might want to wait until after roll call and morning briefing. Say, nine?"

"That'll make it six our time." I thanked him and hung up. "Luca, if it's okay with you, I'd like you to stay with me in Pt. Richmond. It will be easier than having you on the island."

"Fine, Lieutenant. Allow me to pack some items and inform my sergeant."

"Take your time. I'm going to see what Nate has dug up and ask about this Larry Kimballs."

Harley was no worse for his adventure in the bay, and I let him help me up the steps to the colored barracks. Nate called the men to attention; some rose a little slowly from their bunks. It was nothing I could call them on, but it was there: a lack of respect tinged with suspicion.

Nate motioned me aside with an angry flick of his head.

"I was on my way to find you. They've already made up their minds. They took one of the men to lockup."

"Who?"

"One of the white cooks said Larry Kimballs was outside last night, and a lieutenant who's had it in for him got the okay to lock him up. No one has seen him since they took him away."

"He fought with the victim."

"The men told me. Fusco made an obscene gesture when he saw a photo of Kimballs' sister. The men were already angry about the Italian POWs holding dances and going to parties while they're stuck here without passes."

"Are they being punished for something?"

"Yes. For being colored. Not much they can do to change that."

This was not going well.

"Look, Nate, we need to find out what happened so these men aren't blamed for something they didn't do. And you don't have to add *again*. Let's do our job."

He nodded, tight-lipped.

"We need the men to cooperate. I promise you nothing will happen to them."

He shut his eyes and nodded again.

I looked at the men destined for the horror of the Pacific and thought of the Negro Marines who had beat off wave after wave of Japanese trying to steal our ammunition stores the night of the banzai attack. And then there was Luther, the cook who had saved Harley.

I tried to look the soldiers in the eye, but they didn't make it easy. "I've been where you're going—my dog and I were wounded there. We'd both be dead if a cook hadn't saved our lives. With a frying pan." That got a few smiles, and the men looked at me, realizing that I knew what their lives were like and had reason to want to help them. "I don't want any of you to be blamed for something you didn't do, but I need your help." There was silence. "Anyone want to tell me what started things?"

One of the men spoke up. "We were already piss . . . annoyed with the POWs, and then they wouldn't shut up about going to see Lena Horne. It was the last straw. A few of the guys decided to teach them a lesson—so they wouldn't be so comfortable sitting at the concert."

Ducked heads and smiles from the men.

"They waited until midnight and snuck up to the Italian barracks. They were gonna beat on them, not kill them. Just wanted to let off some steam."

"Some of them dagos probably killed our friends in Africa, and now they'll be here, sittin' in the catbird seat, while we're dying in the Pacific." This from a man with a swollen eye.

"One of them Larry Kimballs?"

"*Sheeit*, no. Kimballs don't like fighting."

"He got into it with Fusco."

"He punched him for being rude about his sister. You would've too, sir. But then it was over."

"Where was Kimballs during the attack on the POWs?" I turned to another man who had been watching the exchange and didn't have any visible cuts and bruises.

"Here, patching up people as they came back in. He never left the barracks. We tried to tell that lieutenant who came and took him away, but he didn't want to hear it. Thinks we're lying to help Kimballs. We didn't sleep all night, what with people going to the infirmary, and the brass tearing us new . . . Anyway, no one left the barracks after it stopped raining."

"MPs will get statements from each of you. In writing. Put down what you know, where you were, who can vouch for where you and other people in your barracks were." I held up my hand to stop the mumbling. "I'm not asking you to rat on anyone. I don't think this murder had anything to do with you, but we need your statements to prove that. We need a time table, and going over the night might help you remember something important."

We had barely made it out the door before Nate asked me if I thought they had done it.

"It's early days, Nate, but I don't think they did. I have to call Harry—Captain Buonarotti—and have him get Kimballs back to his barracks. And we need to talk to the cook who saw Kimballs outside. What was he doing out there? He could be involved."

"He'd have to be pretty stupid to say anything if he was involved."

I didn't have the heart to tell him how much successful police work depended on criminals' stupidity.

"If Kimballs is charged, the other men might be, too, and after Port Chicago, they don't think they'll get a fair shake. If that happens, the riots will make the mess in Detroit last year look like a Sunday-school picnic. Sir."

39

Point Richmond

Anywhere, Anytime in America

The muted sounds of "Moonlight Serenade" filled the kitchen. Jonah listened to his landlady hum along, her back to the door.

"Excuse me, ma'am." Mrs. Standish looked up from the biscuit dough struggling under her rolling pin. Strands of gray hair escaped her hairnet and stuck to her flushed cheeks.

"Breakfast'll be ready in half an hour, Jonah. In the meantime, there's coffee and some cinnamon buns on the table."

"Thank you, but I ate breakfast this morning. I can't believe you make breakfast for every shift. Why do you do it?"

"You workers are helping to bring my boy home. It's why I opened my home to you. Besides, it's easier to work than to lie awake at night worrying about him."

He thought about the mothers all over the country worrying about their boys, and about his own mother, who was gone now.

"Did you see anyone outside my room today, ma'am?"

"Is there something wrong?"

"No, no. Someone left me a message. I wondered if you had seen anyone."

"I've been in this kitchen since six a.m. and haven't been upstairs all day. When Patty comes in tomorrow, I'll ask if she saw anyone."

Jonah sat in his room and flipped through his notebook, hoping for a clue about who might have left the note under his door.

Come to the brickyard at 1:00 a.m. I have answers to the questions you've been asking. Come alone.

Come alone. Who in the hell did he have to take with him? Only Oliver, and he didn't think the Marine was up to a meeting at the brickyard yet.

Maybe he was getting close to something. Negro servicemen weren't attacking these women. The sailors were convenient scapegoats. Monica's friend Zora had come back from Detroit angry with men in general and dead set on getting the attacker. She wanted to check with another one of the victims, someone who thought she knew who he might be. Jonah thought the guy should be praying that the police got him before Zora did.

The note meant someone had noticed him asking questions. Good guy or bad? He thought he had been subtle, joining conversations at lunch with the hands on the welding crew or after work at the Double R Restaurant. Maybe someone had figured out what he was doing. Could have seen him at the deeds office in Martinez. In case he got in trouble, he had better call in. Do something with his notes.

As usual, the Double R was fit to bursting, like everywhere you went these days. Guys in hard hats clustered together by trades: the welders, the electricians, the crane men. A group of Pullman porters seemed to be celebrating a birthday. There were white groups and colored groups; no mixed groups, even though the Double R was one of the few places in Richmond open to everyone.

Jonah slid onto an empty stool at the counter. Still warm. Nothing was unused long enough to cool down. There was no day. No night. Even the movie theaters were open twenty-four hours. Gave people some place to sleep until they found a room. He didn't see Ralph. He was pretty sure the ex-boxer had figured out his secret and wondered if he had shared it with his wife. Probably not. He seemed like a man who could keep a confidence.

"Ralph around?"

"Nope. He needed a night off. He'll be in tomorrow morning."

He ordered the chili and corn bread and walked over to the pay phone.

"Leonard, it's me."

"Jonah! What's up?" His editor sounded happy to hear his voice.

"I got a note to meet someone tonight."

"Who? Why? Where?"

"Writing the story already?"

"No, you ass. Wondering if it's a setup."

"It could be from someone who was at the fire that killed those children, or someone with information about the attacks on women."

"Or someone who wants to stop what you're doing."

"It feels a little hinky, but how will I find out anything if I don't take a chance?"

"Depends how big a chance you're taking." Leonard cleared his throat, a sign that he wasn't sure he should say something. "Remember what happened to that fellow that worked on your crew. The one they found hanged."

Instead of putting him off, remembering how he had failed to help Regis Simmons made Jonah more determined to get to the bottom of things.

"I think I can handle it, but to be on the safe side, I've sent you my notes." He lowered his voice and tucked the receiver under his chin. "I think I'm close to finding out who was behind the cross burning in 1941, and why it wasn't burned in front of the house the professor was buying. I'm working on the second cross burning. I think they're connected, but I haven't finished checking out the neighborhood where the minister wanted to rent. I've been asking around—some Negroes are moving into Richmond without any trouble, but someone is *persuading* them to stay out of this lily-white area."

He glanced around to make sure no one was listening. "My source in the police department said they found used flashbulbs near the road where the first cross was burned. Regis told me he gave negatives of the cross burning to Peter Wright. Others, too, of Klan meetings."

"You can't trust anyone in the police department."

He pictured Leonard holding the candlestick phone, pacing back and forth as far as the cord would stretch. "I don't think he's one of them; he was Oliver's partner and he trusted him."

"That means nothing. Do *not* do this. I'll call my contact at the Justice Department, see if we can get more information before you go ahead."

"I know what I'm doing. Look, I gotta go; someone is waiting for the phone. You have this number if you get anything from your contact. If not, I'll talk to you tomorrow. Same time, same station."

He hung up, grateful for the woman who quickly picked up the phone and jiggled the hook for the operator. If Leonard tried to call back, he'd get a busy signal.

Jonah shivered in the wind coming off the bay. Part chill, part uneasiness. He felt as if he were a million miles from anyone who cared about him. He parked at the gate and walked toward the brickyard. Spooky place. The lights of the city across the bay were glimmers of brightness in the black. He longed for the warmth of a bar, the jujube traffic lights blinking in the hours that belonged to the nighthawks. This space devoid of human energy was not for him. No moon, no streetlights, just fathomless darkness. He was an idiot for coming here.

He turned around and ran back toward his car, shining his flashlight on the uneven ground. Something rustled. A barrel rolled in front of him. He jumped over it and brought up the flashlight. A white hood. The flashlight bobbed as he ran; black and white flickered like a magic lantern show. More of them. They circled him. A torch flared, and the night became timeless. It could have been any place, any time, in America.

"Hey, snoop."

"Were you looking for us?"

Jonah turned slowly, hoping to find a way out, to make his mind work through the fear. He struggled for the words his heart told him wouldn't help. Might as well go out proud.

"And I guess I found you." He tried for nonchalance. "Didn't take much to smoke you out. And I didn't come alone. The cops will be here soon."

Laughter surrounded him, and a nightstick flashed in the light of the flames.

"This'll teach you to mind your own business!"

The beating didn't take long. Six against one. Jonah felt them going through his pockets, his clothes, taking his wallet and money. One of the men swore and said he was going to search Jonah's car.

They dragged his semiconscious body up the hill and tied him to a fence. They stretched his arms out and twisted the barbed-wire strands around them.

"See how long it takes him to get out of that!"

"Goddamn it." One of them had pricked himself. "Hurts like a bitch!"

Jonah slumped forward, his feet twisted on the ground. He groaned, tried to speak. The one who had pricked his finger turned back.

"Want some more?"

Jonah screamed when the club slammed through his shins.

His legs were separate from him, but he felt searing pain when he tried to move. *Shins. Arms. Pain everywhere. Chest. Head. Don't push. Don't push.* Last time he had tried to push himself to stand, he must have passed out. His breath came hard, as if something were pressing on his chest. His head lolled forward. The night fog left the bay, climbed the hill, and swirled around him.

He drifted off the fence, rode the currents into the sky, into the cold clouds. So different from home's sweltering nights. It was summer, frogs calling, a mockingbird squeaking like a screen door. The last lazy summer, long before the war. He and his mama were talking on the wooden porch swing, the chains catching and sticking on each backward arc. *Click, thunk, click, thunk.* She brushed back the hair from his forehead, tried to smile. He could see what she was thinking—as if he were in her mind.

Please, God, make him stay. That was what she thought, but she said, "I can't say I fault you, Jonah. There's little for you here, where folks know your kin. I'm afraid of what lies ahead if you do this way. How hard it'll be." But she knew he was used to hard, to taking chances. He was the daredevil, the first one in the river in the spring when petals from the serviceberry still eddied against the banks.

"I don't see I have a choice, Mama. If I leave, I can send money home. There's no work here I want to do."

She could see his mind was made up—see it in the set of his chin, the only way he resembled the man who had fathered him. *Don't waste your breath. And don't make it harder for him.* She could feel his power. Part ambition, part smarts, lots of parts of anger. Who knew what would happen to him if he stayed? He wasn't going to be a man who stepped off the sidewalk for long. Still, her heart ached to keep him with her. She cleared her throat, letting him know a story was coming.

"When I was a girl, my daddy worked for a man with lots of land and animals and a big pond. He decided to raise geese for people to eat, so he got himself a dozen babies. Now, he didn't want them to fly off, so he had to make a choice: he could clip their wings every now and again, or he could pinion them, cut off the last part of the wing, here." She laid her fingers across her wrist. "If he clipped them, he'd have to keep doing it, or they'd fly one day, but if he pinioned them, they'd never fly again. So he picked what was easy. He cut off their wings at the wrist."

"He took away their God-given gift of flying?"

She had watched Jonah leap from sheds and wagons, willing himself airborne since he was a child. She knew he longed to fly, to rise in circles, feel wind rushing past as he dove from a tree.

"He wasn't a God-fearing man. The geese pretty much grew up swimming on the pond and waddling on the banks. Then, one Sunday when the family was away, I heard a ruckus. A goose landed on the pond. The others beat the water and called in a way I'd never heard before. I stopped behind a bush to watch, though I don't think they'd have noticed me, they were so worked up. I counted the geese, wondering if there were more visitors, but there were only twelve geese. While I was looking on the shore for a thirteenth goose, the one causing the commotion ran across the water and took flight again, circling the pond and calling to the other geese. They ran across the water, like him, and beat their wings frantically, but they were water bound, couldn't lift their bodies into the air. It tore at my heart.

"The one who could fly landed again, and the other geese surrounded him. I realized then that there was no visiting goose; the goose that could fly was one of the original flock. Somehow his wing had healed from the cutting, or maybe it wasn't cut off all the way. I don't know. But he could have flown away and didn't. He tried to join the flock again, but they attacked him. I think he woke up some deep memory in them—some ancient longing they carried from the centuries of geese they come from. They drove him from the water and wouldn't let him back at first, but after a bit they settled down, and maybe they aren't the brightest of birds, 'cause they seemed to forget they were upset with him."

"What happened to him?"

"He stayed with the others, even though he could have left. I counted the geese every day, and there were always twelve. They were almost ready for market, and a few weeks later they carted them off. The goose who could fly must have gotten away before they rounded them up, because the next day, I heard honking and ran down to the pond to see one goose circling and calling, and then he flew off."

"It must have been him. It's not natural for a goose to be by itself."

"No, Jonah, it's not."

"Mama, I understand what you're saying. I do. But I have to try."

The fog seemed silver now, summer far away. Jonah tugged at his arm to free it from the wire, but the barbs dug deeper. He tried to stand.

Thursday

October 26, 1944

40

The Edge of Darkness

Theo Wright pedaled through the fog, his knees poking outward on either side of his sister's bike. Zoe couldn't ride a boy's bike, so when her tire had worn past more patching, he had given her one of his. He had raised the seat as high as it would go, but she still teased him that he resembled an ungainly grasshopper.

His father's leather briefcase thumped against his back when he stood up to pump. It held his sketchbook and pencils he needed for his job. And other things. Theo liked getting up early to go to work. He cherished the quiet on the edge of darkness, whether the darkness washed from charcoal to a shell-like pink morning or deepened from periwinkle into an indigo night.

That morning he planned to sketch at the ferry building, to capture the intensity of the workers as they teemed off the boat. Tomorrow he'd focus on the buses that took the workers to the shipyards.

Dried grasses showed a hint of muddy gold as the sky lightened. He slowed, unwilling to overtake the barely visible figure at the top of the hill. He stopped and balanced, one foot on the ground, but the figure didn't move on. He coasted a few feet closer, then sped up when he realized it was only the back of a discarded scarecrow hanging on the barbed-wire fence. It was oddly beautiful. Even a bundle of clothes was sublime in the right light. He memorized the vision as he approached it. It would make a beautiful charcoal sketch.

He glanced back and lost his balance. It wasn't a scarecrow. He dropped the bike and took a tentative step toward the fence. Something seemed familiar, something that caught the thin morning light. A row of mother-of-pearl buttons glowed against the torn shirt. It was Ralph's friend Jonah from the Double R.

What should he do? Did he have to tell? Talk to strangers? He stumbled around in a circle, rubbing his forehead. Then the wind riffled the grass, and something shiny caught the light. Theo entered that special space where all that existed was the possibility of art. He skirted a boot that lay on its side and picked up the object that had caught his eye. When he turned back, it was as if he were seeing the body for the first time.

What should he do? He could go home. He should have stayed home. He wanted to go home to Zoe.

Zoe. What would she tell him to do? He sighed and got on the bike and headed to the ferry building.

After he called Ralph, Theo made himself go back to the hill to wait for him and the police, but when he got to the curve in the hill, the fence was bare except for pieces of Jonah's shirt. He stopped, relieved that Jonah was gone, but then he saw him lying on the ground. He was so busy figuring out what to do, that he didn't notice Wade Slater until it was too late. He caught Theo's bike before he could get away and grabbed his jacket. Theo almost fell when Wade suddenly let go and looked all around.

"Did you hear that whistling, kid? Did you hear it?"

Theo shook his head no.

Ralph slammed his car door and ran to Theo. He shielded him from Slater's sight while he explained that Theo had called him and asked him to call the police.

Wade pushed Ralph aside. "Hey, kid. Hey!"

Theo didn't respond. Wade grabbed him by the shoulder and whipped him around. Theo flinched and pulled back.

"Did you see anyone? Pick up anything from the ground? Give me that briefcase."

Theo shook his head and clutched the briefcase, his eyes cast down.

"Look at me, damn it!"

"Theo, are you all right?" I forgot about my new limitations and tried to jog up the hill. That didn't work. I limped after Harley who raced to my nephew and leaned against him while Luca climbed to the body by the fence.

A man turned around. He looked relieved to see me.

"Are you Ralph?"

He nodded. The right side of his face was scarred, the chestnut skin puckered around the eye.

"Thank you for calling us. Theo thought I was still on Angel Island. I know he didn't want to call the station, but why did he call you?"

"He thought he recognized him"—Ralph nodded toward the fence—"and thought I knew him, and thought . . . I really don't know why." He faltered. "Theo comes to my restaurant. He's comfortable with me."

"How did he know who it was?"

"He recognized the buttons on his shirt."

"Buttons." I looked at the sky, as if the key to understanding Theo might be there.

Then a car door slammed, and Doc Pritchard climbed up the hill to Luca.

I asked Theo what he was doing out there at that hour.

He shrugged.

Ralph spoke for him. "He was on his way to Ferry Point to sketch the workers coming from the city."

"Are you sure it's your friend, Ralph?"

"I'm afraid so." He cleared his throat and said it again, almost to himself.

"What's his name?"

"Jonah. Jonah North."

I felt it in my gut. Another good man gone, and then Doc Pritchard shouted for help to get Jonah to the hospital. He wasn't gone. Not yet.

"Does he have family we should notify?"

"I don't think so." Ralph hesitated.

Wade got in his face. "What do you mean, you don't think so?"

"Nothing. I didn't know him that well."

I was sure Ralph had been about to tell us something before Wade bullied him—his only interviewing skill. What was he doing there? Ralph's call had come into the station while I was calling Newark. Wade hadn't been there, so how did he know about Jonah?

"Ralph, would you mind taking Theo and his bike home? I can't leave yet, and I think he's a little shaken." I wanted to get Theo out of there.

"I'll take him." Wade reached to snatch the briefcase, but jerked back when Harley moved between them, ears forward and eyes fixed on him.

"Hey, Wright, call off the dog. I'll throw the briefcase and bike in my car. I'm going back to town anyway."

Theo huddled over the briefcase and shook his head.

"He's too upset to talk to you now. Besides, he's already told you he didn't see anything." I wasn't letting Wade have another shot at him. "What are you doing here, anyway?"

"What are *you* doing here? You're not on the force anymore, and even if you were, *I* investigate homicides, remember?"

"Well so far this isn't a homicide. It's a beating, so it's mine." I hadn't seen Wade since the day he had tried to kill Roan's dog. I was unsettled by how badly I wanted to hurt him.

Wade shoved his hands into his pockets. "Easy to see what happened. We all knew one a them 'teach the new guy a lesson' beatings was gonna end up this way sooner or later. Probably some Okie didn't know his place, or maybe he was messing with somebody's girl."

"Let's wait until we talk to him before jumping to conclusions. We need some men to comb this area before the winds pick up, see what they can find."

"I'm just saying. Mix those Southern rednecks and those up-pity Nee-groes, and all it takes is some skirt in an overall to set them all off." He chuckled at his own joke. "A skirt in an overall."

I ignored him and turned to Luca.

"Let's pick up Nate and talk to Ralph Robinson before we go back to the island."

"Hey, Wright, it's not your case. Butt out. You're not a detective anymore. Probably never will be again. What a shame." The good-old-boy humor had disappeared. He smiled.

41

We Have a Problem

Wade watched the briefcase slipping away. He might have gotten it for Sandy if it hadn't been for the whistling. He hated it—that same strange melody coming out of the fog, from an alley, by his house. Eerie, like a message written in the air.

Sandy had been frantic when he shook him awake at The Stop that morning.

"Wake up. We have a problem." He told him about Jonah. How Regis Simmons had been on his crew and that Jonah had been snooping around property records and that they hadn't found anything in Jonah's car or rooming house. Sandy knew Jonah had something. Maybe he had left his notes in a locker at the bus station. There had to be a key or something. Now he wanted Wade to see if there was a key on the ground. Or in his shoe.

Sandy had been seeing too many movies.

"I'm done helping you. Uncle or no uncle. You're going to get us all thrown in jail. If I hadn't gotten to the Simmons hanging before Doc Pritchard did, you'd be looking at a murder inquiry. That Pritchard notices everything."

He was tired of cleaning up their messes. First Sandy hired a fool to run Peter Wright off the road, and the idiot had taken the immunity papers Regis Simmons had signed and left the briefcase in the car instead of taking it to Sandy. He had thought the wife was dead, too. Luckily for her, she couldn't remember anything about the weekend.

Sandy and his men had strung Simmons up in his garage figuring he'd talk to save his life. Instead he'd taunted them, told them he'd given Peter photographs of them and the man who'd paid Sandy to set the fires, and now someone else had evidence, too. Then he'd jumped off the chair and broken his neck before they could get more out of him. Sandy told everyone no one had paid him anything, but Wade knew he was lying.

"This is different. This guy was alive when we left him. Get over there. Be the big hero and rescue him."

"Sandy, I'm done. Send someone else."

"Anyone else would seem suspicious. But you're a cop. No one would question you."

"No."

Sandy leaned back. "You'll help me, or I'll make sure everyone knows how close you and your mother were." His eyes narrowed, and one corner of his mouth turned up. "Get my drift?"

Wade couldn't think. He was fifteen years old again.

"Oh yeah, she told me. She and I were pretty 'close,' too. Her way of taking care of family. Can't say I blame you for running away from that sick bitch."

Sandy patted him on the cheek and left.

He cringed, hating the memories, his mother. He had known it was wrong, that people wouldn't understand, but he had felt special, as if he mattered to her. They were a family. Until she disappeared for a few days and came home bragging that she'd been with a man, a real man. Not a crybaby mama's boy.

He'd grabbed some clothes and slept in the back of The Stop where Pappy the bartender made up a bed for him. He didn't need to be nice to girls at school after that. He got what he wanted from the women who hung out at the bar. Didn't even have to pay them. Hell, some of them paid *him*.

He had thought all women were the same, and then he'd met Phyllis and everything had changed. He'd still have her if she hadn't met Wright. He'd wanted to smash Wright's face then, the way he had wanted to this morning.

People acted like it was the end of the world because some kids got killed. And now *this* kid was getting in the way. If the key wasn't on Jonah, and it wasn't on the ground, the kid had to have picked it up. Probably put it in his briefcase. If there even was a key. Either way, Sandy wanted the briefcase, and if Wade got it for him, he'd give him enough money to make a new life in Colorado, with or without Cora.

He knew someone had paid Sandy to set those fires, and that's why he was frantic about the briefcase. One way or another, he was getting his hands on it. If Sandy didn't pay him what he'd promised, Wade would have the goods on him and the guy behind the fires.

42

Whiter Than You

When we left the police station, Nate jumped in the front seat. Apparently, in his eyes, an American corporal out-ranked an Italian captain and a K9 hero. Luca looked amused and seemed happy to sit in the back and gaze out the window. We sped up Cutting Boulevard to Eighth Street, and Harley leaned into him, eyes closed, almost in a trance, while Luca scratched behind those impressive ears.

There were people everywhere. They had pitched tents in empty lots and built shacks out of cardboard. Long johns and a flowered dress fluttered on a line strung between two cars. Every now and then, a pot of flowers brightened the front of a garage.

"Oliver, there are two boys in pajamas in the doorway of a chicken coop. Madonna. I hope they cleaned it before they allowed them to sleep there. There are children everywhere. Don't the children go to school?"

"Yeah, but the schools are operating in two shifts, so during school hours, half the kids are running wild, and the rest of the time, they all are. Some of the kids have never been to school, and even with double shifts, each class has twice as many pupils as it had before the war. My nephew and niece go to a Catholic school, and even that's overcrowded."

"You're Catholic?"

"No." I shifted into third. "Their mother is. Anyway, all these kids running around with no supervision make it hard to keep some kind of order. Must have been like this during the California gold rush, but without the children."

We pulled up in front of Ralph's Restaurant. It filled a triangle, its front door at the narrow end. It was rounded on the corners and faced with white tile. A sign curved from the roof almost to the top of the door; pink, yellow, and blue neon stripes bordered the vertical letters that spelled out *RALPH'S RESTAURANT*.

The room widened toward the back, taking the shape of the block it spearheaded. Metal napkin holders dotted the linoleum-topped counter on the right side of the room.

Nate walked along the cork-faced walls, looking at the sketches thumb-tacked at precise intervals. All the same size paper. All signed with a blocky *TW*.

"These sketches are alive; you can feel who these people are, not just what they look like." He called us over.

In one drawing, I could almost hear the laughter from the full-faced man whose head was thrown back. In another, a woman ate up a letter with her eyes and her heart.

"Theo comes in the afternoon and sketches the customers. If they admire one, he leaves it by the register for me to give them when they pay their bill. Which reminds me." He went behind the counter and pulled out Theo's briefcase.

"We got Theo's bike out of my car, but he forgot this. I thought he was waving good-bye, but he must have wanted me to stop."

I ran my hand over the worn leather. "I'll take it to him. Thanks, Ralph."

I introduced Nate and Luca. "We're working together on another case, but I wanted to talk to you before we go back to Angel Island. Find out what you know about Jonah."

"Sure. How about some coffee, something to drink?"

"We're good," I hadn't consulted the others and stifled a smile when Luca rolled his eyes.

I opened my notebook. "When did you meet him?"

"He came in near the start of the war. We hit it off, used to talk sometimes when the restaurant was slow. He's a welder at the Kaiser shipyards. Learned how to weld at the ferryboat college. He rode back and forth to the city until he got it. He used to come in with some of the other welders." Ralph got quiet.

"What is it?"

"Well, he seemed educated. Better educated than most of the tradesmen who come in. But, you know, you can't make too much of that. The money is good, and maybe he needed a job that paid well."

"Educated how?"

"Well-spoken. He liked to talk about books. And poetry. He gave me a book of poems by that Englishman who wrote the novel that was banned—*Lady* something." Ralph frowned. "Anyway, that's what we mostly talked about."

"What else did you talk about?"

"He asked a lot of questions. I was never sure what he really wanted to know. Kind of indirect, if you know what I mean."

"He must have given you some idea."

He hesitated, then plunged in. "He seemed to be nosing around about the attacks on women. Asked me if I thought the Negro servicemen were doing them."

"Did you?"

"No, and not because of my color."

"Then why?"

"Look, I don't want any trouble with the police. Right now, I've a mind to trust you because of your nephew, but what I tell you can't get back to the real police. Sorry, the active police. You know what I mean."

"Why not?"

He scrunched his battered eyebrows together and looked at me like I might be a bit slow.

"Seriously, Ralph. I want to know."

"Take a good look at me, Lieutenant. Slater will probably be watching me because I was there this morning. I don't want to be rousted every time I get in my car."

Nate nodded. "It's open season on us, sir. Go down to the jail on Friday nights and see who's in the cells—cops are picking Negro workers up as soon as they cash their checks. If they pay the cops, they can go on their way. If not, they spend the weekend behind bars and get labeled drunk and disorderly."

I tried to keep from showing how angry I was. And embarrassed. "I won't say anything to anyone else. Tell us what you know."

"Some of the older folks say it's someone doing the same thing he did before. The prostitutes that hang out by Tapper's Inn and the Savoy can't talk about anything else. They're scared. Figure one day he's going to go too far and someone's going to die. And I gotta tell you what I told Jonah: the girls say it's not Negro sailors doing it. No matter what the police think."

"Jonah was investigating on his own?"

"Yeah. He wanted to know how he could talk to some of the working girls. I told him, the normal way. But then he asked if I knew anyone who would talk to him, especially someone who hung out by the Pink Kitchen, where the last attack was. I set him up with a woman I know, Auntie Josephine. She knows a couple of the girls."

I smiled.

"What's so funny, Lieutenant?" Nate was on guard again.

"Nothing. I know Auntie Josephine."

Ralph cracked a grin. "Ain't she just something? And that's not all he was interested in." He gestured toward the pay phone hanging on the wall. "He used the phone over there. Said he couldn't make calls at his rooming house."

"And?"

"You can hear people's phone conversations in my office. Something with the heating ducts. Let me show you. You go in my office, and I'll pretend to talk on the phone."

We did as he asked and could hear him clearly.

"Interesting. So, what did you hear Jonah say?"

He erased the blackboard where the daily menu additions were listed and banged down the eraser, causing a chalk-dust explosion.

"You might think this sounds crazy, but those of us who live here don't think it's anyone's fantasy."

"For God's sake, Ralph, will you please tell us!"

"He was talking about the Klan."

"Attacking the women?" I shook my head. "That makes no sense."

"No, not that. Beating the colored workers. And he seemed to have uncovered proof of some connection between the Klan and the hill fire." He seemed relieved to have said that. "I'm trusting you because of Theo. There is no one else on the police force I would tell. Especially that Slater."

"Proof? What kind of proof. The whole town thought the Klan set the fire that killed the Fleming children, but there could have been other reasons Negro shipyard workers were beaten, and besides, Jonah's white."

"Didn't matter what color you were if you were a newcomer." Ralph wrote on the board, his back to the men. "Besides, I don't think so." He turned around and seemed to regret what he had said.

"You don't think so, what?" I knew I sounded a bit testy. I leaned against the counter and extended my left leg.

"Nothing. It doesn't matter."

"You started to say something. We want to find out who did this to him. Cough it up."

"I don't think he's white. I think he's passing. I'm only telling you because it might help you find who did this to him."

Nate chimed in. "Wouldn't be the first person to jump the color barrier that way. And don't look so skeptical, Lieutenant. Hard to believe, but some Negroes are whiter than you." Nate almost managed to hide his smile.

"So how do you know that someone is passing?"

"Can't explain it. Little things. And they're more relaxed with us when there are no white people around."

"But he didn't come out and say it." I was finding it hard to believe the fair-skinned man wasn't white.

"He didn't have to."

"If you could tell, then so could other people. Why wouldn't someone have exposed him?"

Nate and Ralph shared a look. "Anybody making it on the other side, we just leave them be. My cousin passes. Has a dark wife and a mixture of kids. They live in the Negro section of town. He drives his car and parks by the bus line, gets on with the white passengers, and goes to his job."

"He never has friends from work come to his house?" A hard way to live.

"He works white, lives colored. His worlds don't mix. He's lucky he's able to stay with his own people outside of work. Other folks go all white. Must be a lonely kind of life."

"You think Jonah did it for a better job?"

"Not exactly."

"Ralph, this is like pulling teeth."

"I think he's undercover. I think he's a reporter for a colored newspaper."

"Why do you think that?" Nate was intrigued.

"One day he was waiting for a call and asked me if I would take a message. Said he had told the other person not to leave it with anyone but me. It was from the *Pittsburgh Courier*."

"Which is what?"

"A Negro newspaper."

"Never heard of it."

"Pittsburgh, Pennsylvania, not California."

"That doesn't make him colored."

Nate and Ralph shared that look again, like whites didn't know jack about the colored world. Nate took up the explaining.

"It's not likely a white man would be working for a colored paper. Even if he wanted to, they wouldn't want him. But a colored man who could mix with whites could find out a lot that colored reporters couldn't begin to get near and go places they couldn't go."

"Are you saying there may be more to his beating than the normal animosity between the locals and the newcomers—something to do with his investigating, maybe even something to do with his being Negro?" I pulled myself up on a stool.

"My guess is no one white knew Jonah was colored."

"Maybe not. I sure didn't." I shrugged. "But why do you think the Klan has anything to do with the other beatings?"

"Just talk. Some of the old-timers remember when it was happening to Mexican workers. Down in LA, they lynched the ones who wouldn't toe the line, but here they were beaten and hung by their clothes on poles or fences. The Klan let it be known it was them doing it."

"So why aren't they advertising now?"

"They are. People say they're wearing their bed sheets and pointy hats for the beatings and hanging people on the fences like before, like Jonah. But people are afraid to say more. If we know, someone in your department has to know. Someone who's been here awhile."

"They could think it was a coincidence."

"Maybe," Ralph clearly didn't want to get into it with me.

Nate rolled his eyes.

"Was anyone beaten this badly before?"

"No. But some were never the same. Mostly they disappeared with their families. The rest of the Mexicans fell in line. Chinese, too."

I looked at my watch. "We need to get going. Anything else, Ralph?" *As if that weren't enough.* "Oh—do you know where he lives?"

"Mrs. Standish's place. On Nevin."

Ralph watched us walk to the car, then called after us. "Wait up. Maybe you want to see this."

He went back in and came out with a piece of paper.

"Theo gave me the sketch," Ralph said. "I asked him not to do any more of Jonah, but I couldn't quite throw it away."

Theo had drawn a three-quarters profile of a white man looking pleased about something. There was nothing remarkable about his even features and wavy hair, except that in the sketch a dark-skinned man with Jonah's light eyes looked back at him from a mirror.

43

The Three Musketeers

If Jonah had found evidence linking the Klan to the Fleming children's deaths, I might finally be able to find out who had killed my brother. Would that help my father? Peter's death had made him a tremulous old man. He sat in his study, poring over scrapbooks of Peter's triumphs or gazing out the window, no longer joining his friends for cribbage. He mourned Peter's death as if it had happened yesterday.

I handed the keys to Nate.

"Nate, you drive. Let's check Jonah's room to see if he left any notes that might tell us whether Ralph is right about him. Then we'll go to the station, call the *Pittsburgh Courier*, and see if Newark has called us. We'll grab something to eat, talk to Doc Pritchard, and go back to the island. Captain Buonarotti had Kimballs released. We need to talk to him."

"'Grab something to eat.' It sounds so American." Luca smiled.

"Maybe I'll surprise you."

Nate seemed annoyed at the banter. "I think Ralph knows what he's talking about."

"Do you know of this newspaper?"

"I never paid any attention to it until they banned it from our base."

"Banned it?"

"Yes, sir. Banned it and other Negro newspapers. Sometimes we managed to smuggle a copy in, but if we got caught, we paid for it. Same with certain authors—Langston Hughes, for one."

"Sounds like the fascists were running your base," Luca said.

"We should let the paper know about him if he's working for them," Nate suggested. "You know, there's a column called 'A Thorn in Their Side' that often talked about things affecting Negroes in the Richmond defense industry."

"Who wrote it?"

"John A. Thorn." He hesitated, then reached into his shirt pocket. "Here. One of the columns."

I unfolded the cutting. "It's an anagram. Jonah North, John A. Thorn."

Luca leaned forward. "Could you read it out loud?"

I scanned it. "Nate?"

"Sure."

I cleared my throat and tried not to worry about the man who had helped me in the alley and written to me. I read:

Detrimental to Morale

By John A. Thorn

You would think the gates of heaven had opened after the Selective Training and Service Act of 1940 passed. Negro men clamored to enlist in record numbers, wanting to do their part and escape their dead-end lives. They believed they would be treated like everyone else—trained and sent overseas to fight the Nazis.

What they didn't know was that the act also gave the War Department final authority to implement it, and the fix was in. It announced there would be no intermingling of colored and white enlisted personnel. To do so, in its words, would be "detrimental to morale and the preparation for national defense."

The military can convince men to jump from aircraft, dive in submarines, and land on enemy-held beaches, but they want us to believe they are incapable of convincing those same men to sit down to eat with a Negro, share a row in a theater, or crap in the same latrine.

No matter where Negro servicemen go, Jim Crow rules. Even though bases are on federal territory, commanders bow to "local customs" and will not admit colored men into white training courses or schools. What the Negro soldiers want to do is fight, not cook and clean for white soldiers.

At Pearl Harbor, Dorrie Miller, a messman, carried several wounded sailors to safety, then grabbed an antiaircraft gun—one he had not been trained to fire—and downed Japanese aircraft. He was the first Negro to receive the Navy Cross.

Despite segregation and discrimination, our men are willing to sacrifice their lives in this war. You would think the government would want these men—all able-bodied men—overseas fighting. But then, they don't think of us as men, do they?

For the second time in an hour, I felt ashamed. I thought about an investigation into the beating, perhaps death, of a Negro journalist and the kind of furor that would cause. Some sort of racial incident might be unavoidable, but maybe we shouldn't be avoiding anything. Maybe the country needed to face what it was doing to the Negroes. Then I thought about what the country was doing to the Japanese. Not the same thing.

A flag with a blue star hung in Mrs. Standish's window. She had someone in the war.

We waded through a sea of dogs in the front yard. Looked like she hadn't taken Jonah's advice about not attracting all the strays in Richmond. She seemed a bit taken aback at our group. I explained why we were there while the dogs flocked around us. An English mastiff seemed drawn to Nate, who danced away from ropes of saliva hanging from the dog's jowls.

"Howard, come here." Mrs. Standish lifted a cloth from the porch railing and wiped the dog's mouth. "Better come in quick. Won't be long before that sweet face needs wiping off again."

She led us into the kitchen, where pies were cooling on the counter. "I'm not sure if this means anything, but yesterday Jonah asked me if I had seen anyone by his room."

"Why?"

"Someone had left him an anonymous message."

"Had you seen anyone?"

"No, but later I remembered a police car driving away from the back garden."

"Did you see who was in it?"

"No. I'm sorry. That poor boy. He has such lovely manners."

She pulled keys out of her apron pocket with her thumb and index finger. "Here's my master key. You can go up on your own, I hope. I need to get these biscuits in the oven. It's the third door on the left."

I watched Luca close his eyes and inhale the scent of warm apples that filled the kitchen.

"You go first." I gave Luca a little nudge to bring him back to reality.

He and Nate floated up the stairs while I thudded after them one step at a time, climbing with my good leg and swinging the other out and up to meet it. I moved as fast as I could, but when I reached the room, they were inside.

"I think it's been forced." Nate pointed at the latch.

Someone had emptied the contents of the dresser, slashed the mattress, torn the carpet from the floor and the blind from the window, and taken the knobs out of the bedposts.

Nate looked around at the chaos. "This wasn't a robbery."

"No, I think someone was searching for something." I leaned on the wall. "Someone who either didn't care if Jonah found out or thought he wasn't coming back. Maybe the note he asked his landlady about lured him to a meeting with someone who thought he had something that could hurt them."

"Perhaps the same thing we search for, and I do not think they found it."

"Why do you say that, Luca?"

"The destruction. It has the feeling of someone angry, frustrated."

"Same thing with this broken picture?" Nate picked up a framed Currier & Ives print.

Luca waggled a hand. "No, I think they broke *that* to see if something might have been concealed between the print and the backing. So, something thin—paper, perhaps."

"If Jonah was John Thorn, then he must have had notes, articles, things he was writing. Maybe a typewriter. Where is it all? It wouldn't be behind a picture frame." I looked around at the mess. Whoever had done this must not have been worried about someone hearing them.

We searched through the piles, not expecting to find anything.

Nate gave up and sat on the windowsill. "They must have taken his papers but were still looking for something else."

"Perhaps they did not find anything here. Perhaps Jonah suspected something and hid his notes elsewhere before he went out that night. Perhaps the men searched for a key." Luca opened a hand and tilted his head.

"Let's go break the news to Mrs. Standish. She's going to find it difficult to replace all these things. And expensive."

We drove up MacDonald Avenue where men and women of all colors bustled in the street. The stores seemed to be filled with merchandise, even during a war. Luca pointed out a sign in a window that read: NO NEGROES, NO MEXICANS, NO DOGS, and wondered out loud how they felt about Italians. I didn't have the heart to tell him.

"You are fortunate. I know your people are dying overseas, and I understand the tragedy of that, but so far, your country hasn't been invaded or bombed. If Italy had made peace with the Allies as soon as it removed Mussolini, it could have cut short the killing and bombing there." He sighed. "I can't wait to see the end of this war."

The three musketeers, as I now thought of us, walked into the police station. Slater pushed past us. We heard him greeting another policeman.

"Hey, Butler, I have a joke for you. A cripple, a dago, and a jungle bunny walk into a police station . . ."

I gripped Nate's arm. "Ignore him. He'd love to get you for something, and we have work to do."

I sat down, finally, and picked up the phone to call New Jersey again. This time, Sergeant Doran answered.

"Did you get my message about Carlo Fusco?"

"Aye, what's he done now?"

"You *do* know of him."

"He was in a lot of trouble here in '29 or '30."

"I'm afraid he's gotten himself killed."

"Well, now, still making trouble for the police one way or t'other."

"What can you tell me about him?"

"He ran with a bad crowd that brought in booze from Canada, which wouldn't have made them much different from a bunch of the other Eye-ties here, but then they killed an off-duty officer."

"I'm sorry. What happened?" I pantomimed to Luca and Nate to sit down or get some coffee. This was going to take a while.

"It was right around all the fuss about Sacco and Vanzetti. There were demonstrations, bomb threats, all kind of anarchist shite going on. Fusco's friends decided to rob a bank. We were shorthanded; our men were being sent all over the city to try to keep a lid on things. Later we wondered if some of the calls had been diversions to keep us spread thin. Anyway, a poor beat cop was on his way to see the doctor and happened on the robbers leaving the bank. He drew his gun and tried to stop them, and one of them shot him."

"Fusco?"

"No. The bullet didn't kill him outright. He told us it was one of the gang we'd picked up before, but we never got him. We heard Fusco ran back to Italy with a load of cash. Guess he hadn't counted on another war."

I was disappointed. I had hoped for something to shift suspicion from the Negro troops.

Doran went on. "The shooter was a man called Nic Criscilla. We suspected him in a number of beatings. He was tight with Fusco."

"Well, thanks for your help. I'll see what more I can find out about him here."

"Good riddance to the bastard." Doran hung up.

"Looks like a dead end." I recounted the conversation to Luca and Nate.

"Perhaps not." Luca hesitated. "There are two brothers in my unit who are named Criscilla. It is not a common name. There might be a connection there."

"Let's get back to the island."

"Let's eat first, Nate."

He looked at his watch. "Okay if I catch up with you later, Lieutenant?"

"Sure. We'll see you at the hospital in about an hour. Come on, Luca, I have a treat for you."

44

The Home Guard

Luca was enchanted by the elaborate copper-and-brass espresso machine on the counter. He kissed his bunched fingers and greeted Mrs. Forgione with a small bow. I left them conversing in Italian, while I checked out the "American" side of the café. Four soldiers sat at a table downing biscuits and gravy. They were probably billeted at the St. James Hotel up the street. I stood behind three boys hunched toward each other talking in whispers. One of them noticed me and signaled the others. Suddenly, the burgers required all their attention.

In the café, Luca held a small cup to his nose and breathed in the aroma.

"You can drink it. I'll make you another." Mrs. Forgione gestured toward the machine.

"It makes me both happy and sad."

She patted his hand.

Enough commiserating. I was hungry, and we needed to get going, but first I wanted to know about the boys in the other room.

She waved a hand to dismiss my worry. "The boys are building traps for the Japanese. They call themselves the Home Guard and keep watch on the hills and dig bunkers and signal each other with flags. They're too young to fight, thank God, but they want to do their part. They're harmless."

"Let's hope so." I thought about how much trouble adolescent boys could get into, but it wasn't my problem, and I had enough to worry about. I asked her to sit with us for a moment.

She perched on the edge of a chair.

"I have some bad news about one of your customers. Jonah North." I told her he had been badly injured, that he might not make it.

She crossed herself. "He is such a sweet man." She lifted her glasses and dabbed her eyes with her handkerchief. "When someone wrote 'No Shipyard Trash' on the café window after we opened the American side, Jonah helped clean it off. He's the kind of man a mother would be proud of."

She walked to the niche by the cash register and lit a candle in front of Saint Lucy, her patron saint, who smiled serenely while offering her gouged-out eyes on a golden plate.

"How is Jonah?"

I set my cap on a stack of medical books and tried to hike a haunch up on Doc Pritchard's desk. I cursed my leg and settled for leaning. Locking and unlocking the brace that held my leg upright drew attention to something I chose to believe didn't exist.

"He is a very lucky man."

"Lucky?"

"Lucky he isn't dead. If he had hung on the fence much longer, he would have died from asphyxiation."

"Theo said he looked like a scarecrow, but when we got there he was on the ground."

"Maybe Slater took him down."

"Maybe. He didn't mention it, though."

"Removing Jonah from the barbed wire, I think whoever did it would have cuts on his hands. The detective's hands had none."

Luca seemed to notice everything.

"Why would he have died, Doc?"

"When the arms are extended, the muscles we use to breathe are stretched and exhaling is no longer automatic. One must push the air out of the lungs with the diaphragm. Try it—it requires more effort than you might think." Pritchard motioned to us, and we did as he asked.

"You couldn't do that for long."

"No. Also, only a small amount of air can be inhaled. That puts stress on the heart. Eventually, it gives out. In Jonah's case, it would have given out even sooner. His heart's probably the reason he wasn't in the service."

That explained Jonah trying to catch his breath in the alley.

"Whoever attacked him also smashed something round across his shins while he was hanging on the fence, perhaps emulating the Roman soldiers who broke the legs of the two thieves to bring on their deaths."

Luca made the sign of the cross. An odd gesture in the circumstances.

Nate burst through the door. "Sorry to interrupt, but the base commander's worried about more trouble, so they're taking extra guards to the island. The coast guard cutter's waiting for us."

45

Angel Island

It Was an Accident

At one time, Angel Island had been called the Ellis Island of the West because of the Chinese and Japanese immigrants who had languished there while waiting to enter the United States. Later, it had been a peaceful refuge for me and my friends when we boated out to picnic on the sandy beaches. Now it housed Fort McDowell and rang with the sounds of cadence being called. It was the last stop for hundreds of thousands of men waiting to ship out for the Pacific.

The boat nudged the edge of the pier.

"Thanks for the lift. We're going to need a ride back." I balanced against Harley as we stepped onto the dock.

"Sure." The seaman looped a line around a dock cleat. "We'll be in the area. Last night one of the men in the auxiliary coast guard thought he saw a boat in the shadows near the shore. On the Richmond side. We need to check it out, but the station will patch you through."

In the POW barracks, a young man sat hunched over a table, gluing toothpicks along the strut of an airplane wing. He looked frail, not much more than a toothpick himself. His long fingers held the plane delicately. His face, too, was long and thin, and his collar stood out inches from his neck. I could hardly imagine him lifting Fusco to hang him on the post, but there was the brother. Maybe together they could have done it.

He looked up. The plane crashed to the table.

Luca touched the boy's shoulder. "Cesare, if you want me to speak to you in Italian, I will, but Lieutenant Wright would like to ask you some questions and hear what you have to say. *Bene?*"

He nodded.

I motioned to Nate to stand on the other side of the table, while I dropped into a chair.

"First, tell me where you were last night."

"Here. In the *baracca*."

"Did you leave at all?"

"No." He glanced up at Luca.

"What about when the American soldiers were attacking the barracks?"

"We hear noise outside, but no go out."

I looked to Luca for confirmation, but he turned up his palms and shrugged. "I sleep in another area."

"And your brother? Where was he?" I shifted in my chair. The ride over hadn't done my leg any good.

"Here, with me."

"Where is he now?"

"Work. In kitchen."

"What about your father?"

"My father gone long time ago."

I acted as if we already knew Nic Criscilla was Cesare's father. "Nic Criscilla. A thief and a murderer."

"No!"

"No? He's a murderer, and now you and your brother are, too."

"No. Not us. Not him."

"We know you have seen him."

Cesare shook his head.

"You have seen your father the murderer." I nodded at Luca to pick up the questioning.

He pursued it reluctantly, asking first in English, then in Italian. A torrent of Italian spilled out of the boy.

Luca translated: "His father didn't kill the policeman, another man grabbed the gun, and it went off by accident. Fusco heard them talking about their father, but they told him he left here in '42, because he was afraid he might be picked up. They said they did not know where he was now."

"Do you believe him?"

Luca shrugged.

"Have you seen your father?"

"*No, no.* Never."

"*Ti calma.*" Luca put a hand on Cesare's shoulder.

Nate had been pacing while we questioned the boy. Now he banged his fist on the table, making the toothpicks jump. "Who cares about Nic Criscilla and a shooting in New Jersey? What about Fusco? We need to clear the colored soldiers."

"Nate, it's only day two in our investigation. Calm down."

"You think those soldiers are feeling calm while they're waiting to be blamed for something they didn't do—again?"

"Trust me. I know what I'm doing."

"Yes, sir." Nate looked like he had to bite his tongue to keep quiet.

"Let's find out if the Criscillas have been off the island visiting anyone." I looked around for Harley, who had his nose pressed against a crack in the floorboards.

"Harley, let's go."

He snorted and padded after us.

46

Point Richmond

Because It Wasn't There

The deep mahogany leaves of Chinese pistache trees shaded the entry to Harry's house. We walked under an archway of bougainvillea onto a path blurred by rampant herbs, where the scent of thyme and rosemary enveloped us. We smelled ready for the oven by the time we stepped on the porch. I rang the doorbell.

"Oliver, how good to see you. And you, Nate." Harry turned to Luca. "You must be Captain Respighi. I heard you were helping with the investigation and of what you did on the ferry. It's an honor to welcome you to my home."

"Harry." I took off my cap. "We're here as part of the investigation on the island."

He seemed a bit puzzled but invited us in. I didn't believe Harry could have known about Nic Criscilla; he was such a straight arrow.

"We are about to eat. Join us."

Luca looked like he was going to swoon from the smells coming from the kitchen. I smiled in spite of myself.

"Thanks, Harry. We don't have much time."

"You have time for a bite. We can talk while we eat."

Luca needed no persuading, but Nate asked if he could take my car and visit Mrs. Slater. I could hardly say no after Harry said she would be delighted to see him. Luca looked puzzled, and Harry explained that Cora had known Nate all his life, that she was like an aunt to him. I was sure Wade wasn't pleased about that.

We were pulling out chairs at the table when we heard Harry's son, Steve, calling Nate's name. Their raised voices were cut off by the sound of the door slamming. Harry pursed his lips.

I put off asking about his POW visitors by telling him about Jonah's beating. I repeated what Ralph had told us about the Klan.

"The Klan." Harry's nose wrinkled in disgust. "There have been many such beatings. The group was widely accepted in California, in fact, the *Richmond Independent* defended its right to exist, saying it didn't exactly approve of the Klan's invasion of homes and infliction of cruelties, but that it was just like any other secret society and every freeborn American citizen had the right to join."

He stopped talking when Paola and her sister brought in platters and told us what was on them. Harry's 'bite' included manicotti stuffed with ricotta and homemade sausage, lettuce dressed with olive oil and vinegar, and chicken roasted with potatoes and rosemary. Luca ate, happily sampling course after course. I drank coffee and wondered where in the world he was putting it all.

Harry continued, "During the thirties, the Klan began to merge with groups like the Silver Shirts, a fascist-inspired organization, and targeted all Jews and Negroes, all non-Aryans. Once the war began, we saw less activity. Many Klan members are probably overseas. I imagine some of the men who were involved in the Fleming children's deaths are in the armed forces now."

"I've explained that to my father—but he thinks I should still have been able to find them."

Luca looked puzzled at the reference to my father. Harry passed the bread to him and explained about the fire and my brother's death.

Luca put down his knife and fork. "Did you think his death was not an accident?"

"We considered it."

Harry stopped speaking, as if something had occurred to him, and left the table. He came back with a piece of paper.

"I missed it because it wasn't there. I'm sorry, Oliver. I should have realized this sooner."

"What? What did you miss?"

"This is the inventory of Peter's briefcase. There's something missing that should have been on it: a signed copy of the grant of immunity. Peter put the forms in his briefcase in my office, but they weren't there when we found him."

"Maybe they didn't meet."

"Then there should have been two unsigned forms. They aren't on the list of items from Peter's office at home, either. No. Someone had to have taken them from the briefcase." He didn't meet my eyes.

It wouldn't have made any difference if he had realized sooner. "Don't be hard on yourself. Think about it. We already knew."

"Yes, I suppose we did."

I didn't want to talk about Peter's death so I dove into our reason for being there. "Harry, we're here about two POWs who visited you, Cesare and Tomaso Criscilla."

"They're Isabella's stepsons. She asked if she and her husband could meet with them here."

"Why here?"

"They live too far out for the boys to have gotten back to the island by their curfew."

"And your brother-in-law's name?"

"Dom Caputo."

"How are they Isabella's stepsons?"

"They're Dom's boys." Harry seemed to think that should have been obvious.

"They have a different last name."

"He used to be called Criscilla, but when he came here, he said Immigration put down his mother's name instead of his father's." He shrugged a shoulder, as if to indicate Immigration was responsible for many such things.

"Could his first name have been Nic?"

"Nic, Dom—they are both short for Dominic." He shrugged again.

"Do you know where we can find him?"

"First tell me what's going on."

"I'm afraid he's wanted for murder in New Jersey."

47

An Indelible Stain

Nate was so angry at Steve that he slammed the door of the house that had been like a second home to him. He could bear his bitterness toward Steve and his sister, Anna Maria, as long as he didn't think about what they had shared. The memories of them riding their bikes down Tewksbury hill or fishing for perch off the pier only made him miss a life that he could no longer dream about, a life that didn't exist for a Negro. Maybe it never had.

He cranked the wheel into the hairpin turn that put him in front of Cora Slater's house, directly above the Buonarottis'. He probably could have walked, but the hill was a killer. Cora came to the door in her gardening apron.

"Nate! Look at you." She brushed her hands on her apron and hugged him. "Come in, come in. Let me wash my hands. I was making some herb pots to take to the church bazaar."

"I've meant to come by."

"It's fine. I know it's been hard for you."

"Hard? You think you know how hard it's been for me?"

She flinched, and he felt ashamed that he had unleashed his anger on her.

"I'm sorry. I should leave."

"Come." She took his hand and led him into the kitchen and sat him down in his old place, the place where he had done his homework and eaten cookies while his mother did the laundry and visited with Cora when her husband wasn't around. She poured him a glass of milk and set a piece of cake on the table.

"Talk to me, Nate."

Maybe it was the chocolate cake, maybe it was the feeling of being home, Nate wasn't sure why, but once he started talking he couldn't stop. He poured out his anger at not being trained to fight, at being used as a servant. He told her how he and his friends had written letters to the Negro newspapers, to Mrs. Roosevelt, to the NAACP, to their churches. He found himself telling her something he had barely acknowledged to himself: How it felt to realize that in the eyes of the world, Negroes were tarnished by an indelible stain, a stain that marked them as inferior, that penetrated to the soul, to the heart of being, and could never be removed.

He told her that once he understood that, he stopped answering Anna Maria's letters, letters that reminded him of a time when he thought anything was possible. She had written letter after letter—at mail call he had hoped for them, but for some reason, as much as he wanted to, he couldn't write back. Her last letter had said if he didn't answer, she would stop writing.

He showed Cora a photograph he had kept hidden when he was in the South. In it, Anna Maria stood between him and Steve, laughing, her arms linked through theirs, her dark hair hidden by a sun hat. It had been one of those perfect summer days, wind off the bay, the smell of sweet peas all around them. Their last summer day at Keller's beach.

"Anna Maria grabbed my hand when we ran into the water, then dropped it. I felt it too, a shock, like she was electrified. After that, we saw each other in a new way. She kissed me good-bye when Steve and I left for the Army. I'd never felt so happy. And then the South, and I realized we could never be together."

He carefully tore the photo into pieces. "It's over. She means nothing to me."

Cora cupped his face in her hands, tried to tell him life would get better, that he was loved.

He was too defeated to argue.

48

Angel Island

You're a Fugitive Now

Tomaso Criscilla had seen the coast guard cutter land, and had watched Captain Respighi and the others head to the POW barracks. He'd been worried that they might connect Fusco to him and Cesare ever since his body had been found. He crawled under the building to listen. Cesare was sweet but a bit slow. God knew what they would get out of him.

When the dog's nose blocked the crack in the floor, snuffling and sniffing the air under the house, Tomaso froze. Thankfully the men had ignored the dog and left. Once that detective found out he and Cesare had been to Uncle Harry's, they'd find Dom.

That damned Fusco. He had started this, and now they were stuck in it. He should have done what Fusco wanted. He smoothed out the paper with the number of his father's friend.

He wasn't sure why he cared, but he had to warn him. Maybe the girl in the PX would let him use her phone again.

Tomaso hated boats, all kinds of boats, yet here he was, huddled under a stinking tarp, flinching at every smack against the waves. He groaned, realizing that once he had warned his father, he would have to get back in the boat.

It slowed, and he felt his father's friend jump over the side and pull it close to shore.

"Come on. Before someone sees us."

The boat was still a few feet from land. He shook his head. He wasn't getting wet.

"*Maneggia!*" The man pulled the boat closer to shore.

"Tomaso, what's happening?" Dom appeared next to a tall gray plant with flowers like blue torches.

"Carlo Fusco was murdered, and the police were questioning Cesare."

"Carlo Fusco. Haven't heard that troublemaker's name for years. What's Cesare have to do with it?"

"They said Fusco was in a gang with a man called Criscilla, so they suspect us of killing him and they're going to find out we were at Uncle Harry's and they'll know your new name. I came to tell you to leave now before they find you and send you to New Jersey."

"Not without my father's gun."

"Leave it. It killed someone. If you don't go, they'll arrest you."

"I can't. We're not far from Harry's. It's almost dark. I can climb the hill and get the gun without anyone seeing me. Then you and I will go away."

"Me?"

"Yes. You're a fugitive now, too."

"No, I'm not. I'm going back to the island and pretend I don't know what's going on."

"We'll talk when I get back."

He grabbed a net from the boat.

Clumps of blackberry bushes and wild fennel shielded Dom as he scrambled up the hill to Harry's house. He had known the time would come when his past would catch up with him. Without the war, maybe things would have worked out, but at least now he had his boys, and he could go back to Italy and make a life with them when the war was over. It was better than nothing.

He crawled along the bushes and crept into the honey house. The clouds moved, and moonlight glinted off the barrels. He wrestled the ones in front of the *lampante* oil to the side. He had barely gotten the lid off when the honey house went dark.

"Who's there? What are you doing?"

He swung around, the heavy net in his hand, and lashed out at the shape in the doorway, knocking its head against the stone wall. The boy fell to the ground, unconscious. Dom swore. He had to grab the gun and get out of there. He turned back to the barrel, and all hell broke loose outside. He dropped the net, jumped over the body, and fled down the hill.

Wade had seen Wright's car parked in front of his house and had come in through a side door, expecting to catch him with Cora. Instead he found her with that Hermit boy. He hid in the shadowy hallway and watched the tender scene in the kitchen: Hermit swearing he didn't love the other girl, Cora picking up the pieces of the photo. She held them, then dropped them in the wastebasket. When he heard her going upstairs, he slipped into the kitchen and picked the pieces out of the basket, dumped them on the table, and fit them together. Hermit with a white girl. Of course. The Buonarotti girl. And Cora there to comfort him. The older woman and the younger man.

He had suspected there was something between them. No wonder she suffered that Hermit woman around the place all the time. It gave her access to the boy. She was no better than the rest of them. He had seen her with Wright, and now with this one, and who knew how many others there'd been? He stuffed the photo pieces into his pocket so he could throw them in her face. Let her know he was nobody's fool.

He looked out the window into the back garden, biding his time until she came down to give him his supper. Someone was by the honey house. He sneaked out onto the dark porch to see what was happening, tripped over Cora's damned clay pots, and swore when he crashed into the garden tools propped against the railing.

A figure ran from the honey house and headed for the bushes. Wade sprinted through the gate that opened into the Buonarottis' yard. A body lay on the ground. Ah, the young master of the Buonarotti house, apple of his father's eye. Hurt. He quickly scattered the photo scraps around Steve's body. Felt the pulse. Not dead—too bad. His boot drew blood on Steve's cheek. He stomped his chest and enjoyed the sound of a bone cracking. He raised his boot again but lost his balance on the loose gravel.

He was about to kick the boy again when light spilled across the path. He ducked behind the honey house and tried to control his breathing.

49

I'm Taking This One In

When Nate went back to Harry's house, Paola grabbed his arm and took him into the kitchen and scolded him as if he were a child. She told him he was the only one who had changed. That he had hurt his friends who had never cared about the color of his skin and didn't care now. The only thing they cared about was his letting it destroy their friendship. She shooed him out the kitchen door in search of Steve, who had gone through the backyard to Cora's house to try to reason with his angry friend.

Nate climbed the path, wondering if Paola was right. He remembered the times he and Steve had sweated in the sun, picking bushels of pear-shaped tomatoes for Paola and Anna Maria to put up in Mason jars. The house had smelled like tomatoes, and only tomatoes, for days while the women sweated in the kitchen until they had canned enough thick sauce to last until the next harvest. He remembered how Anna Maria had screamed when he and Steve had chased her with bits of the sticky honeycomb they had pulled from the honey extractor.

He glanced toward the honey house. Someone lay in the doorway. Steve. He ran to him, and when he bent over to feel for a pulse, someone grabbed him from behind. He shouted for help and struggled to get free.

"Now I've got you."

The voice sounded familiar. He tried to twist around, but his attacker shoved him into the wall and stunned him, then whacked him across the back of the head with something. It was the last thing he felt.

"What's going on out there?" Harry and Luca ran up the path, with me trailing behind. Paola had been working by the open kitchen door and had called Harry when Nate cried out.

Wade spun around to face the men. "I heard a fight and ran down to see what I could do."

"Oh my God, it's Steve. And Nate." Harry turned to him. "What happened? Who did this?"

"Harry." I gestured toward the kitchen, where Paola stood in the doorway, and he ran back to head her off. Harley trotted to the bushes alongside the garden, then followed a scent back to the honey house where I was helping Nate to his feet.

Wade pointed at Nate. "I caught this one kicking him. Easy to see what happened."

Nate groaned. He raised his hand to the back of his head; it came away bloody. He looked at Wade. "Why did you hit me?"

"Paola's calling an ambulance." Harry had run back up the hill and hovered over the boys. "How bad is it?"

Luca knelt beside Steve, pulled a small flashlight out of his pocket, and tried to examine him. "His pulse is weak."

"I'm taking this one in." Wade pulled Nate away.

"The hell you are. Get your hands off him." I faced him down. "This is an Army matter. Did you touch anything?"

"Of course not."

"You're involved, Wade. You need to leave. Someone will talk to you later." I turned to Nate. "Can you walk?"

"I'm fine. Take care of Steve."

Luca pressed the clean part of his napkin against the cut on Steve's cheek. He flicked the flashlight at the feet surrounding him, glanced up at Wade, then turned back to his patient.

Wade swore and stomped up the path and through his gate. He barked something, and I looked up the hill to see Cora break away from him and run toward us.

"Nate, Nate! What happened?" She stopped when she saw Steve lying on the ground. She shook her head in denial, then looked at Nate in disbelief. "What did you do?"

"How could you think . . ." Nate turned to Harry. "I need to sit down."

Cora reached out for Nate. "I'm sorry. I know you would never hurt Steve. That's not what I thought."

"Of course not, Mrs. Slater." Nate leaned on Harry and walked toward the house.

She looked down at Steve, her brow wrinkled. "But how did . . ."

"You need to leave, Cora; this is no place for you." I pointed back toward her gate.

She walked away hesitantly, then stopped and looked back at Steve. She shook her head at me and opened her mouth to say something. I turned back to Luca.

"Oliver, we need a paper *sachetta* for the photo fragments. And someone to search for footprints here and around the grounds."

Luca had taken charge of the crime scene. I would have teased him, but I didn't have it in me. I headed to the house to see what I could find.

I limped back with a paper bag and kitchen tongs, and Luca gathered the photo scraps. If we could get fingerprints from them, we might find out who tore them up. I hoped it wasn't Nate.

The ambulance attendants lifted Steve onto a stretcher and carried him away.

"That is curious, no?" Luca pointed to the ground. "There are no scraps where the boy lay. It looks as if they were thrown around him when he was already on the ground. If the photo had been torn up during an argument, you would expect them to be under him, also. But maybe not."

Raised voices came from the house. Harry threatened to commandeer the ambulance and drive it himself if they didn't put Nate in with Steve and take them to the same hospital for the same care. I thought the whole hillside must have heard Harry bellow, "Forget it, I'm coming with you. Both these men are soldiers! Keep it up, and you'll be wishing you still had your deferments!"

The ambulance wailed away, and we turned back to the scene.

"What do you think happened, Luca?"

"You know how it seems."

"Yes, as if they had a fight and Nate came out the winner—until Wade showed up." I looked up at the Slaters' house. "Convenient, Wade being here."

"I am not inclined to believe his account of events."

"Tell me why."

"One"—Luca made a fist with the thumb standing up—"there is something cruel about him. I have known men like him. They enjoy causing pain. Usually to someone they have power over." Luca raised his index finger. "To make him a suspect, we have two—his interest this morning in the briefcase of Theo."

"Wait a minute. What does that have to do with Steve?"

"I do not know. Not yet. But I think if we open our eyes, we will see something that is there in front of us."

As if taking his own advice, Luca walked into the honey house. "Oliver, why would there be a fishing net in a house for honey?"

"Good question." I felt the net. "It's still wet. Maybe Steve surprised whoever brought it in here." I looked around the little building. "What's in here that someone would want?"

"And why would you need a fishing net to get it?"

"Because it's in one of these barrels."

"*Guarda*. This lid is pushed aside." He slid the lid off the barrel, then gestured to me as if offering me the honors.

I shook my head. Luca tasted the oil. He wrinkled his nose.

"It is *lampante*. A fishing net might well improve the taste." He removed his jacket, rolled up his shirtsleeve, and dipped the net into the oil. Something clunked. He caught it and eased it up along the side of the barrel.

"*Eccola*." The net contained an oilcloth bundle tied with laces.

I took out a pocketknife and cut through the laces, preserving their knots, then folded back the oilcloth to reveal an unusual gun.

"This gun does not bring back good memories." Luca seemed reluctant to handle it. "It is a Bodero, the revolver most of us were issued in the last war. In Italy."

"And who do we know who is from Italy?"

"In addition to me and a large number of Italian prisoners— who, I must add, no longer have weapons—perhaps the father of Cesare and Tomaso. We must inquire whether he knew this oil was here and would probably never be used."

When we were back in the car with the photo scraps, gun, and fishing net, Luca raised a thumb and two fingers.

"And three—there is the blood on his boot. Brand-new boots, I think."

I was confused for a moment. "Oh, you're still talking about Wade. But he was there, at the scene."

"The blood was on the top, not the bottom. He was standing over Corporal Hermit outside the little building. The blood did not come from him or the ground around Steve. No. When I put the light on it, it was bright red and wet." Luca held up the bag. "It would be interesting, would it not, to see whose fingerprints are on the photo?"

I glanced at the bag. "I'm not convinced that he would do something like this. He cuts corners and can be rough on people, but hurt Steve? And why lie about Nate?"

Luca shrugged. "What if Nate interrupted the beating? Perhaps Wade was afraid Nate had seen something. And is he not a Klan member? You say they hate Negro people."

"I don't know if he's a Klansman, although most of the Slaters are. I think he tried to distance himself from his family, tried to make a life on the right side of the law. I don't like him, or how he handled Theo, but from what I've heard, he was a good detective. He probably would have gotten the chief's job if it hadn't been for his family's reputation."

"Oliver, it is possible that not being promoted because of something he had no control over pushed him to the side of his family."

"You mean he decided that being one of the good guys hadn't gotten him anywhere? Maybe." I had seen what he had tried to do to Roan and Emma.

"A pity we cannot compare his prints to the photo."

"Ah, but we can. The chief had me take all the officers' prints for elimination purposes. Tomorrow we'll see what the photo scraps tell us. But now let's go bring Theo his briefcase. He's probably lost without it." I shifted to ease the pain in my leg. "We can sleep there."

"What about Nate and Steve? Maybe they can tell us something."

"I guess we can swing by the hospital now." It would be a while yet before I could put my aching leg up.

"*Bene.*"

Friday

October 27, 1944

50

Rather an Awkward Man

Theo fell on his briefcase as if he had been parted from it for a year instead of a day and ran outside to his studio, leaving his half-eaten toast on the kitchen table. Luca watched the briefcase reunion, noting the lack of contact between Theo and Oliver. Only the briefcase mattered. He thought of the sketches on the wall in Ralph Robinson's restaurant. The Wrights must know of Theo's condition. Had they tried to help him? Not that help would be easy.

Before the war, he had met an Austrian pediatrician, rather an awkward man, who planned to publish his study of a condition he had named after himself: Asperger's syndrome. Theo exhibited two of the symptoms Dr. Asperger had described—a deep, well-developed talent, and social awkwardness. Granted, Luca had observed Theo only in rather unusual circumstances, but that he had not sought comfort from his uncle after finding Jonah was unusual.

Luca seemed to be studying Theo in a clinical way.

"He's not been himself since his father died, Luca. He's always been extremely shy, but he's become more withdrawn."

"Does he have friends he can talk to?"

"Not really." I poured another cup of coffee, offering more to Luca, who declined. "He mainly talks to Zoe, his sister. And his mother. The briefcase seemed to comfort him. That and Harley."

"What is in it?"

"Everything that means anything to him: paper, pencils, his sketchbooks, all the bits and pieces he picks up along the way to put into his art. He notices every scrap that he can use for art but can completely miss a parade going by. I'll ask him if he would like to show you some of his creations. He's usually willing to do that. Not that it matters if you like them or not. As long as he's satisfied with them, that's enough for him."

"Oliver, it appeared to me that Wade Slater showed too much interest in the briefcase. *What could it have to do with anything?* I thought. Now that you say it is where Theo puts things that interest him, it occurs to me that he wanted to find out if Theo had picked up something from the place Jonah was beaten."

"He wasn't at the station when the call came in from Ralph, but he was at the scene before we were. He must know why Jonah was beaten and what whoever searched his room was looking for. Hell, it might have been Wade himself."

"We make many assumptions, Oliver."

"Let's talk to Theo and take a look in the briefcase." I rubbed my eyes. "I had a hard time falling asleep last night, wondering whether Wade could deliberately kill someone. I still—"

"Hello, I'm Zoe." My niece held out her hand. "You must be Captain Respighi. Can I get you something? I thought I might make waffles. Do you have them in Italy? I got some butter and two eggs from Mrs. Forgione's cousin. That should be enough for all of us, and there's still maple syrup from the tin Uncle Oliver brought us back from New England. Do you know New England? I wonder if it's like old England. Someday I'd like to see it. Well, both, really—old England and New England. And Sherwood Forest. Oh! Uncle Oliver the phone is for you."

I abandoned Luca and answered the phone.

"Do you think they have maple—"

"Zoe, take a breath. I'm sorry, honey, but we can't stay for waffles."

Luca appeared to be genuinely disappointed about the waffles. "Thank you for the offer. Perhaps another time, *bella.*"

"*Bella?* What does that mean?"

"That you are a beautiful and enchanting young woman. *Arriverderla.*"

Zoe was momentarily silenced. I quickly kissed her and told her to keep an eye on her brother.

"Uncle Oliver! Wait! Did you bring Theo's briefcase, or does that Detective Slater have it? Theo's driving me crazy about it."

"Slater?"

"Yes, he came here yesterday." Her face clouded. "He didn't believe Theo didn't have the briefcase. He was pretty scary. I'm glad Mom was here. She told him Mr. Robinson drove off with it after they got the bike out of the car."

Damned Wade. "I'm leaving Harley here with you."

When he heard his name, Harley's eyebrows moved up and down like a seesaw and his eyes tracked back and forth between Zoe and me.

"Sorry, fella. You need to watch Theo and Zoe."

Luca and I waved good-bye and hurried to the car.

"You are disturbed, Oliver. Who was that on the phone?"

"Harmon. Ralph Robinson's restaurant was broken into last night."

"You think it was Slater in search of the briefcase?"

"I don't know. Maybe someone thought Jonah left his notes with Ralph. I think Jonah should have a guard at the hospital. Also, a woman named Zora was attacked last night; she's in a coma."

I told Luca everything I knew about the attacks, including the gap in the thirties and the ones that started after Pearl Harbor. We agreed that someone might have moved away and returned. Or been in prison for a stretch.

"I have read that such attacks are sometimes caused by a stressor."

"A stressor?"

"Perhaps the man is acting out his anger against another woman or women—his mother, his wife, someone who controlled or hurt him. If the stress diminished, he might be under less pressure to act out. If the stress increased, so would the need to act out, but it would be unlikely that he would be quiet for years. That kind of personality would probably be more volatile." Luca waggled a hand. "Perhaps it is a combination of things. If you ever have a suspect, you could find out if he has lived elsewhere and if similar things happened while he was there."

I wondered about Chief Anderson. I would have to ask Mrs. Forgione when he was in Los Angeles. Although it was hard for me to think he might be the attacker. Graft was one thing; violence quite another.

"Harmon also said Dr. Pritchard finished the autopsy on Fusco."

"Why did an Army doctor not do it?"

"They wanted an independent autopsy—no hint of collusion or cover-up allowed. A high-powered attorney from the NAACP

is in town, making waves about the Port Chicago verdicts—
Thurgood Marshall—and the Army is on its best behavior."

"So, what is our plan?"

"First, let's stop by the hospital and see the doctor; maybe
Steve will be able to talk to us this morning. Then we'll take
the gun to the lab."

"They will need .422 caliber bullets to make a test."

"And we still haven't dusted for fingerprints on the photo
scraps."

"We also might want to see Mrs. Forgione this morning."

"I can't think of any reason to see her." I tried to keep a
straight face.

"*Allora*, she is related to the Buonarottis and perhaps can
tell us if the father of Dom was an officer in the Italian army."

"Why do we need to know that?"

"Because officers were given guns with a fixed trigger guard,
like the one we found. The model for enlisted men had a col-
lapsible trigger guard." Luca smiled innocently. "I believe we
will have difficulty obtaining records of the First World War
from the Italian government."

"Yes, and while we're there, you might find time for an
espresso."

"And perhaps a pastry."

51

Hard to Swallow

We found Doc Pritchard in the morgue.

"What's the cause of death, Doc?"

"Drowning. An assisted drowning. He is bruised on his back and arms, as if he were held face down in shallow water. I found sand in his mouth and throat passages and water in his lungs.

"Drowning? Not asphyxia?" Luca asked.

Pritchard nodded, but told us that wasn't the interesting part. He shook the metal pan he held. Something rattled.

"It's a button from a field tunic." I picked it up. "What's the interesting part?"

"I found it in his stomach."

"He ate it?" Luca wrinkled his nose.

"It's metal." Pritchard smiled. "Had to be hard to swallow."

I didn't think it was the time for feeble jokes.

"Then it's from one of the soldiers. Our uniforms have plastic buttons." Luca pointed at his jacket. "You must admire Fusco for giving us a clue. The men said he was shrewd."

"I think a surprise inspection is in order, Luca."

"I also have something to show you on the Buonarotti boy. Follow me."

Pritchard paused at the door to a stairwell, then continued down the hall to an elevator. I felt my face flush. Luca glanced at me and fell in step with the doc, giving me a moment to collect myself.

The elevator had been more spacious than Steve's room which contained four beds.

"All the hospitals are filled to overflowing, even with the ship-yard injuries going to the Kaiser facilities." Pritchard squeezed between the beds.

"Am I going home, sir?" Steve didn't look like he could get out of bed.

"Not quite yet. May I show Lieutenant Wright your bruise?"

"Sure."

He lifted the gown that covered Steve's taped ribs and rolled the boy onto his side.

"The bandage obscures part of the bruise, but observe this pattern." He traced the partial outline of a boot.

Luca and I took turns examining the bruise. Pritchard indicated he'd explain later.

"I'll be back tomorrow morning, and we'll see about discharging you." He told me to ask my questions.

"Did you see who hit you last night?"

"No." Steve paused, as if reliving what had happened. "I was on my way to see Nate at Cora's. I'd hoped she could help smooth things over between us, but I heard someone in the honey house and went to see who it was. Next thing I knew, something came out and hit me in the head. Then I don't remember anything, except when I was coming to, I heard someone near me, and then someone kicked me. I don't remember anything else."

"Did the person who hit you also kick you, or did two different people hurt you?"

"Pretty sure it was two. The first one stepped over me and left. I was about to get up when someone kicked me."

"Did you and Nate have an argument at the honey house?"

"No. We argued at my house before he went to Cora's."

"Could he have been the one who kicked you?"

"I didn't see who did it. But I told Detective Slater I don't believe Nate would have done that." He began to get agitated. "He kept saying I was wrong."

Pritchard motioned for us to leave.

I spoke over my shoulder. "If you remember anything else, don't tell anyone but me. Not even Detective Slater."

In the corridor, I asked Pritchard why he had wanted us to see the bruising.

"It reminds me of the bruising on Jonah North. He had been stomped by a boot with the same tread pattern."

"How is he? Can we talk to him?"

"He's rather weak. Give it another day or two."

"How can you be sure about the boots?"

"The bruise has a defined pattern within the sole area. Quite distinctive. I have photos of the bruises on Jonah. When we compare them with photos of Steve's bruises, I believe we will find them to be almost identical. It suggests a link between the two beatings." He considered what he was about to say. "I think this bruise is a bit larger, but then, I could be mistaken."

Right. Pritchard would think he was mistaken when pigs could fly.

Luca raised his leg and showed us the bottom of his boot. "Nate would be wearing Army boots like mine. The pattern does not resemble the bruise."

Pritchard nodded his head in agreement.

"*Dottore*, have you mentioned this information about the bruise to anyone else?"

"Not directly, but that rather arrogant detective chanced to come in when I was photographing it."

52

Her Days Were So Empty

A thin line of silver shone between the black of the bay and the deep gray of the sky. Cora sat on her back porch, gazing out toward the water, willing the silver line to widen, willing an end to the endless night. When she had returned to the house after seeing Steve on the ground, Wade slammed out the front door. She had pretended to be asleep when he came back, and as soon as he'd begun snoring, she'd gone downstairs, first tossing and turning on the sofa, then finally making coffee and sitting in the dark on the porch.

She kept asking herself the same questions. Were those photo scraps the ones she had thrown in the wastebasket? If they were, what were they doing around Steve? Did Nate come back in and take them, then fight with Steve about them? Could he have hurt Steve? He had been so angry the day before.

Voices floated up from the road. Women on their way to catch their ride to the cannery or the tank plant. They walked past every morning, speaking in soft tones, mindful of their sleeping neighbors. Cora envied them their sense of purpose, even more their friendships. Sometimes she caught bits of sentences: "And then he . . ." or "all white orchids . . ." or "not since March . . ." She wanted to know what he had done, or what the white orchids were for. She wanted to laugh softly with them and complain about their manager, to eat sandwiches from a lunch pail and drink lukewarm coffee.

She had heard them talking about the newspapers and letters they put in the tanks before they were sent overseas. A surprise for the men. She had waited for them one morning while Wade was sleeping and asked if she could do something for the boys. Now she knit socks to put in the tanks. She had enough free time to make them when Wade wasn't around, and she saved a bit here and there from the grocery money to buy her supplies. She knit wishes for good luck and safety into them and imagined one of the boys pulling them onto his blistered feet and feeling good that someone back home cared about him.

Her days were so empty. Her mother had told her again and again that a woman had to have money of her own, but Wade had nagged and cajoled her until she had quit nursing. He thought that maybe if she stopped, she would get pregnant.

She had known it wouldn't make a difference, and it hadn't, but it never seemed like the right time to ask him about going back to work. When nurses were in short supply because of the war, she'd brought it up again and at first it had seemed as if he would say yes, but a few weeks later, he had told her not to bother applying. No one wanted a nurse who had quit and then hadn't cared enough to keep up her training.

Her hand went to her chest, to touch her locket. For a moment, she had forgotten it was gone. Wade must have taken it. How else could it have gotten out of her jewelry box? The locket had something to do with the way he'd changed, but he couldn't have known who had given it to her or why she wore it. She had waited for days for him to explode, to accuse her. The blow-up never came, but he treated her as if she were a stranger, as if he had never loved her. She was too afraid to ask if he had taken the locket, but maybe she should have.

It had been her touchstone; the gift Oliver had given her when he had asked her to wait for him—on their last day together. She had taken it off when she went on her nursing shift because she wasn't ready to talk about it with her friends yet, but she kept it in her pocket, reminding her of him. She had been glad it had been in her pocket that night. The man who had attacked her had stolen her mother's opal ring right off her finger, and he would have taken the locket, too, if he had seen it. Funny, how the locket reminded her only about Oliver loving her, of the good part of the day. Not about what happened later. Not about her ignoring his letters and refusing to see him. Now that she was older, she suspected she might have underestimated him, but he had been young, too. She'd never know.

Maybe she would walk to the café. Edna might be there, and she could find out how Nate and Steve were, but if Wade woke up while she was gone, he'd be angry. Besides, she needed to talk to him. It was time for some answers.

53

A Long Time Ago

"Fusco was drowned." Luca pursed his lips. "Where could he have been drowned? And why?"

I braked for a short man in a cowboy hat that had to be fifty gallons if it was a quart. "It appears there was a fight, maybe near the bay. He was killed on an island, after all."

"But it is unlikely that he would have been down by the water. We are not permitted there."

"I don't think breaking a minor rule would have meant much to Fusco." The clutch slipped, and the car stalled out. I ignored the horns behind us.

"We must determine why he would have been there. To meet someone?"

"I would have thought the island was off-limits to any kind of boat traffic, Luca. The bay's heavily guarded."

"I understand the defenses are against submarines and big ships—against threats from outside the bay. I know the fishermen of my village would be able to evade detection around islands in our waters. Perhaps it is the same here."

I remembered how my friends and I had sailed and rowed in the bay. All the caves and hidden beaches we had found—and we had been kids just fooling around. Imagine what the fishermen must know about the shores and the currents. Something else to check. That and civilian suppliers to the island.

A large man pushed open the door of the lab, grabbed me, and lifted me up.

"Hey, Oliver, it's good to see you. I heard you'd been wounded in the Pacific. Where's Harley?" The man nudged me aside so he could see behind me.

"He was wounded, too, but he's fine now. Saved my life. Him and a cook armed with a skillet. But it's a long story for another day, Rob." I gestured toward Luca. "This is Captain Luca Respighi, of the Italian army. We need your help with a gun we found in a barrel of olive oil."

Rob nodded his head in approval. "Storing it there was smart. Kept it from rusting. Let's have a look."

He walked to a workbench. "Let's see what you have."

I set the oilcloth bundle on the table and unfolded it.

"A Bodero. Designed in the 1870s and used until 1912 by the Italian military, and sometimes the police. It was replaced by the Glissenti, but many soldiers still kept the Bodero. This one was designed for an officer. You see the trigger guard? The enlisted men's guns didn't have one. The trigger folded up into the gun."

"Would this kind of gun leave marks that could tell us if a particular bullet was fired from it? We think it might have been used to kill a police officer in New Jersey."

Rob launched into a well-rehearsed lecture about rifling and lands and grooves. Luca seemed lost in thought.

"Luca!" I interrupted Luca's musings.

"What?"

"I can only imagine what you're daydreaming about, but even here I would bet it has something to do with food."

"Forgive me. I did get distracted there for a moment. I was remembering wild boar hunts and the wonderful food the animal gave us. Wild-boar sausage, *pappardelle* with mushroom and wild-boar sauce . . ." He realized we were not interested and gave a tiny bow with his head. "What were you saying, Signor Cowrie?"

"That if the New Jersey police recovered the bullet, there's a good chance you'll be able to identify it." He rummaged through a box of ammunition.

"I believe it takes .422-diameter bullets," Luca volunteered.

"Have you used one of these guns?"

"In the last war."

Rob broke the gun and checked the barrel.

"Whoever your bad guy is, he cared for this gun."

He loaded it, pulled back the hammer, and fired into a tank of water. The bullets slowed quickly in the liquid and sank.

I asked if he could fire the gun without pulling back the hammer.

"Not very efficient, is it? Although it is safe. It would be almost impossible to fire it accidentally." He used a rod to push out the spent cartridges. "My sympathies to you, Luca, if this is the weapon you were supposed to defend yourself with. Having to poke the cartridges out before you could reload would encourage you to finish things with the first six shots."

It took us a while to get to the café. Luca grumbled about food, saying it was a matter not simply of desiring an espresso but of requiring sustenance. I ignored him and wondered if the Newark police still had the bullet that had killed the police officer. If so, I'd send them the bullets Rob had prepared. It wouldn't help us solve Fusco's murder, but it might help the Newark police convict Nic Criscilla. If we caught him.

"*Buon giorno, signora.* How are you today?"

"*Bene*, Captain." Mrs. Forgione glanced at the door. "Are you on your own?"

"Lieutenant Wright will be here shortly."

"While you're waiting, come into the kitchen."

"Wonderful! I have missed the whole music of cooking." He spoke of the sizzle of oil in a pan, the *thunk* of a knife through onions, the *clunk-clunk-clunk* of a spoon against a pot to cleanse it after stirring, the wet *slap* of fish on a board. His hands rose above his head, made circles in the air. And then the smells: rosemary, garlic, sage, oregano.

Mrs. Forgione sat him down at the table. "Tell me, who do you think is responsible for hurting Steve?"

He tasted a bit of salami. "Oliver and I do not think it was Nate."

"Of course, it wasn't."

"Steve does not remember much. We think he was knocked out when he surprised someone in the honey house, and then someone else kicked him while he was on the ground." He tried a spoonful of *pasta e fagioli*. "*Bellissima!*"

"Who do you think kicked him?"

"Between us, I think it was Wade Slater, but we do not know why he would want to hurt Steve."

"Who knows with some people? Wade enjoys causing pain."

He bit into a breadstick. "What happened to create such animosity between him and Oliver?"

"A girl. A long time ago."

He considered that, then shook his head. "No, it seems like something more recent."

"There's also Cora, Wade's wife. She and Oliver were sweethearts for a while. Again, a long time ago."

"Luca, we need to eat and get going." I beckoned to him from the door to the dining room. "But first, Mrs. Forgione, could you sit with us for a moment while we're eating?"

"Of course. Would you like some *cannelloni* for your lunch? And spinach with garlic? It's ready to eat, and you seem to be in a rush."

Luca, nodded his agreement, and we found a table near the fire.

"What did you find out? Does Newark still have the bullet?"

"Yes. It's in evidence there. Sergeant Doran said they had noted what an odd caliber it was."

"And now?"

"As far as we know, this gun has nothing to do with our case, but we'll hold on to it until we wrap up Fusco's murder, and then we'll send it to New Jersey."

Mrs. Forgione brought our lunches and sat down. "I heard about the torn-up photo of Harry's children and Nate."

"Who told you?" No one was supposed to know about that.

"Cora told Edna."

"How did she know about it?"

"I don't know. Maybe Wade told her."

I momentarily forgot about lunch. If Wade had told us the truth, he couldn't have known who was in the photo. Luca and I hadn't known until we had fit the pieces together. And if he couldn't have told Cora, how did she know? She had only seen the scraps around Steve.

"*Mangia!* It will get cold."

"Mrs. Forgione, was anyone in Dom's family an officer in the first world war?" I unfolded my napkin.

"His father. May he rest in peace."

"The commander on Angel Island left a message that Tomaso's gone missing. My guess is that he left to warn Dom that we knew about Nic Criscilla, and then Dom went to Harry's to get his father's gun, and when poor Steve discovered him, he panicked and knocked the boy out." I looked at Luca. "No matter what happens now, Tomaso will be out of the Service Units."

"What if he helps us? If he is returned to the regular POW camp with the fascists, he will be badly treated."

"I don't know. Let's see how this plays out."

"I feel sorry for those boys, having a father like Dom." Mrs. Forgione thought for a moment. "Let me call some people. We're a small community—someone will know where they are."

"I also found out there were many smudged prints along the edges of the photo scraps. Makes sense. Most people try to avoid marring the subject of the photo, but Harmon did find several partial prints in the center. They could have been made by someone who touched each piece while reassembling the photo. He took Steve's prints at the hospital. They weren't a match, but the boy told Harmon that Anna Maria probably sent the photo to Nate. Harmon will take her prints later."

"Perhaps the prints are those of Cora. How did she know what that photo was? She was not close enough to see last night."

"Interesting. Harmon was able to identify two of the prints. Guess whose?"

"Wade Slater."

"Who didn't come in to the station today. The chief thought he was probably out late, interviewing the prostitutes about the attack on Zora."

Luca drained his cup. "What now?"

"First, I'm calling Harry to ask for a guard for Jonah. Technically he's not part of our case, but I know Cavanaugh can't spare anyone to do it and probably wouldn't if he could. And then we pay a visit to Wade. Interrupt his beauty sleep."

54

Damsel in Distress

When we passed the Richmond Natatorium, Luca asked me what it was.

"It's a swimming pool. Someone drilling for oil or gas found an artesian well instead, gave up his dreams of riches, and donated the land to the city. The birth of the Plunge."

"Can anyone swim there?"

"By *anyone*, do you mean you? You haven't had enough swimming to last you for a while?"

"I used to swim every day at my home. In the sea. Not like your bay. No, it was warm and soft, embracing. Like the arms of a lover."

"Do you have one? A lover, a wife, a girlfriend? Children?"

"No. And you?"

"I have a son. Charley. He's in the service." I explained about Elizabeth.

"I'm sorry."

"You know, Charley told me his mother is always with him."

Luca crooked his lips and dipped his head, as if he agreed. "You think it's true?"

"I know my father is watching out for me. He was the one I asked for help when we were in the desert. I do not know about 'true,' but I know I believe it. And that is sufficient." He was silent for a moment. "Perhaps one day you, too, will believe such a thing is possible."

I thought that was unlikely.

We rode through the tunnel out into the sunlight again, and I turned right at Western Avenue and drove up the hill.

"There was someone once. I met her at university, but we drifted apart when I went on to study medicine. She did not want to wait that long to get married, have a family, and I did not want to give up my dream of becoming a psychiatrist. Since then, life." Luca shrugged his shoulders, as if to say, *you know how it is.*

I noticed Luca watching the Buonarottis' house as we passed it. Probably thinking about food again, although he had also seemed somewhat taken by Isabella who had gone to pieces when we'd told her why we had come for her husband. The old damsel-in-distress attraction—seemed even psychiatrists weren't immune to it.

A tall, thin woman stood on the Slaters' porch ringing the bell. She turned, her hand on her chest, when she heard the car doors slam.

She was relieved when I told her who we were. She was worried because Cora wasn't answering the door.

"Maybe she's gone out."

"No. I'm sure she's home. We spoke earlier, and she asked me to come over and help her with a project for the church. This isn't like her."

I didn't see Wade's car. I tried the door, but it was locked.

Luca called from the side of the house. "Oliver, come!"

I went as quickly as I could and found him teetering on a garbage can, shielding his eyes so he could see through a window. "I see her feet on the floor. I think she has fallen."

I smashed the glass in the kitchen door with the butt of my gun, reached in, and undid the lock. Cora looked as if she had been beaten. I blocked the neighbor at the door and asked her to go call for an ambulance.

"Cora!" I knelt beside her.

"Let me." Luca felt for the pulse in her neck. "She has been beaten. Choked, too, I think." He pulled her dress down to cover her.

"Was she...?"

"It appears so."

Could the rapist have done this? It didn't make sense. He didn't go into people's houses. At least as far as we knew. And how had he gotten in? The kitchen door was locked with a turn bolt, but the front door might have locked automatically when it closed. We would have to check that and the windows. Maybe Cora had let him in.

She groaned. "Wade."

"Cora, who did this? Did you see him?"

"Wade."

"We'll find him for you, but tell us who did this."

"Nate. Stop him."

Cora passed out again. I could barely wait for the ambulance. I wanted to kill Nate. I had trusted him. Liked him. Why would he do this? It didn't make sense.

After the ambulance left with Cora and the neighbor, I sent Luca to Harry's.

"We still need to find Dom and Tomaso. Paola can help you reach Harry. Explain to him what's happened and ask him to call the station and tell Wade that his wife has been hurt. If any word comes through about Dom, Harry can help you. Ask him to get Harmon to go with you. But be careful. Dom has killed once—don't underestimate him. I'm going after Nate.

Mrs. Forgione hung up the phone. Just as she'd thought. Dom couldn't stay hidden in their little community. A friend had seen Tomaso and Dom from his fishing boat. He'd found out they were staying with Maurizio, a fisherman, but soon would be moving inland. She'd tell Nate when he came back from the doctor.

She called Paola. If Oliver was still at the Slater's house, Paola could ask him to call her. A busy signal. Probably Anna Maria talking to her friends. While she waited to try again, she heard a familiar voice and peeked around the door. Maurizio was flirting with the girl at the counter while she made sandwiches for him.

She whispered to Mrs. Hermit.

"He's the one hiding Dom and Tomaso. We need to get help, tell someone he's here." She tried calling Harry's again. Still busy. She wished Nate were there.

The bell over the door rang. Maurizio crossed the street and got into a green coupe. Dom looked out the passenger window.

"Come on, Edna. We have to follow them."

"I can't believe I'm saying this, but why don't we call the police?"

"Because they'll get away!" She grabbed Edna's arm. "Can you drive?"

"Drive what?"

"There. The chicken man's truck. The motor's running and I don't see him."

"I drove the truck on the farm when I was young."

"Then get in, and let's go."

"Lucy, we can't!"

"Dom hurt my nephew and your son was blamed."

Edna needed no more urging. Lucy struggled to pull herself into the truck, and Edna jumped into the driver's seat. She pressed the clutch and ground through the gears until she found first. They hopped through the alley and turned left after the green coupe. It was several cars ahead of them, stopped by the wigwag at the railroad crossing where a long freight train lumbered out to the bay.

Edna had the driving fundamentals down, but no practice. Lucy had to give her credit—she only stalled once. They rolled down the windows and listened to the chickens cackling behind them. Soon they were crawling up MacDonald.

"I think I'm getting the hang of it."

Lucy's feet didn't touch the floor. She bounced in her seat, grabbed at the dash, the door, anything to keep her balance. When they stopped at a light, a man grabbed a crate of chickens and ran. She wagged her hand in the air.

"*Madonna.* Now I owe the chicken man for a crate of chickens."

"And that highway robber didn't give you any coupons for them!"

They laughed, perhaps a bit hysterically, as what they were doing sunk in.

"We stole a truck and we don't know how many chickens."

"We didn't steal them, Edna. We're taking them for a ride."

Traffic began to clear. Soon they were only two cars behind. Lucy caught a glimpse of another man in the back seat of the car. Probably Tomaso.

"Dom knows you, Lucy. Get out of sight."

Slimy produce and God knows what else littered the floor. "I'm not going down there." She snatched a bandanna from the rearview mirror and tied it over her head. She would wash her hair when she got home. More than once. "He knows you, too."

"He won't recognize me." Edna winked at her. "We all look alike."

The coupe climbed into the hills, and Edna struggled to hang back without stalling the truck. The car pulled onto a dirt lot. Lucy turned her back to the window as they passed the men and drove around the bend. The truck stuttered.

"Edna, what are you doing?"

"It's not me. I think the truck is running out of gas."

With that, the truck stopped. Edna tried the ignition; it ground but wouldn't start.

"We need a phone." She jumped out of the truck and gave Lucy a hand down.

Lucy looked into the back. "I think the chickens are cold and want to go to sleep."

They found a tarp in the truck and pulled it over the crates, Lucy hopping up and down to reach her side. She hushed the chickens. "Shh. Go to sleep. You should be happy you went for a ride in the fresh air. You could be in someone's oven."

"What now?"

"We have to call Harry. Tell him where Dom is."

Edna pointed at The Grand Canyon Chateau sitting like a dowager aunt on the hill above them. "I heard they're closed for remodeling."

"Let's hope their phone is still in order." Lucy smoothed down her dress. "You stay and watch in case another car comes. I'll go find the phone."

"I should come with you."

"No. Keep watch. If a car comes, you can get its license number."

She climbed the road to the chateau, now respectable after its rowdy past as a speakeasy. No one was there, and the door was locked. Paint buckets and ladders littered the porch. She hoped she wouldn't have to use one to get to the open window on the second floor. She walked around the building and tried the windows until one slid upward. Luckily, the bottom sill was only a foot above the porch floor. She crossed herself, hiked up her skirt, and climbed in.

55

Desolation Filled Her Soul

Cora lay in the ambulance, her eyes shut against the world. Her throat hurt, the way it had once before, and she began to sink into that deep, quiet place far from pain, far from men who hurt her. She had counted on Wade's iron core to protect her from shadows and dark rooms. She had never imagined he could turn his coldness toward her, but she'd shivered when he said her name.

"Cora."

She had been in the kitchen, her back to him. Water leaped from the glass she held.

"Wade. I made stew. You must be starving."

Her hand shook as she set the food on the table. He shoveled food in his mouth while looking up at her. She turned away to wipe the counter.

"Sit down."

"Just let me finish—"

"Pretend I'm your darkie boyfriend. You sat with him yesterday. Held his hand."

Cora's bone-deep tiredness undid her. She didn't care anymore. Didn't care if he berated her, if he hit her, if he called her names. She was tired of trying to please him—and she was angry. Edna had told her the blow to Nate's head had threatened his eyesight. Even if Wade thought Nate had fought with Steve, hitting him with his gun was unforgivable. She scraped the chair on the floor, then sat and faced him.

He waved his spoon at her. Sauce splattered her dress. "Don't try to deny it. I saw you."

She wondered what he had seen and heard that could have made him so angry.

"You saw me consoling a boy I've known for years."

"He's a man." He stared at her. "As you well know."

"I'm like an aunt to him. He was telling me about the service." *And how it made him realize how limited his future would be.* Cora fussed with the salt and pepper shakers that had belonged to her mother. Feeling the cool glass against her palms, she remembered the desolation that had filled her soul when she had found herself without a future, at least the future she had imagined.

"What about the white girl? Did he tell you about her?"

"They were children together. It was puppy love. He's not interested in her anymore." She could not have him making trouble for Nate over a white girl.

"No, he showed you that when he tore up the photo. He's only interested in you now."

"The photo? How did...? *You* put the photo scraps around Steve. You hurt him and tried to blame Nate."

"And why not? Why shouldn't he get what's coming to him?"

"For God's sake, Wade. He's a boy!"

"Quit saying that!" He leaped up and pulled her off the chair. His fingers dug into her forearm, and she sank to her knees.

Her mouth twisted with loathing. For his bullying, his jealousy. He must have seen it. He slapped her, then grabbed her hair and pulled her head back so he could look into her eyes. Tears flowed down her cheeks.

"Oh, am I hurting you? Well, you deserve to be hurt, the way you hurt me. Lying about Wright, and now about Nate, who deserves even worse. Coming into my house, eating my food, touching my wife." He pushed her away and grabbed his gun. "There'll be no one to rescue him today."

"Wade, stop! Stop!"

The backhanded blow knocked her head against the cupboard. She fell to the floor and grabbed his leg.

"Wade, you can't. Please. Please leave him alone."

He kept moving toward the door, dragging her behind him. Cora begged him to listen, to stop.

She had to stop him.

"I'm his mother, Wade. I'm his mother!" Oh God. What had she done? "Do you think I would make love to my own son, that he would make love to me? Do you think we're sick?"

He froze. Then he turned back to her and grabbed her face, half lifting her off the floor.

"His mother?" He squeezed her face. "He's a nigger. He's that Hermit woman's son, you lying bitch!"

"I gave him to her to raise." She fell to the floor when he pushed her away. "He's why I didn't want to leave Richmond. I wanted to tell you, but I couldn't."

"So you've been lying to me all this time. And Edna, too? Shows how good a liar you are." He stalked back and forth, then turned to her and bellowed, "So, are you lying now, or just been lying as long as I've known you?" He squatted back down, his face inches from hers. "Who's the father? That nothing Edna married?"

"No."

"Then who? Tell me." He grabbed her throat. "He's not your son. You're saying that to protect your lover!"

"I was raped. I got pregnant. The rapist must have been Negro." All she remembered of having the baby was pain and darkness, almost dying in her bed. For a long time, she wished she had. She didn't care that the midwife said she would be barren. *Barren*—a good word for her. Edna and her husband took the baby and raised him as their own. Cora lay in bed for weeks, not caring about anything, too depressed even to miss Oliver.

"So, you want me to believe that you were raped and Nate is your son because the man who raped you was Negro."

Cora was exhausted. "Yes."

Her nose dripped blood onto her dress. She looked up at a cold smile.

"Cora, I don't think you understand."

"What?"

"I *know* you're lying. Maybe you had a colored baby, but it wasn't because you were raped."

"I *was* raped. At nursing school."

"But that's not when you got pregnant."

"My God, Wade. It was. Why won't you believe me?"

"Because the man who raped you wasn't colored."

Cora froze, terrified of something she didn't want to hear. "How . . ."

"Remember this, Cora?" He yanked her off the floor and wrapped his arm around her throat. "I was sorry about what I did to you. But not anymore. This time I want you to know it's me." She groaned. "*Now* do you understand how I know you're lying?"

Cora didn't struggle. Finally, he increased the pressure on her throat and the pain ended.

56

Instinct and Need

Pappy hung a hand-lettered sign in the window of The Stop: *CLOSED DUE TO DEATH OF OWNER*.

As he turned away, he saw Wade hurrying toward the bar. Strange that he should show up today of all days. He unlocked the door.

"Come on in. I was just fiddlin' in here. Thinking about Roy. Be good to have some company."

"Did you hear that?"

"Hear what?" Pappy's brow creased.

"That damned whistling. I hear it all the time."

"I don't hear anything, but my ears aren't that good anymore. Come on in."

A half-full bottle of Jameson sat on the bar. Pappy filled another glass.

"To Roy." Pappy lifted his glass. Wade hesitated, then threw back the shot.

"What'll happen now that Roy's dead?" He nudged his glass over for a refill. "You still be the manager here?"

"Yep. The new owner doesn't want to change anything." No one needed to know who the new owner was. "So, how you doing, Wade? Haven't seen you for a while."

"Been busy. Working on a few things."

He waited, but Wade didn't say more. Years of bartending at The Stop had fine-tuned his ability to read the men who came in to celebrate their joys or drown their sorrows. Wade was quiet. Of course, there was no one else there to stimulate his arrogance, but *thoughtful* was not a word Pappy normally associated with him.

He busied himself wiping bottles, polishing glasses, and sipping whiskey.

Wade cleared his throat. "You knew my mother, didn't you?"

"Sure. She came in here a lot when Wade Senior was away."

He glanced at Wade's reflection in the mirror behind the bar. Sure was taking his time getting to what he wanted to say.

"He hated me. Sometimes I wondered if he was really my father. Maybe I was adopted."

Pappy turned around and smiled. "I saw your mother pregnant. You weren't adopted."

"Then maybe Wade Senior wasn't my father. Was there any talk at the time?"

"Let's not talk trash about your mother."

"So, there's some trash to tell." He seemed gratified. "Could someone else have been my father?"

"Your mom got around. Wade Senior was gone a lot, and when he was here, he wasn't good to her . . . and she liked a good time."

"So maybe he wasn't my father."

"Maybe not."

"Any idea who was?"

He polished the glasses, playing for time. He had wanted to tell him for a long time. Maybe now. But he seemed in a strange mood. Instinct and need battled inside him.

"I take that as a yes."

Pappy leaned on the bar toward him.

"Look, Wade, maybe you're better off not knowing some things."

Wade grabbed him by the collar, hurting him. "Tell me, you black bastard!"

So that was how it felt to be on the receiving end of his rage. "You want to know? She was spending a lot of time with Roy Lane before you were born."

"Roy Lane was white." He smiled.

Pappy hesitated. *Does he suspect? But why? What the hell. Today's not the day for lies.*

"Yep. He was as white as you." Pappy leaned both hands against the bar. "And as black as me."

Wade's smile disappeared. "What are you saying?"

"Roy was my son."

"Your son?" His glass stopped halfway to his mouth.

"And that makes you my grandson."

"Your grandson? That can't be!"

"It is."

"Why didn't you say?"

"Because I figured you would rather be a white orphan than a black bastard."

The weight of telling Wade settled over him like a shroud. Roy had told him he was sure he was the boy's father. Of course, it had been an accident; Roy never would have risked having a baby. Might have been awkward if he'd turned out dark. But now he thought maybe it would have been better if Wade had looked more like him and less like Roy.

"I told him to tell you when you were old enough to under-stand, but he wouldn't do it. Chances are, you never would have found out, and life would have been easier for you—like it was for Roy—if people thought you were white."

"I *am* white!"

Pappy pressed his lips together.

"Did my mother know that Roy was colored?"

"Of course not. Think she'd let a Negro touch her?"

"Who else thinks he was my father? Or that he was colored?"

"Wade Senior probably knew he wasn't your father, but I don't think he cared who was at that point. No one knew Roy was colored. Some might have suspected he was your father. He and your mother were quite an item. She wanted to marry him, but he wasn't the marrying kind."

He wondered what was going on in Wade's mind. "What made you ask? Why now?"

The answer was slow in coming. He tilted his head sideways at Pappy, as if what he was about to say amused him. "My loving wife said I spawned a black bastard of my own."

"You have a child?" Pappy didn't know what to make of his expression.

"He's a black bastard!"

Pappy winced. "Still a child."

"Not to me, old man."

He watched calculation and anger harden Wade's dark eyes.

"This is between us, Pappy. No one ever hears it. Understand?"

"Doesn't it matter to you that I'm your kin? Why do you think I watched out for you when you were young? Why Roy let you sleep here?"

Wade put the whiskey bottle to his lips. Drained it. Slow. Considering. Then he shattered it on the bar and thrust the neck in Pappy's face.

"You are nothing to me. Don't ever forget that."

Pappy flinched at the jagged shards pointed at his eyes. Wade threw the weapon at the mirror and walked away. Pappy called after him. "You might want to know what Roy died of."

He faltered for a second. "What's it to me, old man?" The door banged shut behind him.

He lifted a chair off a table and sat down. What had he done? He had thought with Roy gone, he could tell Wade. Burying Roy today had made him stupid enough to look for kin in that boy. He had thought his grandson might want to know he was loved, that he was connected to someone by blood, but maybe it was too late. He wiped his hand down his face. He'd have to tell him sometime. He needed to know sickle cell was hereditary. But not today.

57

She Looked Like a Bride

My headlights lit up the dried stalks of wild licorice along Garrard Boulevard. When I was a kid, I'd made whistles from their hollow stems—couple of lifetimes ago. I tried to slow my breathing, to calm down. Did I believe Nate could have hurt Cora? To get back at Wade? Maybe Nate had been in love with Cora and she had rejected him. Too many questions. None of it made any sense.

I slid to a stop in Carlton's parking lot. The neon treble clef sputtered and flickered, repeating itself against the black window. The first time I'd walked into the club, I'd felt as out of place as a cotton ball in a coalscuttle, but over time I'd begun to blend in. Sort of. Nate hung out there, often lingering at the bar long after most of the other patrons had caught the last bus home. It was worth a look.

I wended my way to the bar through a cloud of smoke and noise. Louis tipped a spouted whiskey bottle over tall glasses, and the colors swirled, dark ribbons in lighter pools. I asked if he'd seen Nate, but he said no and the few people he asked said the same.

"It's a little early for him. For you, too, come to that."

"If you see him, will you call the station? Something came up in our investigation."

"Sure, Lieutenant. I'll let you know."

I wondered about that. Louis had busied himself polishing a clean glass when he answered. I'd felt awfully white.

After Wade left The Stop, he headed home, ready to discover his poor dead wife, only to see an ambulance pulling away from his house. He parked farther up the hill so he could watch what was happening. Wright said something to that dago prisoner, then got in his car and tore away. He waited until the POW walked behind the house, then followed Wright. He hung back, headlamps off.

How had they found her so fast? He'd been gone less than an hour. He'd made sure she had no friends, so he knew no one would have just stopped by. Had she told Wright what had happened? The ambulance had used its siren, so she must still be alive.

He slowed down when Wright stopped at Carlton's. He sure as hell wouldn't think Wade would step foot in that jigaboo joint. Maybe he was looking for the Hermit kid. He sat in his car and waited to see who would come out of the club. It reminded him of waiting for Cora twenty years ago.

He had hidden in the shadows cast by the bay trees and watched her walk across the courtyard to the student nurses' quarters. She looked like a bride, carrying the wildflower bouquet she and Wright had picked that day. Wade had run across them earlier, not far from Keller's beach, and had watched Wright court her, turn on the Wright charm. Her hair caught on a branch, and when she loosened it to roll it up again, Wright stopped her, gathered the golden strands, and buried his face in them. She closed her eyes and tilted back her head. He kissed her throat, then her mouth. Wade followed them to the nursing school and watched Cora hurry to the hospital for her shift. He waited outside, catching glimpses of her through the windows. He was in no hurry.

It was dark when she finally came out, waving good-bye to a few girls who headed in another direction. She took off her nurse's cap, and that spun-gold hair tumbled to her shoulders. He thought about burying himself in her hair. He felt the heat in his face and the shiver through his body. The campus was still, still and dark.

When she opened the door to her room, he slammed into her from behind, his hand on her mouth, his forearm against her throat. He kicked the door shut and shoved her across the bed. She struggled and twisted, and he increased the pressure on her throat until she went limp in his arms.

He thought it would be simple: ruin her for Wright and be done with it. Instead, he lost himself with her, didn't want to leave. Someone laughed outside her door, and he realized he had to get out of there. He slid her window up and tumbled out onto the grass, his fly unbuttoned. He still wanted her. Had promised her he'd be back.

He could almost feel it again: the excitement, the power Cora had unleashed in him. He had tried to find it again, that first exhilarating thrill. It hadn't felt the same with the throwaway women, but he knew there'd be little police time wasted on them. He kept looking for a special one. And then Cora appeared like a gift when he was wounded, and she had been his—until Wright came back.

I limped away from the club. Where else might Nate be? Maybe someone at the station had heard something. I walked along the embankment to ease the stiffness and pain in my leg before I drove back. The band played *'Round Midnight*, and the music got louder, then softer, as the door opened and closed. I wondered how Cora was. Maybe I should've gone with her instead of running off half-cocked, but she had asked for Wade. Her husband. Not my place to go. But I could find the bastard who had hurt her.

I heard a sound behind me and tried to swivel, but my leg didn't know how to do that anymore. The revolver missed my head and hit my shoulder as I fell. Wade Slater loomed, trying to do to me what he had done to Nate. A lucky swing of my cane caught him on the wrist and knocked the gun from his hand. When he reached for it, I jabbed at his eye. He grabbed the cane, and when he tried to wrest it from my hand, I kicked him in the stomach. he fell, and we grappled, neither getting the purchase needed to gain an advantage. Then we rolled off the embankment onto the rocks and sand below.

58

Keep the Women Safe

Luca waited at the Buonarotti's for news of Oliver or Cora. Harry had just walked through the door when the phone rang. He nodded at Luca to answer. "Buonarotti residence."

"We found Dom." Harry's aunt sounded triumphant. "Is Oliver there?"

"No." What to tell her? "He is searching for Corporal Hermit. Cora Slater was attacked today. We think the corporal did it."

"How could you think that? Nate would never hurt her. Besides, he was at the café all day. He should have been in bed, but he came down to the café to patch a wall."

"Why did Oliver and I not see him when we were there."

"Oliver had told Nate to stay in the hospital, so when he heard you, he thought it would be smart to stay out of sight."

"He was there all day?"

"He left at four thirty to go see the doctor, and then he was going back to the café to finish up. He's probably there now."

Luca agreed with Mrs. Forgione's view of Nate. The young man was angry, but Luca sensed he had a gentle heart. He thought back to Cora's words, something for which his training suited him. "I am an idiot! We asked her who had hurt her, and she answered 'Wade'. We thought she was asking for him. We did not realize she was answering our question. I must find Oliver."

"First you have to come here before Dom escapes. We can't stop him by ourselves."

"Stop him? Where are you?"

"At the Grand Canyon Chateau. Mrs. Hermit and I are watching him."

"*Aspetta*. Wait. Wait."

Harry clenched his jaw when Luca told him what his aunt was doing. He spoke in a calm, measured voice, but Luca felt the receiver shake by his ear as he listened in.

"Aunt Lucy, you need to get away from there. We think Dom has killed once. He's not going to hesitate to hurt you if you get in his way."

"Harry, we can't leave."

"Yes, you can."

"No, we can't. The truck won't start. We think it ran out of gas."

"What truck?"

"The chicken man's truck."

"Is he there, too?"

"No." Silence. "We borrowed it."

"Oh my God, Aunt Lucy. We'll sort that out later. Right now, you need to hide. We'll be there as soon as we can. If Dom leaves, don't try to stop him."

"We'll see."

Luca grabbed Nate from the cafe and ran to the police station where Harry stood only inches from Harmon. He gripped Harmon's upper arms and stared into his eyes.

"The most important thing is to keep the women safe. If you have to put the women in danger to capture Dom, let Dom go. You only succeed if the women are unharmed. Do you understand?"

"Yes, sir. Save the women." Harmon pulled his gun and spun the cylinder.

Harry raised his eyes to the ceiling, then turned to Luca. "I know *you* understand. Make sure to keep them safe. I'm going to the hospital. Good luck."

While the police car crawled up MacDonald Avenue, Luca told Nate what he and Oliver had found at the Slaters. The boy seemed torn between saving his mother and going to Cora. A rainbow of lights glowed through the fog that swirled among the servicemen and defense workers who crowded the street. Shoe-shine boys called out at the entrances to dark alleys, where a customer could slip in unnoticed if he wanted to pay a little more for a special polishing.

Harmon cut over to Nevin to make some time and get away from a truck blaring about women wrestlers at the carnival in South Richmond. The sounds faded as the car traveled the side streets, winding its way through quieter neighborhoods where the distance between houses lengthened and scarecrows waved empty arms over victory gardens. Soon the car ascended from the fog and raced to the Grand Canyon Chateau, somewhere at the back of beyond.

"Pull over by the chicken truck." Luca pointed.

Edna and Lucy popped out from behind some bushes. The men shook their heads and shooed them back under cover.

"They're in that little building. We think there were only three men in the car. We haven't seen anyone else go in." Mrs. Forgione whispered rather theatrically.

Luca thought she was enjoying this far too much. He hated to encourage her. "Mrs. Forgione, Mrs. Hermit, you both have been splendid. *Brava!* Now you have to stay out of the way. If anything happened to either of you, Harry would never forgive us." He guided them into the shadows.

Grasses rustled as the men crept behind an old, abandoned building. Harmon put an ear to the door of the shack, then reluctantly agreed that it made more sense for Luca to eavesdrop, since he spoke Italian—a suggestion Luca had made earlier. He listened, then waved the other men to the side.

"They wait for a car to take Dom and Tomaso to Reno. Tomaso does not want to go, but Dom says he has no choice. There are only three voices. What do you want to do?"

"We should probably take them before their friends show up. Especially if you think the boy doesn't want to be part of it." Harmon seemed confident.

"What if they're armed?" Nate touched his holster.

"You have a gun; I have a gun. Let's go in, weapons drawn, and maybe we'll be able to avoid any shooting."

Harmon's logic escaped Luca. Shooting seemed much more likely if weapons were brandished.

"On three, I'll hit the door, and you two follow."

"Try it first." Luca shrugged, as if to say he could be wrong. "It is for the garden. Perhaps it does not have a lock inside."

"Right." Harmon pressed the latch and burst into the building, followed by Nate and Luca. He shouted, "Police!" and leveled his weapon at the men. The two older ones sat at a table, cards fanned out in front of them. A hand slipped below the enamel top.

"Hands where I can see them." Harmon waved his gun.

Tomaso sprang from a cot, yelling, "Dom, no!" and knocked Dom's chair over. Dom's shot went right though the eye of Betty Grable, who had been flirting with them over her shoulder, and left her dangling from a thumbtack.

Nate grabbed the gun and yanked Dom to his feet. They cuffed the older men and asked Tomaso if he would cooperate. He had fallen all over himself and his father in his desire to help, so they believed him when he said yes. He had knocked the pistol from Dom's hand as he aimed at Luca, the only one without a gun.

59

The Man of Her Dreams

I came to slumped against a rough surface that stank of petroleum and iodine. When I raised my head, my face scraped against a thousand sharp edges. It felt like a grater, a grater with razor-thin ridges that sliced my hands when I grasped the piling I straddled. Handcuffs dug into my wrists.

A match flared.

"Feel like a last smoke, Wright? Can't offer you a last meal or a blindfold."

My stomach clenched at the gloating tone in his voice. He was going to kill me. Maybe. Or maybe I could talk some sense into him. I shivered in the cold water.

"Okay. You've proved your point. You're a better man than I am. Now take off the cuffs."

He laughed—one angry explosive breath. "I didn't need to handcuff you to a piling to prove I'm a better man."

"Take these off."

Wade stood at the water's edge. My lap was wet now, the water like ice. I tried to pull myself up and yelled at him to let me go.

"Yell all you want. No one's going to hear you over the music and the water. You're under a pier!"

"For God's sake, Wade. Cora's been hurt. You should be with her."

"Cora. Is she all you can think about? Even now, when you're about to drown? I should shoot you, but I'll enjoy knowing you're sitting here in the cold with the water rising around you, struggling to free yourself, thinking about how if you hadn't taken the only person I wanted, then thrown her away, you might not be drowning in the darkness. Alone."

"What are you talking about?"

"I'm talking about Phyllis. Remember Phyllis? Oh, probably not. She didn't mean anything to you, did she?"

"She was lovely. What happened to her was a tragedy."

"*What happened to her?* Like you had nothing to do with it." He stepped toward me and raised the gun.

"I *didn't* have anything to do with it."

"You threw her away like so much trash when you met Cora."

"Phyllis knew there was nothing serious between us." *Jesus, we're arguing like teenagers.*

"It was serious for her. You're the reason she's dead. It wasn't enough that I loved her." He sounded hurt, regretful. "She didn't see me, didn't look at me the way she looked at you, the man of her dreams. I wasn't good enough, even after you threw her away."

"Wade—"

"Shut up!" He kicked me in the knee.

Pain shot up my leg. I tried not to throw up, to fight through the nausea and lightheadedness.

"Only fair for me to take something from you."

Is this how I'd find out who killed Peter? Fat lot of good it would do me, and my father would never know.

"You killed Peter?"

"No."

"What are you talking about?"

"Cora."

"Cora? You didn't take her from me. That was over long before you met her."

"Really? Then why did she keep your locket? The Wright family heirloom. You should ask her sometime why she left Richmond. Oh, right—you won't be able to, because the crabs will have your tongue. Now I have to say good-bye and get that damned briefcase from your nephew. Hope I run into your niece. I think she fancies me."

I struggled against the piling. "I'll kill you."

"I don't think so. It's over for you, Wright."

He raised the gun.

60

The True Patriots

Harmon siphoned gas into the chicken truck and got it started. Figuring out how to get all the vehicles, the women, and the prisoners back to the Point was like the problem of the fox, the goose, the grain, and the rowboat. Finally, Luca decided Harmon should take Dom and his friend to jail in the police car, Nate should drive Tomaso back in the green coupe, and Luca would take the women home in the truck, then join Nate.

After they had secured the truck and the coupe behind the police station, they took Tomaso to Nate's car. Luca sat in the back with their prisoner.

As soon as the doors shut, Tomaso began talking. "Can you help me, Captain Respighi?"

"I will do what I can. Perhaps the fact that you kept your father from shooting me will persuade the army to let you stay with the Service Units. But now, tell us what you know about Carlo Fusco. Did he know about your father?"

"Yes. I noticed him staring at Cesare. As if he knew him, but he never said anything. Once I met Dom, I understood."

"Cesare does look like him. I imagine Fusco saw the resemblance, especially since he knew Dom when they were young."

"One day, after we had been to Uncle Harry's, Fusco heard us talking about our father. We convinced him we didn't know where he was, but he said if I didn't help him, he would tell the police that Dom was wanted in New Jersey."

"Did you help him?"

"I was going to, and then I thought, *let him tell*. Dom ran away once; he could do it again."

"And then?"

"It worked for a while. Then he told me someone in the mess was stealing food from the fascist POWs and the buyer was coming to the island that night—the night he died."

"Why would they talk in front of Fusco?"

"He pretended not to speak English. The Americans got used to him being around and ignored him."

"How were they planning to transport the food off the island?"

"He said a supply boat was in on it. They smuggled things back and forth all the time, but that night a smaller boat was bringing someone to inspect the meat."

"What happened that night?"

"Fusco needed proof of what they were doing. He said no one would believe him without it."

"Do you think Fusco wanted to blackmail them?"

"Who knows with him?" Tomaso paused, considering the idea. "I think he was truly angry about them taking the food from the fascists. He thought they were the true patriots. He wanted me to go down to a little cove where they were meeting and be a witness. He thought the Army would believe me more than him because I had gone over to the Americans." He looked away.

"But you didn't go?"

"No. I wanted to be able to go to Uncle Harry's and I wasn't going to risk my privileges for Fusco and the fascists."

"Do you know where the people taking the food were meeting? They were taking a big risk—the island is a military installation."

"There's a cove people use when the island is fogged in."

"Did Fusco tell you who else was involved?"

"Not a name, no, but there was a cook—a fat cook. Fusco said the cook was getting fat while the prisoners starved."

"Getting fat can mean making money." Nate explained the Americanism.

"Maybe, but I don't think so." Tomaso sounded tired and confused.

Luca almost felt sorry for him. "We will get you settled, then look for Oliver."

61

A Rowboat with Arms

Wisps of music floated from the blues club, a rich contralto that glided through the black night, caressed me as my body leaned away, then back, swaying with the movement of the waves. It was soothing until water splashed into my open mouth, and rivulets snaked into my lungs. I coughed, tried to get my breath. I dragged my torso out of the water and slumped against the piling. The singer's words teased at me.

Skylark. I would like to soar away. From the pain. *No, she said "lane." Or "rain."* My head hurt, my leg was ice and fire, but I wasn't dead. Why had he hit me with the gun? Why not shoot me and get it over with? Maybe he had been afraid someone would come to investigate the sound of a shot. Or maybe he planned to come back after I had drowned and take off the cuffs. Make it look like an accident. Or maybe he enjoyed knowing it would kill me if I couldn't stop him from harming Zoe and Theo.

Well, the hell with that. I hugged the mussels and tried to inch my way up the piling. I bent my left leg and pushed, but I couldn't get high enough to drag the braced leg up. *Trigonometry. I am a triangle.* Or was that geometry? The water reached my waist. How much time had gone by? I heard a car door close, laughter, people heading toward the warmth of the club. I cried out, but the sound disappeared into the swell of the music as the door opened.

At full tide, the water would rise at least as high as the mussels that clung to the piling, and they were over my head. If I could stand, maybe my head would be above water at full tide. I strained to see the tidemark on the piling, but it was too dark. I bent my good leg and pushed, but I couldn't drag my other leg up. It wouldn't bend, and I couldn't reach the brace to unlock it.

Think, Oliver. Try something else. I rolled onto my bad hip and dug my heel into the mud and sand, then bent my good leg and pushed, rolling farther onto my bad leg, using the piling like a pivot point. I swung about a foot above the water before I slid down again. That would work, but first I needed to rest. Maybe as the water rose it would be easier.

I closed my eyes, listened to a buoy clanging in the bay. I loved the sound of the buoys, the deep song of the lighthouse. Seagulls had rested on the swaying markers as my friends and I sailed by them. *Ding, ding. Ding, ding.* I wondered where it was. You could hear the bells long before you could see the buoys. Sound traveled far on water. That meant something. Should mean something. But what?

The fog in my brain cleared for a moment. Obviously, I had to make a noise, but yelling had proved futile, and I was tired. Very tired. I reached above my head, about to pull myself up again, and the handcuffs clinked. I raised my hands and hit the cuffs together. If I hit them just so, the ringing echoed and traveled along the water. *Dot dot dot dash dash dash dot dot dot.* If I could keep it up, maybe someone coming out of the club would hear me. Maybe the coast guard, if they were still hunting for the boat they had told us about the day before. *Dot dot dot dash dash dash dot dot dot.* Wartime. Everyone knew the Morse code distress signal.

I closed my eyes and continued my monotonous song, soon losing track of the dots and dashes.

I had drifted away. When I opened my eyes, an empty rowboat floated under the pier. The boat had arms that pushed it along the pilings. I closed my eyes again. My brain must have shut down from the cold. I felt a bump and raised my head. *The Japs.* They had finally gotten me.

"Be quiet, Oliver. I'm going to get you out of here."

They do speak English well. Gunny was right. And he knows my name.

"Do you have a key to these cuffs?"

I wondered whether Wade had thrown the key away when he took my cuffs.

"Oliver?"

"Pants. Right-hand pocket."

He tied off the boat and slid over the side. When he had unlocked the cuffs, he pulled me away from the piling and helped me to my feet, still under the cover of the pier. I staggered, close to hypothermia, maybe past it. I shook in the cold air, from the chill, from shock—I didn't know which. I looked at the man supporting me.

"You really are Japanese." I shook my head. "I must be hallucinating; you're all gone."

"Not quite. Besides, I'm American. Not that it makes any difference." He smiled.

I wondered why he wasn't angry, why he would help someone whose country had imprisoned his people.

"They haven't found you?"

"No. And don't worry. I'm not a spy. I'd have enlisted, but the government would have put my father in a camp. He wouldn't have survived." He repositioned his shoulder under my arm. "I could've been fighting in Europe or breaking Japanese codes in the Pacific. Instead I'm hiding out and caring for my father."

I shuffled my feet through the sand and rocks, trying to help my rescuer, who breathed heavily under my weight.

"Who did this to you?"

"It's too complicated, and I'm too tired." I could barely talk through the shivering. "How did you find me?"

"Your SOS. But someone else may have heard it, so we need to hurry—I have to get back to my father."

"If they see you, they'll probably shoot you. Were you the boat they saw the other night?"

"Yes. I was pretty sure they had spotted me, so I hid until they left. Usually I don't go out, but the person who brings us food and medicine didn't come. When that happens, he leaves supplies at a prearranged spot, so I went out tonight and picked them up. I was heading back when I heard you."

"How did you know my name?"

"We have a mutual friend. Besides, when you came home, you were a bit of a local hero."

"Can I do something for you?" I looked down at my pitiful condition. "Not now, of course, but later?"

"The person who helps us knows you. He told me you helped him once. If we ever need you, he'll let you know. Actually, there *is* something you can do. I can't ask anyone else."

"Name it."

"Will you try to find out if something has happened to him? To Roan?"

"Roan? Why . . . Oh. All right. But how will I reach you?"

"I'll be here a week from today at two in the morning if it's foggy. If not, I'll come on the next night that is. If Roan shows up within the week, he'll let you know you needn't come." He took a deep breath. "Are you ready? I need to get you up the embankment before the moon breaks through again."

"What's your name?"

"Just Tom."

I leaned on Just Tom, who supported me while pushing and pulling me up the slope. I swayed on the walkway, looking for my cane. If I fell, I wouldn't be able to get up again. It might be easier to crawl to the club anyway. Car lights swept across the lot, barely catching Just Tom's back as he disappeared over the rocks.

62

Pulling Things Out of a Hat

Louis Carlton took one look at me and hustled me into the bathroom. I tried to thank the customer who had taken me to the club's backdoor without asking any questions.

"We need to warm you up and clean you up. I don't think a hot shower can hurt, and it'll help with the stink. You're covered in that damned oil from the refinery." Louis turned on the taps and waited for the water to get hot. "I'll dig up some clothes for you."

"I need to call someone."

"Hurry up and get in there. You're not going to do anyone any good if you pass out. You need some help?"

I'd had all the help I could stand for one night. "I can manage."

I struggled out of my clothes and held on to the wall with one hand while I washed with the other. The brace chafed like hell, but I left it on. A little more water wasn't going to hurt it.

I was leaving the shower when Louis returned with some athletic clothes.

I couldn't imagine the dapper man sweating, not with his marceled hair and the uptown look he cultivated.

"Here. They belong to a waiter who's training to be a boxer."

"I need to call someone."

"You said that before." Louis pushed the phone to me. "You might want to take that brace off. Wet like that, it's gonna rub you raw."

"I need to be able to walk, so it stays."

"Wait." Louis rummaged in a desk drawer. "Take it off and wrap this around your leg before you put it back on." *This* was a cashmere scarf. "I had plans for that. Cute little number comes in here on Tuesdays." He winked.

I did as I was told. The soft warmth felt good, but soon the brace's wet padding would soak through it.

I called Jennie, willing the damned dial to go around faster. A busy signal. *Get off the phone!* I was afraid to call the operator to break into the conversation—not until I knew what was going on.

I called Harry's house, wondering for a moment why I wasn't calling the station. He picked up on the second ring.

Before I could explain what I needed, he told me Nate had not hurt Cora—that he had an alibi.

If I'd trusted Nate instead of tearing off after him, I wouldn't have ended up handcuffed to a piling. I told Harry what Wade had done, and that he might be going after Zoe and Theo. Louis was hanging on every word.

"Were there any witnesses? Did anyone see?"

"Do you think he would try to kill me in front of a crowd?"

"It would be your word against his."

"Harry, do you think I made this up?"

"Oliver, I believe you. I'm thinking what to do next. Give me a moment."

I needed to move, to get to Theo and Zoe.

"Harry!"

"My brothers are here. I'll go with them to Zoe and Theo and figure out a reason why on the way. If we run into Wade, I'll pretend to know nothing. In the meantime, come to my house. No, that won't work—Wade could see you from his house. Go to my Aunt Lucy's. I'll meet you there, and we'll figure out what to do about your failure to die. I must go, Oliver. I'll see you at my aunt's house."

"Harry, he has a gun. Be careful." I realized I didn't have my gun. Did Wade take it? Or was it in the bay?

"Don't worry."

By now I was more than ready to leave, but Louis seemed to have other ideas.

"Drink this." He held out a mug. "It's soup." He put a gun on the desk. "You might need this. It's registered, and I have a permit, Mr. Policeman." He walked to a closet and pulled out a crutch. "I ain't sayin' you need it, but you might want it."

I glared at him. The guy was like a damned magician pulling things out of a hat.

"A customer left it. Said he could walk out on his own steam." He waved the crutch. "And he did."

"Oh, all right." I pulled myself up, leaned on the crutch. "Look, Louis, do you think you could keep it quiet that I was here? Until I work some things out?"

"Sure. The guy who brought you in won't talk, and I don't think anyone noticed you coming in the back. But take care, Oliver. That Slater is one mean son of a bitch."

"What do you know about him?"

"Come back when this is over. See how it shakes out."

"I have another favor to ask."

"Go on."

"Can you drive me somewhere? On the QT. I need to leave my car here. The keys are in it—someone will pick it up."

"Let's go."

I was quiet as we drove to Mrs. Forgione's house. Harry and his brothers should be with Zoe and Theo by now. Wade seemed to be spiraling out of control. What did Theo have that he wanted so badly? And how did he intend to get it without implicating himself in something? *Remember, he has to think you're dead. So far, he's free. And he'll want to stay that way.*

Wade floated up the hill, window rolled down, one elbow on the doorframe, feeling like a teenager out for a cruise. The clouds boiled in the sky, raced along the horizon. Bits of moonlight peeked through and dappled the darkness.

He went into his house. Cora was gone, but he felt her presence in the shadows of lies that filled the room. He missed her, even though she might not be dead. He missed his idea of them together, her sheltering against him on the ferry to Sausalito. They had driven for hours to the lighthouse at Point Reyes, laughing as they climbed down the hill, hoping to catch sight of the whales on their migration up the coast. Cora had huddled against him, and he had wrapped her inside his jacket. She hadn't been able to find a thing to eat on the restaurant's game-filled menu. What is the difference between eating a rabbit and eating a lamb? he had asked her. Then she said she didn't want to eat lamb, either, but insisted they stay. She'd charmed the chef into making her a plate from the side dishes.

Charmed the chef the way she charmed everyone. A charming little liar.

He changed his clothes, stuffed the wet shirt and pants into the laundry basket, and remembered the Hermit woman. What was he going to do about her? And his laundry?

He was hungry again. He walked through the blood and mess on the floor and filled one of those colorful bowls with stew. While he ate it cold, standing at the sink, headlight beams swung out of the Buonarottis' driveway and moved down the hill. He belched. Time to call the station so they could tell him about Cora. Time to cry about his wife.

63

Take Care of Nate

We stood on Mrs. Forgione's porch pretending Louis wasn't holding me up.

"Come in, come in."

"I can't stay, ma'am." He waved and skipped away from my attempts to thank him.

"Oliver. Come, sit down."

I refused the arm she offered. Bad enough I had the crutch.

She looked heavenward for patience with me. "Sit down. I made coffee."

"How is Cora?"

"The doctor thinks she'll be fine. She gave me a message for you. She said to tell you Wade knows about the locket and to take care of Nate."

Take care of Nate how? The coffee warmed me, and I then realized I had been drinking a lot, and that the bathroom was probably upstairs.

"Do you have any idea where Luca and Nate are?" I kept forgetting Luca was my prisoner. I should know where he was.

"We—they—found Dom and Tomaso. Dom is in jail, and Luca and Nate are taking Tomaso back to Angel Island tomorrow. They're staying overnight at the coast guard station. If you want to wash your hands, there's a bathroom through that hall. We put it in when Enrico broke his leg. But when you come back, I want to hear what happened."

I returned to an ice pack and an adamant Mrs. Forgione. How to tell her how hopeless and angry I had felt, trapped in the cold, terrified about what Wade might have been doing to Zoe and Theo? And Jennie, who had been through enough. Imagining Charley hearing that his father was dead.

"Sitting here, warm and dry, I find it hard to believe what happened tonight. Except for the pain in my leg—and my head."

"Harry said we're pretending you're missing?"

"I'm not sure whether that's the best thing to do. I'd like to talk to Luca about it."

"I'll call the coast guard station."

Luca was examining me when Harry arrived and assured us that everyone at Jennie's house was fine, and his brother was on guard duty. Luca said I would live, which was funny since I was already dead. I told them what Wade had done, Nate told me about their adventure with Dom, and Mrs. Forgione pretended to lock her lips with a key.

Harry shook his head at my questioning look. "Don't ask."

"What do we do now? I can't be dead forever." I shifted the ice bag on my knee.

"Although that is customary." Luca looked up from the brace he was blotting with a towel.

"What do we do about Wade? He tried to kill Oliver, hit me with a gun, and probably was the one who beat Steve." Nate sounded calm, but I could see that he was barely containing his anger. "We need to stop him before he hurts anyone else."

"I think he already *has* hurt someone else—Cora." Luca looked around at us. "Oliver, think back to what we asked her."

"It was a lifetime ago, Luca. How can I remember?"

"I remember it clearly. You said, 'Who did this to you?' And Cora answered, 'Wade.'" He raised a hand to stop my protest. "You assumed she was asking for him, but she was answering your question."

"Then why did she say 'Nate'?"

"You said, 'We'll find Wade for you, but tell us who did this.' And she answered, 'Nate. Stop him.' I think she was afraid for Nate and asking us to stop Wade."

"That makes some sense of what Mrs. Forgione said: that Cora wanted me to take care of Nate. Why was she afraid for you, Nate?"

He got up and turned toward the window. "I think Wade was eavesdropping when Cora and I were talking yesterday, while you were at the Buonarottis. He may have misunderstood. My mother told me how jealous he was, even before the war, and that it might be better if I stopped going to visit Cora. I'll kill him if he's the one who hurt her and Steve."

"Everyone needs to calm down." The pencil Harry had been taking notes with snapped in two. "Why do you think Wade is the one who hurt Steve?"

Luca spoke up. "There was blood on his boot. On the toe, not underneath. Dom told us that he swung the fishing net at Steve and knocked him down, but then he heard a noise and ran down the hill. I believe Wade saw Steve on the ground and, for a reason I do not know, kicked him. When he heard Nate leaving Paola's kitchen, he hid, then seized the opportunity to hit Nate and try to frame him."

"And there's the print on the photo scrap when he said he hadn't touched them," I added. "The torn-up photo of Nate, Steve, and Anna Maria that was strewn around Steve."

"But *I* tore up the photo when I was talking to Cora. I left the scraps in her kitchen," Nate said.

"Another reason to believe Wade was the one who hurt Steve. He had access to the photo scraps and scattered them around him so it appeared you had done it." Luca shrugged.

"But I would have explained. Steve would have said it wasn't me."

"He does say it wasn't you because he doesn't believe you would hurt him. But he didn't see who did it." I shook my head. That was a mistake.

"I would have said I'd left the photo scraps at Cora's."

"I think something was going to happen to you when you tried to escape."

"But—"

"He was dead set on taking you away."

"But Cora would have said . . ." Nate gazed at the wall as if a sad movie played on it.

"What is it?" Luca asked.

"When she saw the scraps on Steve's body, she asked me what I had done. So maybe she wouldn't have said I couldn't have done it." Nate scuffed his boot on the floor.

"Nate, it was reasonable for her to wonder. You might have gone back for them. And you were angry." Luca tried to console him. "But it might explain what happened between her and Wade. If he heard you and Cora talking and then found the photo, he could have leaped to the wrong conclusion."

"Which was what?" Harry asked.

"That Nate had given up Anna Maria for Cora."

"That's crazy." Nate was incensed.

"Yes. But regard his other actions. Not those of a healthy mind, surely."

"How could he get away with hurting Cora?" Nate stumbled over the words.

"She's his wife. He won't feel threatened by that." Harry raised his hands, palms forward, as if to say, *don't blame me—I'm merely stating the facts.*

Luca interrupted. "But handcuffing Oliver to the pier? It was insane—not literally. Which brings me to something I have been wondering: Why does he hate you so much?"

"He blames me for a girl's death."

"Phyllis Brennan." Mrs. Forgione looked up from her rosary. "Wade adored her. And she adored you. But then you broke it off, and she was devastated. The whole Point knew." She tilted her head to the side. "I'm sorry, Oliver."

"I met Cora. I didn't think about how Phyllis would take it."

"What happened to Phyllis?" Luca asked.

"Her body was found near Keller's beach. Everyone assumed she had fallen—or jumped. It was kinder to believe she fell."

"Or maybe she was pushed."

"Nate!" Mrs. Forgione spoke as if Nate were twelve years old.

"An interesting idea, Nate. Wade is pathologically jealous. If she rejected him, perhaps he snapped. Perhaps that was the catalyst to all the rest."

Luca's theory made sense to me.

"When we were by the bay, he said it wasn't enough for Phyllis that he loved her. He said I took something away from him, so he took something away from me." The men looked puzzled. "Cora."

"But she married him years after it was over between you two." Mrs. Forgione the historian chided him.

"He said to ask her why she went away, and then he laughed, because of course I couldn't, since I would be dead."

"But what happened to make him act against you now?" Harry looked ready to drop.

"I don't know. Wait—Mrs. Forgione, you said Cora wanted me to know Wade knows about the locket. Maybe that's it. Under the pier, he asked me why she kept it. Called it the Wright family heirloom. Maybe that's what did it." I explained what the locket meant, then stupidly shook my head again.

But it was Harry who said, "I'm getting a headache. The past, the present . . . what about the future? What are we going to do?"

"What has Cora said?" I looked at Mrs. Forgione.

"That Nate didn't do it, but she doesn't know who did. She was laughing and crying, and the nurse had to give her a sedative. Shock, I guess."

"There's still the question of Theo and the briefcase. Wade told me he was going to get it from him."

"My head hurts more now." Harry stood up. "I think we need to sleep. Luca and Nate can come home with me."

When the men protested, Harry held up his hands. "*Basta!* We're too tired to think. Oliver almost died; Nate not only plastered a wall but apprehended, with Luca, a man wanted for murder in New Jersey; and I have comforted a wife and daughter who are distraught about Steve, a sister-in-law who has discovered she married a murderer—or maybe not married, since his papers were forged, another legal mess—all after spending the day dealing with the results of the court martial. Plus, I have to settle up with the chicken man. We need sleep. We can meet again in the morning."

"The chicken man?"

"We'll tell you tomorrow, Oliver."

Saturday

October 28, 1944

64

A Failure to Die

The smell of coffee convinced me to try to sit on the edge of the bed. My leg hurt so badly that I almost wished I had let the navy surgeon cut it off. Maybe it would still come to that.

Not a good idea to look in the mirror. The bruise on my temple almost eclipsed the dark circles under my eyes, and my face and arms were crosshatched by small cuts. I washed up, ignoring the stinging as best I could, and struggled into the uniform Harry had brought over the night before. I limped into the kitchen.

"*Buon giorno!*" Luca greeted me with his usual good cheer. "Mrs. Forgione had to go to the café." He yawned.

"Luca stayed up with Paola and Isabella last night. Regular hen party." Nate ribbed Luca.

"After years of being only with men, I was delighted to listen to them talk. Isabella was furious about her criminal husband, then sad, then furious again." He rubbed his bald head. "I hid my delight; it would not have been well received, but to be with women overcome with emotion was exhilarating. It reminded me of home, my sister and her friends lamenting betrayals or rejoicing together."

"You think of Isabella as a sister, then?" Nate glanced at Harry.

I smelled bread burning. "Luca, the toast."

Harry seemed grateful for the interruption. "Something nagged at me, Oliver, after you told me about Jonah North's beating. As if the name should have meant something to me, and last night I remembered that I had heard it in connection with Regis Simmons's supposed suicide."

"In what way?"

"Regis was a welder on Jonah's crew."

"They knew each other."

"More than that, they were said to be friends."

"So, if Regis was the informer, perhaps he confided in Jonah when he found out my brother was dead."

"Exactly. And that means Jonah's beating may be tied to your brother's death. I'm authorizing you to investigate it and the Fleming children's death for my office."

Nate was fidgeting. I knew he wanted us to focus on clearing the Negro troops, so I asked Luca what they had learned about Fusco's death.

"It appears it had nothing to do with the Negro soldiers." He handed me the toast. "Tomaso told us last night that Fusco had planned to go down to the cove to spy on black-marketeers. It is reasonable to believe he died there. It would have made no sense for the Negro soldiers to take him down to the cove, drown him, then carry him back up that hill to hang him when they could have left him there."

Luca glanced at Nate, who agreed. "They wouldn't have drawn attention to themselves by imitating what happened at Fort Lawton, but someone who wanted to frame them would have."

"Makes sense."

"Luca and I could go to Angel Island and continue the investigation there. If that is still what you want us to do." Nate was raring to go. "We'll take Tomaso back to the island, talk to Cesare again, now that we know what went on, and try to figure out what Fusco discovered that got him killed."

"That reminds me." I told Harry that Doc Pritchard had found a metal button in Fusco's stomach. "Someone is missing a button."

Harry signaled that he would arrange an inspection.

"We also need to find out what Wade thinks Theo has. Then we will have more information, possibly, and what we learn might help us understand what has been going on." Luca looked at me.

"And what about me? Am I alive or dead?"

"Let's act as if nothing has happened," Harry said. "I'll take a statement from you, and we'll hold on to it in case we need it. We don't want to give anyone any reason to impede your investigation into Fusco's death and Jonah's beating. Wade will be the only one surprised that you're not dead; perhaps it'll throw him, and he'll make a mistake. In the meantime, I've had someone pick up your car."

"Thanks, Harry. We never did talk to the *Pittsburgh Courier*. They might be able to clear some of this up until Jonah can talk to us."

"Let me do that. I think you should go see Zoe and Theo and try to find out what Wade is after—if you can find their house." Harry nodded toward the window.

A dense gray cloud had descended on the Point.

65

Being Part of Their Goodness

The thick mist camouflaged Roan and the golden dog Emma, smudged their outlines into the trees above the Wrights' house. He had watched out for the boy and his sister since Oliver had saved Emma. He was back from Guam, but Roan liked the children, liked being part of their goodness. They reminded him of a time he cherished, when he had lived with his sister and his niece Phyllis.

He hovered over Theo like a guardian angel, protective but invisible. The boy hadn't noticed Roan following him on his morning excursions and hadn't realized he was there when he found the man on the fence.

Roan tried to be invisible, but he hadn't been able to help himself that morning. He had to untangle the man from the barbed wire. Unwinding it had cut his hands, but he didn't stop until the man was free and he was able to lay him gently on the ground. Then he hid in the weeds and stood vigil, listened as the morning woke up: quail wings whirring as they broke from cover, crows calling softly as they left their roost, and sparrows chirping from the brush.

The man wasn't dead. Roan knew death, had walked among acres of it in the fields of France. As he had sat on the hill waiting for Theo to come back, the barbed wire became the barricades of his war, and he saw the bodies of his fellow soldiers dangling from them in the yellow haze that rolled across the ground. He was lost in the whistling of shells, struggling to reach the wounded, when an angry voice had scattered his battlefield memories. Roan had looked toward the road.

Theo had come back, and Slater had grabbed his bike and was yelling at him. Roan had been keeping out of the detective's sight ever since he had tried to kill Emma, but he had used the shadows to haunt him again and again.

He had crouched in the fog and whistled the tune that drove the detective crazy.

Remembering that morning must have made him shake, because Emma was licking at his face, bringing him back to her, to the present, to the hill behind Theo and Zoe's house. She didn't like it when he shook. Roan soothed her, crooned to her, and they settled down together in the fog to wait for Wade.

Roan knew he would come for Theo.

Not quite day. Not quite night. Wade felt the same way. Not quite anything. He missed Cora. Even though she wasn't dead.

When he had shown up at the hospital the night before, she had flinched and reached for the button to call the nurse. He put a finger to his lips, sat down on the bed, and told her what she was going to say. If she said anything else, her precious Nate would suffer for it. She had nodded.

At least Wright's gone. Both Wrights. The Slaters against the Wrights, and the Slaters won. Who would have guessed?

All he had to do now was get that weird kid's briefcase, give it to Sandy, take the money, and go to Colorado.

He eased out of the car, careful not to slam the door. The dense fog covered him as he sneaked to the back of the house and headed for the kid's studio. There was a light on. Was that moron already inside working? It didn't matter if the boy was there or not. One more Wright hitting the dust didn't bother him any. If the briefcase wasn't there, he'd go to the house.

The fog muffled the sound of his stalking. It was easy going—until he tripped over something stretched across the path, and all hell broke loose. Damn boys and their war games.

He waited to see if anyone had heard. He crept forward, and then he heard the whistling. Eerie, as if it were dissolving in the mist. He hesitated. A dog barked, and he turned toward the sound. Bells jangled around him, and snatches of color glowed through the fog. Of course. It was the freak and his dog, and this time Wright wasn't there to save them.

"I know what you did. I know and I'm going to tell." Roan was singing in a whisper. Singing and not stuttering. What the hell? Wade didn't answer. He took cover in the brush and crept toward the barking. One good blow with the gun would crush the dog's skull.

Roan darted across his path. Wade lunged and came away with a strip of cloth. He forgot the dog and chased the flying ribbons. He was going to be rid of this nuisance for good. The fog separated, and he could see Roan running exactly where he wanted him. He had almost reached him when Roan suddenly leaped into the air. Wade stopped and watched him stumble at the edge of the tiger pit. He had dislodged some of the grass stalks and palm fronds that camouflaged the hole and the sharp points of stakes that stuck up from the ground. It was ingenious.

The boys must have gotten the idea from Tarzan movies. Too bad they didn't work that hard at something useful. Then again, this was turning out to be pretty handy.

He laughed. Roan scrambled over the edge of the pit and lay on the ground.

"Get up, idiot. Do you think I didn't know what those kids were doing and every place they dug one of their enemy-catchers? Think you could trap me?" He raised his gun. "Shut that dog up, or I'll shoot it."

Roan called to Emma and she stopped barking, but her whimpers filtered through the fog.

Wade walked around the edge of the pit and stood over Roan. "I said get up. You're going to have an accident."

66

Angel Island

Their Worst Nightmare

**" **Tomaso looks green. I think his numerous trips in a boat might be punishment enough for his misdeeds." Luca nodded toward the boy.

"I can understand him wanting to warn his father. Maybe Harry can do something to help him. He helped me." Nate would be grateful to Harry forever.

"Helped you? In what way?"

He wasn't sure where to begin.

"I had no idea what it meant to be Negro in America until the Army sent me to Texas for basic training." He looked over the water. "I think it was a lot easier for the men who had grown up in the South. The rest of us never knew when we were about to do something wrong." He struggled for an example. "Like using a pay phone on the street or sitting on a bench in a park.

It was impossible. No matter where we were, a bigot was watching. The fear was probably the worst part. Knowing that any one of those hate-filled people could destroy us for any reason, real or imagined."

"Did the other soldiers, the white ones, defend you?"

"Not where I was. Steve came to our canteen, but the white officers dragged him out."

"It is like that in Italy. The darker you are, the farther south you come from, the more you are looked down on. I am from Sicily. It is hard to go much farther south." He hurried to add, "I know it is not the same as what you experienced, but the feeling is, the frustration, the hurt. The anger."

"They called us troublemakers. We only wanted what the white soldiers had—a bus ride to town, a seat in the PX. Guess they figured if we didn't have a bus, we couldn't invade the town."

"Why are you smiling?"

"We used to sit in that leaky canteen and figure we were those white folks' worst nightmare—strong young men, educated, confident, ready to die. What was to stop us deciding we could fight for freedom here? I think we scared the hell out of them. Anyway, Steve called his father, and he managed to get me out of there. You might be able to get him to help Tomaso."

"Thank you. I will ask him."

"Would you stay here after the war, Luca? If you didn't have to go back to Italy?"

"I could stay; my mother was born here. But I want to get back to find her and my sister." He looked at the hills around the bay. "I cannot tell you how much I want to see my home again."

Luca looked so forlorn, Nate was sorry he had asked.

An MP waited for them in the harbor. He clutched a sheaf of papers and shifted back and forth on his stumpy legs.

Nate jumped onto the dock. "What do you have? You look ready to do a dance."

"Yes, sir. I mean, no, sir."

Tomaso teetered as if the ground were moving under him and took some tentative steps up the path.

Luca put his hand on Tomaso's shoulder. "Go see your brother. You can tell him what has happened. Is that all right, Corporal?"

Nate nodded and turned to the MP. "Tell us."

"One of the men waiting to ship out to the Pacific was outside the barracks the night of the fight."

"They told us they were all in the barracks."

The corporal raised his eyebrows almost to his widow's peak, as if to say, *what did you expect?*

"After Lieutenant Wright talked to them, they decided to tell what they knew. I told them nothing would happen to them for stretching the truth the first time."

Luca wondered if the commanding officers of these men would take such an understanding view, but perhaps they *would* look the other way. Maybe some good would come of their fear of publicity.

"What did the witness see?" Nate rolled his hand in a get-on-with-it motion.

"His brother is one of the Port Chicago defendants. He didn't want to listen to the talk in the barracks, so he hid in the shadows near the exercise yard. He heard a fight, then splashing and whispers down by the water. He didn't know if it was his friends or the Italians, so he crept closer to see what was going on. A big man pushed the POW's head under the water, then pulled him out and asked him questions. He couldn't hear everything, but he heard the man asking who else knew."

"Then what happened?"

"The big man said something to the other three, then held the man under the water. There was splashing for a while, then nothing."

"Who were the other three?"

"A smaller man—looked like a fisherman, with those high boots—one of the cooks from the camp, and another white soldier."

"Did he recognize anyone?"

"He got glimpses of them. He's not sure about the small man, but he would recognize the big man and he knew the cook."

"Is he fat? The cook?"

"He is. How did you know?"

"It's not important." Nate glanced at Luca. "Then what happened?"

"The men let the POW float in the water while the big man looked in a box. He picked something up and smelled it, examined it with a flashlight. They all argued, and then the fisherman helped the cook and his helper carry the body up the hill. He got in the boat with the big man and the box, then disappeared into the dark. The witness took off back to the barracks."

"Why didn't he tell anyone?"

"He didn't care what those white men did to each other. Besides, if he told, he figured he'd be in trouble for being outside, get blamed for something." The corporal resumed his little dance. "There's more. The inspection Captain Buonarotti ordered this morning turned up a field tunic missing a button. And a pair of wet boots. Guess whose." His smile faded when Nate didn't react. "The cook's."

"I'm looking forward to talking to that cook." Nate's eyes narrowed, and his smile alarmed Luca. He would see that the corporal was not alone with the cook.

At first the cook didn't seem worried. A Negro soldier said he was outside. Big deal—no one would believe him. But when Nate told him they had found his missing button in Fusco's stomach, he collapsed. He wasn't really cut out for a life of crime. He didn't even try to argue that it wasn't his button.

He hadn't signed up for murder, just a little black-market dealing. Those dagos didn't deserve sugar and coffee, or meat. He had noticed Fusco listening to him while he set up the rendezvous with his connection and had begun to wonder if the POW understood English. When Fusco followed him to the cove, they were ready for him.

They had decided to hang his body so the Army would blame the Negro soldiers—the way they had at Fort Lawton.

Nate leaned toward the cook. "Who were you working with?"

The cook turned his head away. "A civilian with connections."

"What kind of connections?"

"A place to sell whatever we took, and someone inside the legal system who knew when there would be inspections—stuff like that."

"Who is he?" Nate tried to hold the cook's gaze.

"I can't tell you. He has a whole group of people working for him." The cook pressed his lips together.

Nate leaned back and smiled. "You're doing time for this. It can be easy or hard. Think about how many bad meals you're going to eat in twenty or thirty years. You want us to want to help you, give us his name."

The men waited. Luca was amused that Nate had gone to the cook's obvious weak spot. Maybe the cook would crack, maybe not. Finally, he spoke.

"Sandy Slater. His nephew's a policeman. But he wasn't here that night. He couldn't fit in the boat with that fat butcher who wanted to inspect the meat before they paid for it."

The cook calling the butcher fat.

"What was the butcher's name?"

"George something."

"Who else?"

"That's all I know. Look, it was just food from the POWs. No big deal."

"It's a big deal when someone gets killed and someone else gets blamed." Nate shoved his chair back so hard it crashed to the floor.

Nate and Luca returned to Harry's office in the Presidio where Nate filled him in. Luca leaned against the wall and watched them and wondered whether there was a restaurant in the Presidio. It had been a long time since breakfast. Even mess coffee would be welcome.

"Finally. Grounds to arrest Sandy Slater and get search warrants for his shop and house. I've wanted to be able to do that for a long time." Harry pulled some forms out and made a list. "Anyone else?"

"The cook said someone in the legal system was helping them, but he didn't know who." Nate seemed like a different person now that the investigation had cleared the Negro soldiers. Maybe he would develop an appetite soon.

"My first guess would be Wade Slater or Paul Butler. When Peter died, we wondered if there had been a leak, someone who might have told the Klan what he was doing, but Peter would never have told anyone in the police department about Regis Simmons."

"Maybe it's someone in the prosecutor's office."

"I've wondered about that since Peter died. The only thing that was unusual was that a secretary burst into my office when we were talking about the informant even though I waved her away. She could have seen the immunity forms. Told Sandy Slater."

"You didn't suspect her then?" Nate's tone wasn't accusing, simply curious.

"No. I suppose I should have, but she had no obvious connection to anyone we thought might have been involved."

"Can you get the warrants without tipping off our suspects?"

"We—the Army—will handle it. There won't be any leaks. I'll add the secretary. Nate, you get the men we need."

It looked like food was going to have to wait. Luca sighed. It seemed inappropriate to inquire about it now.

67

Point Richmond

It Might Be Too Late

When I got out of my car, I heard voices behind Jennie's house. I leaned on my borrowed crutch and made my way to the hill. Something flitted through the fog and moved toward the sounds. I whistled the *forget everything else and come to me now* command. Nothing. It wasn't Harley out there in the gloom.

Getting up that hill wasn't going to be easy, but it sounded as if I didn't have too far to travel. Thank goodness. I belly crawled through the damp, reminded of basic training. At least live rounds weren't whizzing about my head. The wind thinned parts of the fog and I peered up the hill hoping to locate the source of the voices. I froze when Wade pointed a gun at Roan.

A shadowy form wavered in front of me. Then the arc of a bow materialized. Zoe rose from the mist. Before I could move, she told him to drop the gun. Her voice sounded too calm.

"Oh, how precious. Did you think whistling would distract me?" His voice turned ugly. "Put down the bow and get over here, or I'll shoot him."

Zoe held her pose. I willed her to drop to the ground and creep down the hill under the cover of the fog.

"Fine. Which do you think is faster, little girl, an arrow or a bullet? Put it down!"

I crawled closer to him.

Zoe turned to run down the hill.

"Stop, or I'll shoot the freak." He waved the gun, motioning her toward Roan, who was maneuvering away from the pit. Wade turned toward him. "No, you don't. Move over—"

"Waa-ade." I called in my idea of a ghostly voice.

He spun around. Once, then again. "No. Impossible. It can't be you. You can't keep coming back!"

I pointed the bartender's gun at him. "Over here, Wade."

He swung toward my voice and fired. Roan leaped on his back and grabbed for the gun. A second shot echoed across the hill, and Zoe's scream joined the sudden cawing of the crows. Wade and Roan teetered on the edge of the pit, until Roan propelled them into the air. They disappeared into the earth.

Harley flew up the hill and almost knocked me over. Someone shouted, "What's happening up there?" Harry's brother joining the party. A bit late.

"Call for an ambulance. I think Zoe's been shot, and Roan may be hurt. Hurry." I held on to Harley and let him half-drag me up the slope.

Zoe lay face down. Harley nudged her, but she didn't move. When I turned her over, a red blossom spread across her sweater.

Roan found himself on top of Wade, surrounded by a forest of pointed stakes. He pushed himself off and staggered to the side. Blood dripped from his sleeve, and the crowns of the trees spun into a blur, whipping around his head. He called to Emma. Finally, his voice penetrated her howls.

He looked back at Wade, who writhed, pinned to the stakes from the weight of Roan's body and the force of the fall. Wade lifted his head and tried to push off from the ground. Roan picked up the gun, and Wade strained to see what he was doing.

"Go ahead. You won't get away with shooting a policeman." His face twisted as he stretched his arm back toward his leg.

Roan set the gun on the edge of the pit. He had never shot anyone, not even in the war. He could hear Oliver yelling something about an ambulance. Help would be here soon. It might be too late.

He looked at Wade's leg, at the stake piercing it. It was flat and thin, sharp like a knife blade. Roan welcomed the smell of damp earth as he crawled between the poles that supported Wade's body. The stake through his torso might have pierced something vital, but the most life-threatening wound was the one near the groin.

He crawled under Wade and closed his eyes, then put his hand under Wade's leg and pushed upward. He could barely hear Emma barking over Wade's screams. Flesh and muscle clung to the stake, Wade's weight now working against Roan. He lay on his back and heaved with both feet until he ripped Wade's leg off the stake. Wade flailed his arms. He tried to staunch the blood spurting from his leg, tried to wrench his torso from the stakes. He struggled, helpless. He was pinned like a bug.

"Help me."

Roan dragged himself to the corner of the pit and closed his eyes. He buried his face in his arms and thought about Phyllis.

68

Punishment Enough

Doc Pritchard thrust a finger at me. "What is wrong with you, man? Remain there until you are attended to and trust your niece to me."

I wished Pritchard had made one of his bad jokes. Seeing him serious worried me. I waited until Zoe's gurney disappeared down the long gray corridor, then surrendered myself to the nurse. She squinted and wrinkled her nose while she looked me up and down. After she uncovered my knee, she called a doctor. He whistled.

"I'm going to clean up your cuts and wrap your knee. There's not much I can do except warn you that if it becomes infected, you'll lose the leg. If you want to keep what's left of it—and I'm not sure why you do—then come in daily for injections of penicillin, and I'll keep an eye on it. But you need to rest it. No weight-bearing activities."

I nodded. This wasn't the first doctor who seemed to think my leg should have been amputated, but I hoped someday someone would figure out how to give me a new knee, and they couldn't do that if I didn't have a leg. I was willing to live with the pain until then.

Later in the evening, Zoe sat propped up in her hospital bed, her arm in a sling fastened with a giant safety pin. She sipped her chocolate milk shake through a glass straw and told her audience her version of what had happened behind the house.

"I knew something was wrong when I heard Emma barking." She sipped. "I've known that Roan and Emma have been looking out for me and Theo for a long time, so I figured they might be watching the house, too, and I was afraid that something was wrong with Roan, because Emma wouldn't stop barking. Usually they stay quiet and out of sight, like they don't want us to know what they're doing."

Zoe's next sip allowed Jennie to ask why she hadn't woken Mr. Buonarotti's brother.

"He had fallen asleep in a chair, and I thought I could see what was happening and yell if I needed him."

While Zoe's cheeks were sucked in with her next sip, I asked her why she hadn't let Harley out.

"He was whining and pawing at the door, but I thought it would be better for him to stay and guard Theo, because someone might have been trying to trick us into leaving him unprotected. He did give me a dirty look when I told him to stay." Zoe smiled at the dog, who sat by her bed, making sure nothing else happened to her on his watch. "For a minute, I thought he wasn't going to listen, but he did, so I strung my bow and went out to see what was happening."

I was so grateful Zoe was alive that I didn't have the heart to tell her how foolish she had been. It would be punishment enough that she would miss the archery tournament she had practiced so hard for. Pritchard predicted it would be quite some time before she would be able to string that bow again.

Luca arrived with Harry and his Aunt Lucy. The smells from the hamper they carried reminded me that it had been a long time since breakfast. While we ate, Harry told me what had happened on Angel Island and what they had found at Sandy Slater's. Someone had tried to burn some brand-new boots. Enough of the soles remained to tie them to the attacks on Steve and Jonah. Guess Wade had heard the doctor commenting about their unique pattern and tried to get rid of the evidence. They also found a box containing a list of names and the grant of immunity Peter and Regis Simmons had signed. It would be easy to convince a jury that Sandy could only have gotten it from the wrecked car. Harry thought the Slaters must have kept it in case they ever had to justify Regis's death to the Klan, but if they already had that, why Wade's interest in Theo's briefcase?

"I don't think I can sleep until we find out why Wade wanted Theo's briefcase." I pushed myself out of the chair and tried to balance on my new crutches. "Luca, let's go see Theo."

The women stayed behind to watch Zoe through the night. Luca kissed her good hand and told her she was not only beautiful but brave. She smiled at him, then closed her eyes. I pitied the teenage boys who would have to compete with Zoe's memories of the POW.

69

A Disappointment

I didn't think Luca did it deliberately, but he seemed to enchant every woman he smiled at. Of course, the nurses would be happy to get him more padding for the tops of my crutches. I sat in a chair outside Zoe's room while Luca disappeared into a linen closet with a pretty blond nurse.

I closed my eyes and drifted off for a moment.

"Are you proud of yourself?" My father's voice jarred me awake.

"Look at you. What did you accomplish, running off to the war? You left your brother to die so you could come home a cripple. It's what you do best, isn't it—letting down the people who need you? And now you almost got my granddaughter killed."

I tried to push myself out of the chair.

"Judge, Zoe's going to be fine."

The look of disdain on my father's face stopped me. I felt a physical tumbling in my chest. There was nothing I could ever say that would change how my father saw me.

"You know, you're right. I wasn't there for Elizabeth. I wasn't there for Peter. And Zoe almost got killed. You're right."

"Is that all you have to say? You're nothing but a disappointment to me."

"I know." I looked him in the eye. "I guess I've always known."

"You're pathetic." He turned his back on me and almost bumped into Luca, who stood nearby, holding my crutches. I watched my father walk away and felt the guilt return; he was right. I wasn't there for the people who needed me.

"I heard. Forgive me for intruding, but you know none of it is your fault."

"I'm not one of your patients, Captain. Let it go." My voice forbade an argument, but he ignored me.

"If you were one of my patients, I would let you find your own way to the truth, but we do not have time to indulge ourselves."

I reached for my crutches, and Luca backed away.

"I will ask you this: Do you blame your son for your wife's death? From your face, I see that would be unthinkable. So why is it different for you?" Luca held up a hand to silence me. "Because you expect more of yourself than you do of your son? Because you are better than he is? No, I think he is so much like you that he almost drowned trying to save his mother. Does he blame himself that she died? No. Because he has no need to punish himself for surviving. I think he is very much like you, with one significant difference. He was raised by a loving man, not a 'judge.'"

I looked at my feet. I understood where Luca was going with this. I didn't blame Charley, was grateful Charley didn't blame himself. So why did I think if I had been at the lake, things would have been different? Because I could have done what Charley couldn't?

"Think about it, Oliver. And think about whether you could ever speak to your son the way your father speaks to you. I suspect you have never spoken even to your dog that way."

"He was different with Peter."

"Not entirely. I am sure he judged your brother but approved of what he saw. The son who wanted to be like his father. Which only makes it more difficult for the other son, who knows love is possible but not attainable. In a way, your father's disapproval freed you to be the man you were supposed to be, however painful it was. Now you must learn to be as forgiving of yourself as you are of your son."

We looked at each other; then I nodded. "Can I have the damn crutches now? And your bill?"

"*Ehhh*." Luca reached out a hand. "I don't think you can afford me."

Theo emptied the briefcase while Luca and I watched. He carefully lined up pencils and pens, stacked sketchbooks, and sifted through his odd collection.

When Luca asked him if he had taken anything from the place where he found Jonah, phrasing and rephrasing the question until my brain went numb, he reluctantly opened a cigar box and removed one piece of foil at a time, lining their edges up neatly before adding another. He stopped at a piece with embossed writing, set it aside, and gestured toward it. He said it had never been in the briefcase. He had put it in his pocket.

It was the wrapping from a piece of *torrone*, the nougat candy Mrs. Forgione gave to customers. I turned it over. No secret message. I didn't bother asking Theo if he was sure this was the right paper. It had nothing to do with anything. Wade's pursuit of the briefcase had been pointless.

Friday

November 3, 1944

70

A Pattern of Deposits

Almost a week went by before Jonah was in any shape to talk to me. Once he was able to have visitors, Mrs. Forgione and Mrs. Hermit made sure he had at least two visitors every day who brought him food they considered nourishing. Then Auntie Josephine got into the act, and you almost needed an appointment to see him. Luckily, his roommates didn't mind the company. I squeezed myself in between visitors.

"Oliver. Where's Harley?"

"I think I'm getting a complex about him, Jonah. Seems everyone is happier to see him than me."

"He does have the advantage over you in a lot of ways." Jonah still looked battered, but there was mischief in his eyes. Then he sobered. "I heard Sandy Slater confessed."

"To the deaths of the Fleming children, Regis Simmons, and my brother. Oh, and your beating. He probably thought he'd be safe if he took responsibility for everything. Kept insisting no one else was involved."

"We both know someone was behind those fires. After the second fire, I took a couple of trips to the deeds office in Martinez—did you know the Martini was born there when a drunken goldminer left off the *z* in the Martinez Special?"

"That's what you discovered in Martinez? A legend? And you an undercover reporter."

"Ralph told me you know about that. And about me." He shrugged a kind of apology.

When he asked why I was smiling, I told him Nate had said some Negroes passing looked whiter than I did. Jonah agreed that was hard to imagine.

Basically, he had found out what I had, had traced the rental houses back to Trier, the lawyer, but never uncovered who his client was.

"Regis Simmons knew, but he wouldn't tell me even though he was scared to death after your brother died. He told me the proof was in the negatives he had stolen from the Klan photographer and given to your brother." Jonah reached for the glass on the bedside table.

"We never found any negatives. What was in them?"

"Some of the men who had burned the cross and other men meeting in front of a Confederate flag. He told Peter who they were—a few were prominent men who wouldn't want people to know they supported the Klan."

"Maybe that's what Wade Slater was looking for. You were beaten, your rooms were searched, and my nephew was terrorized. But we don't need them anymore. After Sandy was beaten almost to death in jail, he decided not talking wasn't going to keep him safe, so he implicated Trier."

"But we already knew about Trier. How does that help?"

"It gave Harry probable cause to subpoena his bank records. They discovered a pattern of deposits that was traced to two people: former Chief Anderson and a butcher who was involved in black marketeering and the death of an Italian POW. Both owned houses secretly, and Harry convinced Trier to tell us which one was behind the deaths in exchange for a lighter sentence. Attorney/client privilege didn't seem as important to him then."

"Who was it? I'll bet Anderson."

"Your judgment hasn't improved any since the night you decided to keep a late-night rendezvous with the Klan. It was the butcher, but Anderson has his own worries now. His wife found out about his secret houses, and people are more inclined to believe he was a crooked cop. He's not a happy man."

"So, it's over."

"I suppose so. Although there's still the question of where those negatives are."

Thursday

November 23, 1944

71

A Hero

Thanksgiving Day. Darkened windows reflected Harley and me while we slowly made our way up Park Place toward the Café Avellino. I thought I should be thankful that I had graduated from crutches to a cane, but I would rather be thankful for a leg that supported me without one, that wasn't stiff from riding in the freezing cargo hold of an army plane all the way to Washington, DC, and back in less than twenty-four hours.

I had stolen my son away from work long enough for dinner at the Willard Hotel. Just seeing Charley's smile when Harley raced to him and jumped up to lick his face made the trip worth it.

The maître d' seated us at a table for three with a flourish that dared other diners to complain about the dog who accompanied the limping Marine and the man who was clearly his son.

The waiter asked if we were waiting for our guest, and Charley told him she was already there. He poured wine into the three glasses without commenting.

We silently toasted Elizabeth, touched our glasses to hers, and in that moment, for that moment, I believed she *was* there.

The conversation was pretty one-sided. All Charley was supposed to say about his work was that it was boring pushing numbers around all day, so I talked about Jonah and the fire, Luca and the Angel Island POWs. I told Charley about almost drowning, and about Just Tom. He drained his wineglass, then smiled and shook his head. When I looked at him quizzically, he said it was ironic that I had been attacked by a man who should have been my ally, and saved by my mortal enemy—at the risk of the man's own freedom.

Charley told me about a girl he had met, one of the coeds recruited from Wheaton to join their division. He insisted it wasn't serious, but the way he talked about her led me to believe it might be more serious than he knew. I talked about the K9 units' efforts to bring the dogs home from the Pacific and re-train them. The military believed the dogs were unfit to return to civilian life, but we were determined to honor the sacrifice of the twenty-five dogs who had died protecting us on Guam. What better way to do that than by finding loving homes for the ones who had survived?

Charley asked whether I would be able to help with the re-training, what I was going to do when the war ended. I didn't have an answer. So much depended on whether I could still be a detective with my injured knee.

When we held each other outside the restaurant, finding it difficult to say good-bye, Charley said he hoped to be home for Christmas. He wanted to meet my new friends, the ones I had solved the murders with.

Harley and I stopped outside the café. The streets were empty, the bars silent. Smoke escaped from chimneys on the hills surrounding us, weaving through a silver mist that smelled of salt and green. I pictured women cooking in kitchens with steamy windows, children trying to keep their dress-up clothes clean, and men reading the paper in easy chairs. Charley was right: Pt. Richmond was home again.

I hoped Charley was also right about making it back for Christmas. If you asked people what they wanted for Christmas, the answer was the same. For the war to be over, for their men to be safe. Civilians were encouraged by the news that the Allies were nearing Germany, but I knew the military anticipated a massive German attack, a last-ditch effort to buy Germany time to regroup. If that did happen, Charley would be needed at work. At least he would be safe—not like Mrs. Forgione's sons, fighting somewhere in Italy and France. I didn't know how she managed to go on.

The café was closed to the public, but Mrs. Forgione had invited the people she thought of as family to come for a special Thanksgiving dinner. Jonah couldn't make it; he was still recuperating at Ralph's house, probably surrounded by adoring women.

At her husband's wake, the café had seemed exotic, the men at the round table as foreign to me as the crowd at Carlton's. Now I couldn't imagine my life without them, especially Luca, who sat at the round table with Harry. They spoke in Italian, no longer an enemy language.

They were probably talking about finding Luca's mother and sister. Harry was optimistic about the search because Sicily was in Allied hands.

"Oliver, *buona sera*."

"*Buona sera*, Signora Forgione." I still hadn't quite gotten that rolled *r* sound.

"You are becoming more and more Italian every day. Pretty soon you'll be taking time to sit and enjoy your food. Like Luca."

"I doubt anyone could enjoy their food as much as he does."

"Not to be disrespectful, but I think I know someone who does. One moment."

She scurried away and came back with two large knuckle-bones.

"These are for Emma and Harley. They also have something to be grateful for."

The dogs followed her, rather politely I thought, until she laid the bones down in front of the fireplace, then they settled with their backs to each other and got to work.

Someone touched my sleeve. Cora, looking much better than she had in the hospital. After I had sworn Wade was dead, she had told me that he was the one who had attacked her. And why.

She put her hand in her pocket. "Close your eyes and open your hand."

Something cool touched my palm. I knew without looking that it was my grandmother's locket.

"I think this should stay in your family. Maybe give it to Charley one day." When she closed my hand around it, a beautiful opal ring flashed on her finger. "I found it in a box hidden in the garage. There were other things, too. Earrings, a barrette. Will you come by and pick it up? I don't have the heart to go to the police station."

I looked at the ring on her finger, one that looked vaguely familiar from a long time ago.

She read my face. "It doesn't matter anymore, Oliver. As hard as it is to believe, he loved me, and for a while we were happy. He was a damaged man."

"Have you talked to Nate?"

"Yes. Edna and I told him everything. He took it better than I expected. Except for Wade being his father. A man who said he was Wade's grandfather went to see Edna. He told her Nate was the spitting image of his own father. They worked it out, and Nate is happy to have a great-grandfather. And two mothers. Seems he's okay with everything as long as we erase Wade from our lives."

"Why didn't you tell me why you left me?"

"We were young." She shrugged. "But I'm happy you know now."

It sounded final. A chapter in our lives had ended. She touched my sleeve again and walked into the kitchen.

The bell tinkled, and a teenager I almost didn't recognize pushed through the door with Jennie and Zoe. Mia Fiori. It looked as if Jennie had taken the girl under her wing. I felt a rush of tenderness toward all three of them—women to be reckoned with, like my Elizabeth. And Ellie Fleming, who had died trying to save her brother. And Cora, who had carried a secret in her heart.

When the girls asked Roan to play, he pulled a clarinet out of his pack and played the introduction to a song. One by one, the men joined in singing. I was touched and didn't even know what the hell they were saying, but I caught the repeated phrase *Santa Lucia*. Didn't take a genius to figure it out.

Luca left the singers and we sat at a table. Harry joined us with a bottle of wine and four glasses.

Nate straddled a chair and rested his chin on his arms. "It's finally over."

Harry raised his glass.

"Wait. Roan should be here, too."

"He's content there, Nate, with the girls and the singing. He doesn't want us to make a fuss over him, call him a hero."

Mrs. Forgione put a basket of bread on our table. "But he is a hero."

"Yes, of course he is. He saved Theo and Zoe."

"Luca told me *you* saved Zoe. That she would have died if you hadn't been there." She tilted her head toward the musician. "Roan's been a hero for a long time. He never speaks of it, but his sister, Dorothy Brennan, showed me his Silver Star before she passed. Did you know he was a medic in the last war?"

I looked at Harry. He shook his head. I wondered if he was denying, as I was, that Roan knew removing the stake from Wade's leg would kill him, or if he was saying, *no, enough.*

EPILOGUE

Theo looked at the collage on the easel. It was finished. When he sat with it, he had no impulse to add an element, move one, color one, add words, a photo. The calm had settled inside him. He held the feeling in his chest and his head, closed his eyes, opened them. It still felt right.

He had made a large charcoal drawing on a silver-gray canvas. White chalk lightened the fence edge and the grasses on the hill. A figure hid under strips of light and dark tissue paper that overlapped and formed a kind of jagged moon. Different-size buttons tumbled in a milky way of stars against the charcoal sky. They spilled down the sepia hill to the canvas's edge, where they danced like light on the water. A tiny speck of silver foil peeked out from under a bush made of paper, the partial words *Ralp* and *taur* barely visible through the layers of indigo glaze that threw the bush into shadow.

Theo scooted the drafting stool over to his worktable and opened his briefcase. He separated bottle caps, some straight, some bent, some printed, some plain. He disassembled empty cigarette packs, opened and flattened the cellophane outer layer, then the silver paper layer, then the paper part with the name. He knew that as he worked, carefully sorting and organizing them, they would tell him what to do. String, a bird skeleton carefully contained in a jar, some pampas grass fronds from the tiger pit on the hill, and tufts of Emma's beautiful golden fur joined similar items already in cigar boxes.

When the briefcase was empty, he laid it on the table with the overlapping flap extended. He had to decide what to do. He had almost lost everything to that Detective Slater. He had heard his Uncle Oliver talking in the commotion after the gunshots on the hill. Detective Slater had been after his briefcase. Something about what Theo had picked up from the ground by Jonah.

But that had never been in the briefcase. The only thing in the briefcase that mattered was what his father had left him. He loved having it with him all the time, but maybe it was time to find a better hiding place. Or work it into a piece. Not a piece, not yet. He raised a seam inside the briefcase that appeared to be stitched down and slid his hand into the thin pocket between the stiff outer leather of the flap and the stiff inner lining. Their secret compartment, the place Theo left sketches for his dad, and his dad left him used movie tickets, or cigar bands, or lunch-counter receipts. It was their secret, barely enough space for a few thin items. Even Zoe didn't know about it. Theo had discovered it years ago when he was exploring the briefcase. He had slipped a sketch in, then asked his father weeks later if he had found the hidden present.

He slid out a length of film in a paper holder. He loved the film, shiny on one side, dull on the other. When he tilted it in the light, the darks went flat, then glossy. It said *120* under the little holes that bordered the frames. He set it aside and with his tweezers eased a worn page out of the flap. He could picture his father's fingers gripping his tortoiseshell pen as blue words flowed from the golden point, ink glistening until it dried into squares and lines across the page. He closed his eyes and slid his fingertip across each square, each line of words—words his father left him.

AFTERWORD

Readers of *In the Shadow of Lies* often ask whether certain events really happened. Unfortunately, my answer is most often yes. The story is fictional, and the characters my invention, but I have tried to portray accurately the way people were treated in the Bay Area during World War II. It was a dark time, a time of fear—fear of invasion, of social change, of anyone who was different. Fear allowed us to close our eyes to injustices, to accept the excuse that regrettable actions were "necessary" for national defense or national security. We didn't *want* to do it, we said—we *had* to.

Everything I have written about the restrictions against Italian Americans is true, based on real stories told by the people who experienced them. I am most grateful for the people who told their stories in *Una Storia Segreta* and *UnCivil Liberties*, and to Lawrence DiStasi and Stephen Fox, who collected them.

The ugliness Nate Hermit experienced is based on the real experiences of black soldiers. I know good men in the military tried to circumvent the injustice against black soldiers. *Taps for a Jim Crow Army* and *Fighting for America* are two of the sources for Nate Hermit's military experiences. The USO for black servicemen *was* blocked in Pt. Richmond.

Italian prisoners of war lived on Angel Island, collected garbage, and held dances in San Francisco, and the country was divided about their privileges.

An Italian POW was found hanged at Fort Lawton, Washington, and black soldiers were blamed. The entire story of the Port Chicago explosion and the subsequent mutiny trial and verdicts is also true. Black men passed as white reporters to cover stories, and Thurgood Marshall, later to become a US Supreme Court Justice, did go to San Francisco after the verdicts to help the men.

Oliver's experiences on Guam are based on true accounts of the fighting there. The dogs did find men who had been buried to their neck in sand and abused for several days. Incredibly, all the men survived. The banzai attack and the attack on the field hospital happened, although there is no record of a dog's detecting the latter. (For that I plead authorial license.) The Marine K9 Corps saved patrols from snipers and guarded the men at night. Captain William Putney tells their story in his memoir, *Always Faithful*. It is a moving tale of bravery, sacrifice, and love.

In 1924, Ku Klux Klan members marched up MacDonald Avenue in the Fourth of July parade in Richmond. A photograph of them appeared in the *Richmond Independent*. Later, they held an initiation ceremony in the El Cerrito hills. The Klan was active throughout the United States then and continues in some parts to this day. Other references to news and editorials in the *Independent* are also true. The cross burning that killed the Fleming children did *not* happen, but it could have, as cross burnings were common occurrences throughout Klan history.

The references to corruption in the Richmond police department are also fictional.

During the war, college students from more than thirty colleges, including Mount Holyoke, Smith, Vassar, Wellesley, Princeton, and Wheaton, were recruited for secret classes in cryptology. Many joined the navy or WAVES after graduation and worked in Washington, DC, where they deciphered and analyzed the thousands of codes the government received every day.

I could tell only a small part of the story. The time, the place, are filled with stories of people suffering discrimination, abuse, and hardship, but they are also filled with stories of sacrifices, large and small, that touch me. Readers seeking more information on these subjects may refer to the bibliography on my website. http://maryadlerwrites.com/

I cannot express how grateful I am to the courageous men and women who lived through these times and left us their writings, their words, so we might understand and appreciate their sacrifices. I have done my best to tell some of their stories. Any mistakes in the telling are my own.

ACKNOWLEDGMENTS

Encourage: to make someone more determined, hopeful, or confident.

I am not sure if anyone has ever had as much encouragement, from the most unlikely sources, as I have had while writing this book. People I barely know were excited about what I was doing and helped make me more determined, hopeful, and confident about writing it. To writers beginning their journey, I want to say, take heart and share your dream with people who will wish you well and share your adventure with you.

Among the people encouraging me were my first readers, Barbara Brown, Richard Jones, and Steve Osborn, who slogged through early drafts, and Karel Collins, who painstakingly read all of the book's "final" versions. Each of them made the book better and helped me to believe in myself and the project.

When I was tearing my hair out because I had read widely about the battle for Guam but couldn't "picture" it, my husband suggested I look on YouTube (not a place I normally go for information). To my surprise, I found History Channel reen-actments of the battle and, most inspiring, interviews with the men who had been there. The interviews, conducted decades after the war, showed how immediate and painful their memo-ries of that time still were. There are no words to thank them for what they gave, and for what men and women still give, in service to their country.

When I had gotten Oliver into a fix I couldn't get him out of, Chris Stribling, friend and Feldenkrais practitioner, brilliantly demonstrated how Oliver could use his injured leg to extricate himself from his predicament. Thanks, Chris.

I am grateful to Robert Shell, who interrupted his vacation to share his considerable knowledge about guns with a generally clueless stranger, and to D. P. Lyle, MD, author of *Forensics for Dummies*, who generously answered my questions about that subject.

A special thank-you to Jackie Good, who helped me find my voice. My thanks also to the Regional Oral History Office at the Bancroft Library, UC Berkeley, for details about life in Richmond during World War II.

My family supported me throughout this process and heard more than anyone would ever need to know about the history of World War II. Were it not for Brian Callahan, our talented winemaker, there would have been no CRUX wines to sustain us during that time. I give my thanks for and to my daughter Kim, who supplied moral support from across the sea; my daughter Heidi, for years of affectionate stories about children with Asperger's syndrome; my son, Aaron, for his insights about the battle for Guam and all things military, and for his careful reading of the manuscript; my son-in-law, Mathew Hall, for his discerning and insightful analysis of the book and the gentle way he discussed the things that did not work so well for him; and my husband, Richard, for his support, his belief in me, and his willingness to help me in any way he could. Thank you.

I have been blessed to have known and cared for many extraordinary dogs. From the time I was a child, they have protected me, comforted me, made me laugh, and taught me to see with my heart.

There are many beautiful spirits like Harley and Emma in shelters and rescues, longing to accompany you on your journey. If you enjoyed reading about them in this book, please think about inviting one to share your life.

ABOUT THE AUTHOR

Mary Adler escaped the university politics of "the ivory tower" for the much gentler world of World War 2 and the adventures of homicide detective Oliver Wright and his German shepherd, Harley. She lives with her family in Sebastopol, California, where she has created a garden habitat for birds and bees and butterflies—and other less genial critters. Unintended consequences at work again.

She does canine scent work with her brilliant dogs—the brains of the team—and loves all things Italian, especially Andrea Camilleri's Inspector Montalbano and cannoli, not necessarily in that order.

Among the books she would be proud to have written are Fred Vargas's Commissioner Adamsberg mysteries, set in Paris; Maurizio de Giovanni's Commissario Ricciardi mysteries, set in Naples; and Henning Mankell's Kurt Wallander mysteries, set in Ystad.

She reminds herself daily of the question poet Mary Oliver asks: "Tell me, what is it you plan to do with your one wild and precious life?"

She enjoys hearing from admirers of Oliver and Harley and would love for you to visit her website at http://maryadlerwrites.com/. There you will find recipes, photographs, book reviews, and other writings.